Like a Chinese Tattoo

Cullen Bunn

Rick R. Reed

David Thomas Lord

JA Konrath

For more information on this and other Dark Arts Books titles, visit www.darkartsbooks.com or e-mail sales@darkartsbooks.com.

Printed in the United States of America.
First Dark Arts Books Printing, March 2008
ISBN-13: 978-0-9779686-3-3
ISBN-10: 0-9779686-3-4
10 9 8 7 6 5 4 3 2 1

Acknowledgments

This one is for JimmyZ Johnston for last minute proofs and long-standing support; Shawn Lee for being one helluva a script-writing co-hort, especially when deadlines were tight; and, as always, Cindy for the kind of encouragement a lot of other people only dream about.

– Cullen Bunn

Thanks to James O'Barr, Ed Kramer, the Red Lion Pub (and Tina Jens), Bill Breedlove, John Everson, and Jeanne Cavelos. All of you played a part in bringing the stories in this book to life.

– Rick R. Reed

All stories have an origin, a conception. Therefore, every story owes, if not thanks, at least acknowledgement to those who – knowingly or not – contributed to the inception or continuation of its life. And so, I'd like to acknowledge and thank:

My family, especially the girls who called me "Da;" Karen, who slept while I wrote "Da's Boy," but woke up to critique it; The Glimmer Train sisters, Linda and Susan, who said that story was special; and, Jane Castle, who made me feel it was. Bryan Buchemi, who first requested "The White Room;" Martin Mundt and Lawrence Santoro, who first published it; and, For telling me it was special, Mort Castle, who has taught me so much, just by being my friend.

– David Thomas Lord

These stories are for all of my fans. Both of them.

– JA Konrath

Contents

Introduction

The number one question we get from folks is "Why do you guys do these odd little anthologies?" (Actually, that's not true, the number one question is easily "WTF were you thinking with that 'Babies is Smart' story by Martin Mundt???" – but that is neither here nor there.) I guess the supposition is that people have been hearing for so long how anthologies don't sell, and major presses won't do them, and, for all practical purposes, short stories are a dead market anyway, so why even bother? It is doubtful anyone would argue that at least the first two of those are largely true. Of course, one could quibble with the definitions of "sell" and "major," but that's probably even more depressing than just conceding the point.

But, indulge me for a moment, and let's take a short trip back in time...

Many years ago, when I was a little kid hanging out in libraries reading everything I could get my hands on (and, where if you wanted to find out where something was in the library, you went to this strange contraption called a "card catalog" and opened little drawers and thumbed through carefully typed and numerically ordered index cards to hopefully locate what you were looking for. Really. I am not making this shit up.), I stumbled upon a book that would forever change my life.

It was a stark black book with what looked like blood dripping on – and off – the cover. The title said *Alfred Hitchcock's Monster Museum*, and in addition to the dripping blood there were a couple of small black and white photos of Mr. Hitchcock's disembodied head staring out at the reader. Holy Toledo!

In addition to the selection of stories, there were also, what I guess would today be called "multimedia" illustrations which were sort of collages of photographs interspersed with drawn art and, of course, plenty of that dripping blood. (You can actually view a couple of them here: http://trickrtreat.blogspot.com/2007/06/alfred-hitchcocks-monster-museum.html. Never mind the card catalog, the Internet is a great thing!)

If the images weren't trippy enough, the stories were absolutely amazing. The one I still recall to this day (and, apparently, so do many other people) is "Slime" by Joseph Payne Brennan. It's pretty much *The Blob*, but a lot more like the 1980's nasty film version than the Steve McQueen movie. Mr. Brennan doesn't skimp on his descriptions of exactly what the oozing menace does to its various animal and human victims. Holy Toledo redux!

A subsequently procured copy of *Monster Museum* soon became one of the most read, re-read and re-read again books I owned. And, those weirdo illustrations gave me the willies plenty, too.

One of the good things about that card catalog was that the numerical system meant that similar books were grouped together, so soon enough I was able to get my hands on most of the euphemistically captioned "Alfred Hitchcock's stories for younger readers" lineup: *Alfred Hitchcock's Ghostly Gallery*, *Alfred Hitchcock's Haunted Houseful*, *Alfred Hitchcock's Supernatural Tales of Terror and Suspense*, etc. etc. As well, I was also able to find out there were more "grown up" volumes also available, with provocative titles like *Stories to Be Read with the Door Locked* and *Stories Not for the Nervous*.

Alas, none of the other books had retained the services of the illustrator from *Monster Museum*, but the amazing breadth of the stories contained within them more than made up for it. In addition to the "usual suspects" one would expect (Bradbury, Sturgeon, Stout, Ellison, Dahl, Wellman) there were stories guaranteed to permanently stick in a young mind like "In a Dim Room" by Lord Dunsany, "The Distributor" by Richard Matheson and "The Bronze Door" by Raymond Chandler(!).

There was a particularly nasty story I read in one of the books that involved a not very pleasant scientist who lands on a small island and discovers it is populated by giant, man-eating snails. That's bad enough, but the remainder of the story is the grim – exceedingly grim – flight of the scientist from the inexorable giant snails who chase him VERY slowly, but just…keep…coming.

For many, many years I kept that story tucked away inside my head, only remembering the implacable progress of the snails as they pursued the doomed scientist. Thanks to the aforementioned miracle of the Internet (and, more specifically, eBay), I was able to find a copy of that particular book (*Alfred Hitchcock's Supernatural Tales of Terror and Suspense*) and discover – much to my surprise –

that the "snail story" was not only properly titled "The Quest for 'Blank Claveringi'" but that it was written by none other than Patricia Highsmith, also the author of *Strangers on a Train* and *The Talented Mr. Ripley* (among many, many others).

In fact, the number of "non-genre" (for desperate want of a better term) authors whose work was found between the covers of those hoary old Alfred Hitchcock books was truly amazing. Because of my exposure to their work, I returned to the card catalog and went on to read many of the writers, both "horror" and non-horror. (Even if, as in the case of Ms. Highsmith, somewhat inadvertently.)

Flash forward a few years, and it was another group of anthology books that put the final piece in the puzzle of where my primary interest would lie. Already a big Stephen King fan, especially of his short-story collection, *Night Shift*, I talked my mom into buying me a paperback that contained, among another 20 or so stories, a Stephen King tale. That book was titled *Nightmares*, edited by Charles L. Grant.

Presumably, if you're reading this book, you are well aware of Charles L. Grant's work as both a writer and an editor. (If not, then carefully place a bookmark here, set this book down and go educate yourself by reading as much of both as you can get your hands on, and then return.) As I type this, I still proudly have exceedingly well-worn paperbacks of *Terrors, Horrors, Fears* and *Shadows* on my bookshelf, the very same ones I laboriously acquired from the local Kroch's & Brentano's though using a combination of allowance and paper-route money.

Nightmares has not only that Stephen King story, but also introduced me to the work of writers like Bill Prozini, Chelsea Quinn Yarbo, William Nolan, etc. And, to this day, whenever I need to be reminded of what may be the most perfect horror short story ever written looks like, I fetch that copy of *Nightmares* and open it to page 187, where "I Can't Help Saying Goodbye" by Ann Mackenzie commences, and am appropriately humbled.

So, probably right now you are rolling your eyes (having returned from that suggested break to brush up on your Charles L. Grant) and saying "What on earth does all that have to do with this book and the original question about anthologies?"

As it turns out, quite a bit. It's no secret that the attention span of the average adult in our culture is shrinking rapidly. A one-second delay when the light turns from red to green by a car in front of us glues many peoples' hands to the horn. If the shopper in front of us has an item with no price and the cashier has to look it up manually, there is more melodramatic sighing from the people in line than in a whole slew of romance novels. If a webpage takes more than one second to load, the exasperation approaches apocalyptic levels.

And, as one can see from the bookshelves in stores ranging from Target to Borders, increasingly if your name isn't King or Grisham or Cornwell, there isn't room for your novel. And, even if there was, who has time to read A. Whole. Novel? And, if there is "no market" for short stories, how can readers find new voices to encourage them to read (and buy) more books?

So, in addition to the fact that we love short stories here at Dark Arts, there is also the lofty hope that perhaps people will read some of these stories and be inspired to look for more from their favorites. For the happily unsuspecting reader, the commitment – money, time, patience – is small, and yet the potential payoff is so huge.

As with our previous volumes, we've tried to capture a range from each author – short fiction, longer fiction, "serious" stories, "humorous" stories, and, especially, "weird" or "disgusting" stories that might not fit anywhere else.

So, from JA Konrath, who is primarily known for his excellent "mystery" novel series featuring Lt. Jacqueline "Jackie" Daniels, we have "The Confession," a particularly nasty story told only in dialogue, "Punishment" which seems like a fairly traditional tale of torture and revenge until its shocking conclusion, and "The Necro Files," one of the most riotous, laugh-out-loud-in-disgust novellas I have ever had the pleasure of reading.

I've been a fan of Rick R. Reed's work since he was one of the first authors to be published in Dell's Abyss line of horror fiction. His visceral writing style combined with his desire to peel back the layers of even the most outré segments of society have given him a niche all his own. Whether the subject matter is disparate as rough vengeance in "Moving Toward the Light" or a new look at one of the most pervasive horror scenarios in "Purfleet," his take is always riveting, and for those of you unfortunate enough to never have encountered one of his (many) brilliant tales of the ongoing scandalous misadventures of Amelia, we have included a sample herein, "Stung."

From David Thomas Lord, who writes some of the most hauntingly beautiful prose in any genre today, we have three stories which truly showcase not only great writing, but an astonishing range of technical skill – whether it be the pitch-perfect dialect in "Da's Boy," the mounting careful construction of a nightmarish metaphor (or is it???) to a shocking conclusion in "The White Room," or – in the longest piece of his here, "The Great White Ape" – an oasis of his trademarked sumptuous descriptive abilities combined with unbearably-building suspense.

I first heard Cullen Bunn read one year at a Gross-Out contest at the World Horror Convention. For the uninitiated, the Gross-out Contest is where writers attempt to one-up each other by writing and performing the most vile, disgusting, hideous, nasty stories they can come up with, and the winner is judged by the fiercest measure possible – applause from an audience comprised of both fans and their fellow writerly colleagues. After the levels of depravity had (or so I thought) been plumbed to their limit, Cullen stepped to the mic, and in quiet, measured tones proceeded to plumb depths that had not even been hinted at previously. Before the winning applause stopped ringing in my disbelieving ears, I knew that one day, if anyone was foolish enough to allow me the opportunity to publish stories, I would have something by Cullen Bunn. What's most impressive, though, is the stories included here that aren't designed to make people run from the room with their hands covering their mouths. The gradually building horror of a novella like "Remains" couldn't be less like the unrepentant, joyful (and hilarious) foulness of "Granny Kisses." (You have been warned.)

It is our hope with this book (and our other Dark Arts titles) that you will be able to discover some talented authors you may not be familiar with, or to perhaps find another, hitherto unknown side of one of your favorite writers. In any case, we sincerely hope you enjoy these stories.

– Bill Breedlove
Chicago, Illinois
February 2008

Cullen grew up in rural North Carolina, but now lives in the St. Louis area. The first collection of his noir/horror comic, THE DAMNED, was published in 2007 by Oni Press. The follow-up, PRODIGAL SONS, will be released in 2008. His fiction and non-fiction have appeared in a number of magazines and anthologies. Somewhere along the way, he founded Undaunted Press and edited the small press horror magazine, WHISPERS FROM THE SHATTERED FORUM. All writers must pay their dues, and Cullen has worked various odd jobs, including Alien Autopsy Specialist, Rodeo Clown, Professional Wrestler Manager (during which time his rivalry with Jim Cornette grew to epic porportions), and Sasquatch Wrangler.

Visit his website at www.cullenbunn.com.

CULLEN BUNN

Tomorrow, When the Demons Come

"What we do today doesn't matter," Marco said, the preamble to a mantra I had heard time and time again. "Nothing matters. For tomorrow, the demons come."

"Don't tell me that." I tried not to let pain show in my voice. "I don't want to hear that. I don't believe it…and neither do you."

A smile played across his lips. He looked at his hands for a few seconds, and the smile slipped away, leaving in its wake a hint of disgust. *Disgust at me?* I wondered, pathetically, hating myself for feeling so doubtful and weak, like a schoolboy in the thrall of a crush. Or was he disgusted with himself? He pressed his palms against his chest. Wiping his hands on his tee shirt, he pulled the wash-worn fabric tight against the muscles of his chest and stomach. Crimson patterns stained the shirt at the passing of his fingers, the bloody outline of his hands smeared down his belly, melting towards his crotch.

"Is that it?" I asked. "Is that all you have to say to me?"

Still, he ignored me, tilting his head curiously from side to side as he examined the blood on his shirt and the pinkish discoloration of his hands, the bright veins of red running through the creases of his flesh.

"How do you do it?" I pleaded.

The smile returned, and he looked up, held me in place with his stare.

"Is it that important to you?" His voice was little more than a whisper. "Do you really need to know my every secret? Do you really want to know how it is that I live with myself?"

A snake of fear uncoiled in my belly. He was turning my own

words against me, taking my curiosity and twisting it into something sad and pitiful, needy and obsessive.

He reached out for my cheek, and I jumped at his touch. I had barely noticed him move across the room. His fingers seared my skin. The smell of his body – rich and meaty and delicious – washed over me. I turned my mouth towards his hand, but he pulled away.

"You don't want to know everything, now do you? Where's the fun in that?"

I blinked, unable to speak. He had drugged me, poisoned me with his touch, with the memory of his past caresses, with the promise of more to come.

I shook my head.

"No."

"Good." He turned from me, walked across the room and shrugged his scuffed leather jacket on over his bloodied tee shirt. He looked over his shoulder at me as he pulled open the door. What might have been love, or perhaps triumph, gleamed in his eyes. "I'm going out for a while. I'll be back before long, but don't wait up for me. Go to sleep."

And he was gone.

I rushed to the window, hoping to get some hint of his destination. He moved along the sidewalk, hunched over to fight back the chill night air, but still somehow graceful. Frosty breath plumed in small clouds around his head. He seemed to be talking to himself, maybe bitching about me—

Stop it, I told myself. *Don't think like that. Ever.*

Marco turned a corner and vanished into shadow.

He would not be back for several hours. Alone, I paced about the creaking, unkempt house for a while, trying to keep my mind occupied, but tormented by the anger and doubt and confusion spinning in my head. My thoughts drifted again and again back to Marco.

And to the locked room.

Marco owned a massive, decaying house downtown, the kind of house that a "working class Joe" might dream of one day restoring but would never be able to afford to renovate. But Marco's parents had left it to him when they died, along with enough money that their son would never need to hold down anything so banal as a steady job. I lived with him in the house, and I had complete run of the place, except for a single room upstairs.

The locked room.

That chamber was forever denied to me. At times I wanted to enter, just to see what was hidden within, even though I knew very well that Marco would have hated me for it.

Finally – thankfully – exhaustion overcame me, and I crawled into bed, pulling the silk sheets around my body, drifting to sleep surrounded by the scent of Marco's sweat.

方 方 方

"Nothing matters. For tomorrow, the demons come."

I always assumed the phrase nothing more than a way to shut me up, or a contrived defense or justification for the things he did to people. Not to me, mind you. He never hurt me, not physically, not intentionally. I was one of the lucky few he allowed to share his life. There had been a half dozen or so in the years before we met, and I never considered what had happened to them, how it came to pass that they stepped aside to make room for me. Perhaps Marco simply grew tired of them, the way he would eventually grow tired of my company.

Perhaps they had each in turn been led to the locked room.

I remember the night I met him. I was twenty-three years old, little more than a frightened boy – shy and unaware. He was beautiful and pale, his blonde hair teased into spikes, an oversized white dress shirt hanging from his lean frame. He seduced me with his jaded eyes and gentle touch – me, virgin territory to him. His every word spoke of thrills and dangers. He was charming and cunning and wise, and he captured me, enslaved my imagination.

To say he ravaged me wouldn't be completely true, but it wouldn't be a lie either. He ravaged everyone. Everyone he spoke to, everyone he glanced at across a smoke-filled room, everyone he brushed up against on the metro. He ravaged them all in some way, men and women, gay and straight. He tore into their minds, their thoughts, their dreams, and left little pieces of himself, shrapnel memories of his passing, behind to taunt them.

God, I hated him, but I loved him, too.

He made love to me. He brought me to heights of pleasure I had not known before, and I gladly followed him into depths of depravity unlike anything I had ever seen or heard or felt. He went down on me in public places, movie theaters, bus stops, and dance clubs. He held me close and read poetry to me from dog-eared paperbacks as he fucked me.

He told me fairy tales.

Late at night, when outside the sirens shrieked and gunshots echoed along seldom-traveled streets, he pulled me against the heat of his body and told me such beautiful stories, tales of creatures personifying twisted human emotion. Greed, with his many grabbing hands; Love, whose beauty was so terrible that she drove those who looked upon her mad; Lust, with wiggling tongues sprouting from his mouth, nostrils, eyes, and ears. And Jealousy – how I loathed her – clad in tangled, living vines, torturing her victims with their own imaginations. All these creatures had a place in his stories. He shared the tales with me in the same way a parent might tell a bedtime story to a restless child.

We drank too much, got stoned. We sipped expensive tequila and shot Jack Daniels, depending on our moods and the day of the week. We pushed ourselves to the limits of alcohol poisoning and held each other when we were trembling and sick. We smoked weed and dropped acid and shot up, and together we expanded our thoughts, our horizons...or maybe we only succeeded in dulling our sense, even for a little while. The end results didn't matter. They were all the same to Marco.

We shared lovers – men, women, girls, or young boys. Nothing as base as age or gender mattered in Marco's bed, where the scent of rose petals clung to the air and every sensation was of heat and pleasure and longing.

But when we were done, he always sent me away. This was the unspoken rule between us. He did not need to tell me to leave, but his eyes commanded me. I would wander from the room, and he would take our lovers away, take them to the locked room.

And there the screaming would start.

He wouldn't let me watch. I was forbidden to enter, no matter how much I begged. I suppose that's how I knew that he loved me.

"You don't want to find out if you have the stomach for this," he once said. "You don't ever want to know."

So I lurked outside the door sometimes and listened and jacked off and when I grew weary of the screams I retired back to bed or crashed on the soiled living room couch. Sometimes I stayed awake long enough to hear the screams change to cries of delight or pleas for help or gurgling sobbing. Sometimes, listening to Marco's playthings, I used a razor to scratch spiraled patterns into the flesh at the back of my hand, letting the blood bead along the tiny white trails of torn skin.

Often, that bitch Jealousy appeared to tease me, bringing her tongue close to my wounds, but never quite suckling the blood away before turning and laughing and dancing into the ether.

Afterwards, Marco would emerge from the locked room, covered in blood, out of breath, and carrying himself as if a burden had been heaped upon his shoulders.

He would leave then, storming out into the night, only to return sometime later. When he returned, his mood was almost always brighter, some might even say cheery. It was unsettling and frustrating. Where did he go and what happened to affect him so? I never asked, no matter how bad I wanted to, and he never volunteered the information.

There were times when I wanted to leave him. Once, while watching the evening news, I saw a picture of a young boy that Marco had brought home flash across the screen, and I considered calling the police. But as afraid as I was of Marco's depravity and the things he did behind the door to the locked room, I was more afraid of losing him.

It turned my stomach, but I started to look forward to visits from new lovers. For months, Marco would bring no one, then he would bring someone new each night for a week, a new and different taste or texture to enjoy, a new cry in the night. That I know of, Marco used no criteria other than a moment of whim in choosing who he would bring home, and I worried that he might one night bring home someone who he shouldn't, someone who might hurt one or both of us.

Sometimes, he would call to me from upstairs, and I would find him standing outside the locked room, a bundle wrapped in garbage bags and packing tape at his feet. Together, we would drag the body downstairs and out to the car, stashing it in the trunk. We'd drive out to the landfill and dump the body, all the while talking about books or music or something equally pointless. Once the body was abandoned to the waste, Marco did not mention them again.

方 方 方

This was our life for the two years I lived with Marco. We lived and loved and reveled in our own depravity. We might have gone on like that forever – I was beginning to think that Marco might very well live forever, and I would have lived with him. But sooner or later, everyone falters, everyone stumbles.

I stumbled late one autumn afternoon. I was not lured by the embrace of another. Marco and the strays he brought home were more than enough to satisfy my sexual appetite. But my curiosity, especially when it came to the secrets of the locked room, got the better of me.

Marco was out, I assumed buying cigarettes and booze, maybe trolling for an evening's pleasure, and I found myself standing at the door to the locked room. I allowed my eyes to creep over the door, noting every imperfection of the wood, every nick and scratch, the way the door hung just a few centimeters crooked in the frame. I imagined that the other side was scoured with scars left behind by clawing, desperate fingernails. Sweat beaded on my upper lip. I wiped it away, licked it from my fingertips as I considered the contents of the room beyond. I believed myself ready for whatever I might find, for whatever horror or god or devil awaited in the room. Nothing I found would change my feelings toward Marco. I belonged to him completely, but I needed to know everything about him, and only two secrets eluded me – the contents of the locked room, and the purpose and destination of his journeys in the early mornings following his activities in the chamber that at that moment waited for me to enter it like a lover.

My hand strayed to the doorknob. What would be the harm in testing it? I knew it was sealed, but the thrill of doing something forbidden tempted me.

My fingers brushed the cold metal knob.

My palm closed around it.

Ever so slightly, I turned—

"What are you doing?"

Marco's voice startled me, and I spun around. He stood in the hallway, watching me. He drew a long breath from one of his cigarettes. The scent of cloves hung around him like a halo. The hollows of his cheeks and the dark circles beneath his eyes made him look like something dead.

"I – I was—"

He didn't wait to hear my explanation. He only shook his head and walked away.

"Marco, wait."

He did not face me, but only raised a hand to silence my protests.

I didn't follow. I didn't try to further explain my indiscretion. A dreadful assurance filled my heart.

Marco would be leaving me.

I knew then and there that I had one chance, just one chance to prove my worth to him – or maybe I needed to prove it to myself.

方 方 方

I found her at the Skin Trade, a trendy little bar on the landing, one of those places where yuppies go when they want to get a taste of the darker side of life. College kids in Polo shirts and Dockers crowded around a chain-link protected stage to stare at a bad Marilyn Manson cover band.

Her name was Kimmy. At least, that's the name she claimed. She was gorgeous – thin, pale, blonde – and there was an air of innocence about her. Marco would like that. She couldn't have been more than 20, but her fake ID had served her well, and she was well on her way to being totally trashed by the time I approached her. She had watched me from across the bar, and I used the veil of smoke between us to hide the mixture of lust and venom in my eyes. She was talking to some guy, a wannabe goth in black jeans and mascara, dancing with him occasionally, but all the while her bleary eyes returned to me as I slouched against the bar, knocking back shots of vodka, waiting, biding my time. When her companion staggered off to the john, I approached her. She looked me up and down, and a pouty smile formed on her lips. I stepped in close, leaning on the table and whispering in her ear.

"That your boyfriend?" I asked, but the words were not my own. I recognized a chilling familiarity in my voice, and the question was whispered in just the right tone to coax the answer I wanted.

"He's an ass," she said, matter-of-factly, shrugging and wrinkling her nose as if the thought of him was distasteful.

"You didn't answer my question."

She shrugged.

"Do you want to get out of here?" Again, the words were not mine, but this time I recognized the phrasing. I sounded like Marco. For a second, this realization shocked me, and doubt welled up inside me. Quickly I tried to grasp what it was that I had lost. I grabbed her hand – gently. "Well, do you?"

She nodded, meekly, but her hand tightened in mine, and I pulled her away from the table. As we pushed our way through the crowd, she looked back, once, and maybe she caught a glimpse of her boyfriend.

It was the last she would ever see of him.

She was indeed twenty, an art major, but taking a semester or two off to earn a little extra money by working full time at a floral shop. This she told me as we took a cab back to the house, all the while the cabby, a dark-skinned man with darting eyes and shaky hands, watched her in the rear-view mirror. Kimmy dreamed of one day working as a commercial artist for ad agencies. She had grown up in a small town, and she wanted to make her parents proud, she wanted to one day have a family of her own, and she hoped that she hadn't hurt Nick, her date for the evening, too badly. Most importantly, she wanted me to know that she had never, ever done anything like this before, and I believed her.

I, on the other hand, only wanted her to be quiet. I did not need to hear about her life. I did not want to. For a second, as I listened to her tell me about her roommate, a dear girl named Stephie, I looked out the car window and saw Doubt, the filthy thin beggar, panhandling along the sidewalk. I placed my hand upon her leg. He skin was cool and smooth. The cabby craned his neck to see if I was copping a feel up her skirt.

"Shhhh," I whispered. My voice was heavy. "We'll be there soon."

She remained silent for the rest of the ride.

When we walked into the house, and she saw Marco lounging

on the couch, she tensed and shot a glance at me. He was stretched out, reading from his tattered copy of Byron, sipping from a glass of dark wine.

"Kimmy," I said, "I want you to meet a friend of mine."

I saw a hint of surprise on his face. He was impressed with me, I could tell. He pursed his lips and tossed the book onto the coffee table. He rose and crossed the room like a ghost, extending his hand to Kimmy. She shivered but offered him her own, which he kissed, ever so lightly.

"Can I get you something to drink?" he asked.

And she was ours.

Later, we gathered in Marco's bedroom, his silken sheets slick with our sweat. Marco knelt at the head of the bed, his perfect body shimmering in the candlelight. He cradled Kimmy's head in his lap, and she grasped handfuls of the sheets and looked up at him through a haze of passion as I wrapped my arms around her thighs and kissed and licked at the warmth between her legs. She gasped and cried out and moaned, and I crawled up her body, thrusting into her. All the while, Marco held her head forcing her to gaze up at him, and he asked over and over.

"Is this love? Is this love?"

I wasn't sure if he was asking her or me, but I saw the way she looked up at him, the way she reached up to touch his face, and I knew that her trembling and whimpering was for him – him!

That bitch Jealousy tittered at me from the corner of the room.

I shoved into her, faster now, wanting to hurt her, and my own sweat ran into my eyes, blinding me. Kimmy begged for more, wailed with increased pleasure. I looked to Marco, but his face was a twisted blur.

"Is this love?" he asked.

When we were done, the three of us lie coiled around one another, still, panting, the closeness of our bodies warming us in the cool night air.

"She's asleep," Marco said.

I was nearly asleep myself, but his voice roused me.

"It's time for you to go," he said to me.

I sat up. "No. Wait. I thought—"

He silenced me with a kiss, leaning across Kimmy's body to press his lips against mine. When he pulled away, he said, "Go."

I could hear her – Jealousy – lurking in the shadows, giggling.

"No. I…I want to go with you…with her…to the locked room."

"I've told you before." Marco said. "That's not allowed."

He touched Kimmy's porcelain cheek. She sighed softly and stirred in her sleep.

"Marco," I said, "please. Just this once."

He looked up at me and muttered, "I said, go!" with such malice that I could only stagger off the bed and out of the room.

Never had I heard such sweet passion…or such horrid torment…as I heard from the locked room that night.

When silence had once again shrouded the house, I lay upon the couch with my eyes closed, pretending to be lost in blissful sleep. But as I heard Marco come out of the room, gather his jacket, and leave through the front door, I jumped up, threw on a pair of jeans, a tee shirt, and leather boots, and followed.

I kept my distance, stayed just close enough that I wouldn't lose sight of him. He walked past packs of people staggering out of bars, passed hooting whores and brightly lit peep show windows. He did not stop, did not even look up, until he reached a small, poorly lit storefront.

The sign out front was written in bold Korean lettering, and I could not make it out. The windows were dark, painted on the inside and dirty. My reflection twisted in the glass. The buildings on either side were dark and deserted, the doors and windows boarded up. Shadows poured off the derelict buildings and flooded toward the storefront, only barely beaten back by the single bare bulb that fizzled and guttered near the door.

Marco stepped inside.

I waited for a few seconds, steeled my courage, and followed him.

The interior room was bathed in a dim red light. Almost suffocating heat clung to the air. I saw no sign of Marco, but an elderly Korean woman waited for me behind the counter. She beckoned, and as I stepped towards her, she smiled and asked in broken English, "Wash your troubles away?"

"I followed someone here."

"Wash your troubles away, yes? Twenty dollars." She pointed to a doorway covered by a beaded curtain. Beyond, a cloud of steam writhed.

I put my money on the table. The woman smiled and pointed to the doorway again while sliding the crumpled twenty off the counter and into her pocket.

I stepped through the curtains.

A heavy wave of heat rolled over me. Before me lay row after row of shallow, steaming pools of water. Buckets and towels were lined up along the far wall. The pools were all empty, save for the last. Through the vapor, I saw Marco, naked, basking in the steaming bath with his back to me.

I stepped closer, intending to speak, intending to reveal myself, but as I did, I noticed something strange about the water in which he lay.

Images seemed to dance through the water.

Here was a reflection of Kimmy, screaming, slashes across her once-beautiful face.

This was quickly washed away and replaced by the image of my own face, crying out in passion.

Then, a young boy, crying for his mother, purple bruises over his frail body.

I looked to Marco. He seemed to be asleep, or in a kind of trance, then back at the images roiling in the pool.

Another young man, weeping and mewling as Marco led him to the locked room.

Suddenly, I realized how Marco lived with himself, lived with the atrocities he inflicted, because somehow the bath was washing away his shame, washing away his remorse, washing away his inhumanity.

Marco stirred, on the verge of waking. I stepped away from him, hoping the shadows and the steam might hide me. He emerged from the bath, the last of his guilt dripping off his body and forming strange, rippling images in the pool. Did he see me? I could not be sure. Nor did I care. The bath held my fascination now.

I glanced at the doorway. The beaded curtain swayed gently, the strands clicking against one another. I saw no other sign of Marco.

I was alone, save for the quickly changing images lapping at the tiled sides of the bath.

Trembling with excitement, I disrobed. I stood above the pool and watched memory after memory play itself out upon the water's surface, but the images vanished so quickly.

I slipped a toe into the bath. The water was warm, soothing.

I checked the door once more. I couldn't believe that Marco had failed to see me. But if he had spotted me, he did not return.

Shuddering, I slipped down into Marco's bath. Every part of him washed over me. I bit my tongue to avoid crying out at the feeling of ecstasy. Tears ran down my face as Marco's memories invaded my pores.

I ducked my head beneath the surface and drank, drank it all in, drank all of Marco into me, every part of him. I drank more of that steaming water than was humanly possible, gulping down all the evil, terrible thoughts that Marco had washed away. I drank it down, lapped it up, like a lover's juices, and the bitterness of it intoxicated me.

Finally, having gulped down my fill, I passed out.

I am not sure how long I lay unconscious in the bath. It seemed an eternity, an eternity plagued by dreams – no, nightmares – that were not mine. I lay there for at least a day, quite possibly more, and when I awoke I found myself in a different room. I lay upon a cold stone slab. My back stung, feeling raw, as if I had writhed against the rough stone during my fitful sleep. A gauzy shroud covered me; it felt like a spider's web as I pulled it away.

Who had brought me here?

At the foot of the slab, I found my clothes, neatly folded. I dressed quickly.

I staggered weakly from the bathhouse. The old Korean woman was not to be found. The place was empty, the pools drained. It looked as if the place was closed, or as if it had never been opened at all.

It was early, the sun only just starting about the task of burning the night's fog away. The city was only now waking, and I passed only one person on the walk home.

A young black man, he did not look up as he passed. He walked quickly, his hands shoved into his jacket pocket. I detected Marco's meaty smell, and the coppery tang of blood, clinging to him.

I turned as he walked past, and the hair at the back of my neck stood on end. I quickened my pace. By the time I reached the house I was almost out of breath from running.

When I entered the house, the smell of blood was even stronger. I rushed upstairs, to the bedroom, where I found Marco.

He was naked and pale – oh, so pale – and he lay upon his silk sheets stained crimson. His throat had been slashed open, and it looked as if his head might fall off if I so much as touched his body.

As I had feared, he had brought the wrong person home to play.

Had Marco seen me in the bathhouse?

Surely, he must have.

And he had brought this man home, perhaps at the urging of a green-robed whore.

I fell to my knees.

This could not be happening. I would not lose him, not now that I understood him so well, so much better than he understood himself.

I don't know what brought me to do what I did then. Perhaps it was some dark urging from the thoughts and dreams and fears that I had consumed.

I rammed my fingers down my throat.

I gagged, and stomach acid flooded my mouth, and I wanted to scream as I felt something tear at my insides and claw its way out of my stomach, up my throat. It felt as if it might rip me open, and chunks of flesh – maybe my own, torn away from my stomach lining, maybe something else – spilled from my lips, spattering the floor. I wretched and choked and wretched again, and the vile stream poured from my mouth, as my body emptied itself of Marco's memories.

I couldn't look, couldn't turn my eyes towards the putrid thing that must have lain beside me. I squeezed my eyes shut, and tears blazed hot trails down my cheeks. My throat burned, and acid tingled in the back of my mouth. The smell – God the smell – was sickening, a mixture of vomit and rose petals and Marco's meaty stink. I could not look, but I heard something moving, something flailing about painfully on the hardwood floor, and soon enough a rattling, raspy breath, an inhuman gasp. And it cried out, this thing lurking beside me, this thing I had brought into the world but, like a shamed mother, could not look upon, and its cry was that of an infant, an infant born of washed away sin, and it was the most unnatural sound I have ever heard.

I could not look.

I staggered to my feet, all the while turning my head from the whipping, spindly thing, lying in a pool of bile. My stomach felt as if it had been ripped inside out. My chest felt as if my ribs might snap through my skin, tear open my heart. I was distantly aware that I had pissed myself, and warmth spread down my legs. Bracing myself along the wall, I stumbled down the hall, to the locked room. My fingers closed upon the dented, brassy handle. I turned the knob.

A dry laugh caught in my throat. The door had never been locked at all.

I only barely crossed the threshold before collapsing, crashing to the bare floor, grunting like an animal as I pulled myself into this room that had been denied to me for so long.

Darkness enshrouded me.

I thought, in those last few seconds before I lost consciousness, that I saw Jealousy and Fear and Exile watching me from the shadows, but they were not real, they were only figments of my imagination, and save for these phantoms the room was empty.

From the hallway, I heard the wet flapping of bare feet against the hardwood floor, but I did not have the strength to turn.

I closed my eyes.

And waited for the demon to come.

Remains

The dead rats danced the day the hired man came 'round.

My father, rest his soul, might have scolded me for saying such a foolish thing. He didn't care much for dreams and fancies – nightmares, either. But that's how it started, way back during those last warm weeks of September, more than thirty years ago.

With dead rats.

Dancing.

My little sister spotted the stranger before I did. I was shelling peas, like Mama had asked the both of us. Sitting on the warped front steps, I snapped pods, scraped peas into a large bowl, and tossed the husks into the yard for the chickens to squabble over. Abbie, on the other hand, did everything in her power to avoid anything remotely akin to a chore. I could hear her crawling around the crawlspace beneath the front porch.

"What are you doing?" I asked.

"I'm *busy*."

"Sure you are." I glanced at the bucket of unsnapped peas. The supply didn't appear to be diminished, despite my efforts. "You know, you're supposed to be helping."

"I'm *busy*," Abbie said again.

"Mama doesn't want you playing under there anyhow. You're gonna ruin your clothes, and there's spiders down there big enough to bite your fingers off."

I grabbed another snap from the bucket and cracked it open for emphasis. Abbie hated spiders, and I hoped to startle her out from under the porch. Considering how hard-headed my little sister could be, though, I should've known better.

"Ain't no spiders down here, Seth, not that I ever saw."

"You sure about that?"

"Yes, I am, thank you very much."

I sighed in defeat. Since scaring her didn't work, I decided to give guilt a try.

"Maybe not, but you should come on out of there anyhow. I wouldn't ever stick you with doing the chores all by yourself."

That was a lie, but as I hollowed out yet another shell, it felt like the truth.

Abbie started humming a lighthearted tune, partly to let me know our discussion was at an end. I halfway considered tattling on her, just to watch Mama drag her out from under the porch and take a switch to her backside. But Abbie and me, we had an understanding – we didn't snitch, no matter what. Sometimes, the agreement bit me in the behind, but a deal's a deal. I kept on snapping peas, and before I knew it, I was humming right along with my sister.

I didn't notice the lone figure approaching our house, but eagle-eyed Abbie spotted him right away.

"Who's that?" It took me a second to realize she'd stopped humming. Her voice was hushed and muffled. "Somebody's coming this way."

I shaded my eyes from the sun and looked down the tree-lined path.

The stranger was tall and lean, dressed in dirty jeans and a button-up work shirt. He carried a bulky duffle bag slung over his shoulder. For some reason, he reminded me of a scarecrow that had crawled down from its perch in the corn field. I couldn't really see his face, because the shadows from the trees seemed to cling to his features. He didn't so much walk as lope, like an animal, and every few steps he paused to glance over his shoulder, as if expecting to see someone following him.

"What's he doing?" Abbie's small fingers jutted out through the lattice work lining the porch. Through the holes in the trim, I saw her big blue eyes peering out from the shadows. "He looking for someone?"

He's on the run, I thought, *from the law…*

Or something worse.

The idea just popped into my head. Unexpected thoughts like that often exploded through my noggin, and I'd been accused of letting my imagination get the better of me more than once. To hear my folks tell the tale, I read too many of those crime and horror comics Mr. Oswald stocked at the drug store. Maybe I did, maybe I didn't. Either way, I'd learned to keep my lips sealed when it came to my wild notions.

But I didn't like the stranger from the moment I spotted him.

Something about him put me on edge.

He gave me the creeps.

"You just stay put." I rapped my knuckles against the porch, and Abbie pulled her fingers back into the shadows. "Stay quiet. Stay out of sight."

For once, Abbie didn't backtalk me. I figured the stranger spooked her as much as he did me. In its time, the filthy crawlspace beneath the porch had served as a fairytale castle and the Lone Ranger's base of operations, an army bunker and a mud pie bakery. But today, Abbie used it as a hiding place.

I continued shelling peas, but I didn't take my eyes off the man as he tramped my way. I couldn't guess his age with any accuracy. He might have been in his late thirties or early forties. His face was weathered from countless hours wiled away in the sun, and his longish hair was more gray than black.

"Afternoon," he said. His voice was deep and gravelly, like road grit coated his throat.

I nodded and scowled at him.

He shrugged his bag from his shoulder. The duffel *thunked* into the dirt. Placing one of his steel-toed work boots on the lowest porch step, the stranger leaned close and draped his arms over his knee. His sleeves were rolled up to his elbows, and I saw dozens of scars crisscrossing the flesh of his forearms – some of them still pink and only recently healed by the looks of it. Dirt had settled into the wrinkles of his face and hands, and his fingernails were crescents of pure black.

"Your daddy home?" he asked.

Underneath the porch, Abbie shuffled in the dirt, crawling back into the darkest of the shadows. The stranger tilted his head. His eyes strayed towards the latticework, and one corner of his mouth rose.

"I'll fetch him," I said.

I put the bowl of shelled peas aside and stood up.

His eyes ticked away from Abbie's hiding place and met mine. His grin came across like a bestial thing. His teeth were yellowed and looked sharp. I backed towards the screen door. I called for my father, and I felt a rush of relief when I heard the heavy tread of his approaching footsteps.

The stranger looked over his shoulder again.

I narrowed my eyes. What are you running from?

He stood up straight when Daddy stepped onto the porch. My father was a big man, tall and broad-shouldered, and he'd worked hard almost every day of his life. He wore his favorite pair of blue coveralls. His greasy cap was folded up and shoved in his pocket, because he never – never – wore a hat indoors. I could tell his hands were bothering him. His knuckles were red and swollen as thick as tubers, and his fingers curled like the legs of a dying spider. Sometimes, his rheumatism flared up so bad he could hardly pick up his fork to eat breakfast. Today was one of those days, and Daddy's voice was laced with a painful weariness.

"Help you?"

"I sure hope so." The stranger kept on smiling. "Word is you're looking to hire a man to pitch in around your place. Figured I'd come by and see about the job, unless you've already brought somebody else on."

Daddy eyed the man for a second or two, sizing him up.

"You ain't from around here, are you?"

"No, sir. I was just passing through when I heard about the job. Thought I could stay around for a while, though, maybe earn some extra traveling money."

"Where is it you're headed?"

The stranger nodded and sucked at his teeth. "No place in particular."

"You ever work a farm before?"

"Worked tobacco since I was a boy, and I spent a couple summers as a farmhand outside of Knoxville."

"I can't offer much of a wage," Daddy said, "barely enough to get by, really. There's a backroom in the tool shed that's got a cot and a washbasin. You can bed down there. We'll feed you three times a day, but you'll have to take your meals either in the shed or outside."

The rule about eating outside didn't sit particularly well with Daddy. As far as he was concerned, anyone who worked the land deserved a seat at our supper table. But he knew my mother would never stand for a stranger sitting alongside her family.

In this case, I was glad for my Mama's ways.

"All that sounds fine," the stranger said. "I don't need much, and it'll be nice to sleep with a roof over my head and get three squares for a change."

Three squares, I thought. *Sounds like something an escaped convict might say.*

Nah. That's just your comic books talking.

"All right then," Daddy said. "Sounds like you've got yourself a job."

The stranger thanked my father and introduced himself as Cole Jensen. He stuck out his hand. Daddy hesitated for a second, then reluctantly reached out to shake the hired man's hand. He winced painfully as Cole's fingers closed around his own. I could have sworn I saw that disdainful smirk wriggle across Cole's face.

"Why don't you go put your bag away?" Daddy pointed to the tool shed. "I'll be over directly to show you around."

As Cole trudged to the shed, I whispered to my father, "You don't need to pay somebody to help. I can handle anything needs doing."

"I know you can. But there's too much for any three people to do, let alone two. Your mama's about to pop with the new baby, and you and your sister have your schooling to attend to."

"I could stay home and help instead."

It wasn't a completely selfish gesture. Matter of fact, I liked school, especially reading and writing. But I didn't like the idea of Cole Jensen lurking around the farm when I wasn't around to keep an eye on him.

"You can help in the mornings and the afternoons. Don't fret. We won't do it all without you."

He rubbed his hands together, trying to work the ache from his bones, and he tapped his foot against the porch steps.

"Abbie, get out from under there before your mama catches you and tans your hide. I don't want to listen to your wailing when your rear end's stinging."

My sister scurried out into the light.

Daddy smiled and said, "Why don't you two take Jerry Lee out to the barn for a while?"

"Yes, sir," I said, all too glad to take a break from field snaps.

"Do we have to?" Abbie whined. "We were gonna go out to the pond this afternoon."

"Don't give me any duff," Daddy said. "You know you aren't

supposed to hang around at that old mud hole. But if you hurry up you can finish your chores and still have some time to play a little before suppertime. The more bellyaching you do now, the less time you'll have for fun later."

Pouting, Abbie made a spectacle of dragging herself away.

Daddy only shook his head. Like the rest of the family, he was accustomed to Abbie's overdramatic antics.

"One day," he said – more to himself to anyone, "that girl will break all the hearts in Hollywood."

I fought back the urge to warn him about the hired man. Daddy was a hard-working man, though, and he toiled in the *real* world, not in a world where boys spied boogiemen in the shadows.

But he might be an escaped criminal…or maybe even a killer.

Daddy wouldn't see it that way.

From around the other side of the house, Abbie called impatiently. "Hurry up, Seth!"

I watched my father greet Cole Jensen by the tool shed. I looked long and hard at the road that bordered our farm. I didn't see anyone coming to haul the hired man away. But I sure wished I did. After a few minutes, I went to join my sister.

Something told me nothing would ever be the same again.

I had never known any home other than the farm. Our house, tall and white and surrounded by Mama's rose bushes…The old shed, with its sagging roof and rotting walls, and its replacement, with its fresh coat of paint and that eyesore of a tractor parked beneath…The cement birdbath, where cardinals sometimes gathered in the mornings…

I loved that old farm.

But the hired man ruined it all.

Spoiled it.

After it was all said and done, I hated the farm.

And I hated Cole Jensen and what he had brought with him.

This is how it happened.

方 方 方

We kept Jerry Lee chained to a post in the back yard. The little rat terrier would get to running and never stop if he got a wild hair. I'd spent more than a few afternoons chasing him from darn near one side of the county to the other. He wasn't good for much, except for one thing, but Abbie loved him anyhow. As I rounded the corner, I saw my sister kneeling down beside the black and white dog. She scratched behind his ears, and he wagged his stubby tail. His tongue lolled out of his mouth.

"Come on, Jerry Lee!" I clapped my hands together. "We're going to the barn!"

As soon as he heard the word "barn," the dog jumped to attention, his muscles tense, his eyes darting and alert.

"Why'd you go and do that?" Abby stood up and put her hands on her hips defiantly. "We were having us a relaxing time."

"We don't keep him around to be your pet."

"You're just jealous because he's *my* best friend."

"A dog like this, he ain't nobody's friend." I unhooked Jerry Lee's chain from the post in the ground. I held one end of the chain like a leash. "You're a dyed-in-the-wool killer, ain't ya, boy?"

Jerry Lee tugged at the chain.

Abbie wrinkled her nose and shot me a raspberry.

"I wish a green fly would land on your tongue," I said.

Jerry Lee pulled in the direction of the barn. He might have been small, but he was strong. I kept a firm grip on the chain. For Jerry Lee, the barn meant one thing.

Rats.

He jumped and yipped as Abbie and I opened the barn doors. Light spilled across the dirt floor, chasing shadows into the corners. The barn was old and dark and smelled of dust. Along the wall leaned a couple of thick, three-foot long sticks. Abbie grabbed them and handed me one as I undid the chain around Jerry Lee's neck. He might have been a runner, but I didn't worry about him charging off while he was on the job. Sniffing the ground, he walked into the center of the barn, like he had done a hundred times before. A low growl rattled in his throat. He stood at attention, waiting.

Rats infested the barn. Big ones. Some almost as big as Jerry Lee. Nothing we did deterred them. Daddy had tried poisoning them with d-con, and for a while we discovered a bunch of mummified rat corpses in the corners. But eventually, they stopped taking the bait. We brought in barn cats, but some of them vanished altogether or – as I believed – were devoured by the rats, and the remaining felines decided to avoid the barn altogether. We lined the feed barrels with metal, but it wasn't long before the rodents gnawed right through. If a rat could gnaw through metal, I didn't want to think what it could do to flesh and bone.

I wasn't worried, though, because my sister and I were armed with the most lethal rat-killing weapon known to man.

Jerry Lee.

Abbie and I used the sticks to jab at the shadowy corners of the barn and behind feed barrels, flushing rats from hiding. As soon as the squealing vermin scurried across the room, Jerry Lee pounced. He clamped the rat in his jaws, gave it a quick shake, and tossed the creature – shattered spine and all – into the dust. On a good day, Jerry Lee could kill three dozen rats in an hour, and he never grew tired of the carnage. The whole time, Abbie wore a look of pure disgust as her favorite pet vented his bloodlust. I hate to admit it, but I almost enjoyed myself, and I made a little game out of scaring the rats into Jerry Lee's waiting teeth.

Once we were done, I chained the exhausted terrier to the yard post again. Panting, he flopped on his side to rest. Abbie and me carried out the gruesome task of scooping up the crushed, slobber-matted rat carcasses, tossing them in burlap sacks, and dumping them in the burn barrels around back. I got the feeling the surviving rats watched us with hate-filled eyes from the darkness, but they didn't dare creep out of hiding. We tossed the last of the dead rats in the barrels, and Abbie mopped sweat and dust from her forehead with the back of her arm.

"Think we can go to the pond now?" she asked.

"You heard what Daddy said."

"He don't really care. Besides, he's too busy showing Cole around."

My stomach knotted up at the mention of his name. Maybe getting away from the farm, even for a couple of minutes, wasn't such a bad idea.

"All right." I shrugged. "Let's go."

She grinned at me and dashed off.

Jerry Lee hopped up, growled, and *chuffed* a quiet warning. He stood defiantly in the circle of dirt he'd worn in the grass from his prowling, but he stared towards the front of the house. I followed his gaze, and saw Daddy talking to the hired man. Cole didn't seem to be paying much attention to whatever Daddy was saying. Instead, he looked back at me.

I jumped when Abbie called out to me.

"You coming, Seth?"

She stood at the edge of the corn field, shifting from one foot to the other, almost like she had to pee. I moved towards her, but glanced over my shoulder.

I realized something that chilled my blood.

The hired man wasn't looking at me.

He was staring at my sister.

Giggling, Abbie raced through the corn field. Tall stalks loomed around us. Soon, it would be harvest time. Not long after that, the field would be beaten flat in preparation for next season's crops. For now, though, a thick sea of cornstalks enveloped us. I followed Abbie as she weaved back and forth between the rows, kicking up dirt clods, making the stalks shake and sway. By the time we reached the pond, I was covered in sweat and gulping down mouthfuls of hot, dusty air. My shirt and jeans clung wetly to my skin.

Situated right in the middle of the field, the pond was ringed by a high mound of dirt. Climbing to the crest of the earthen hill, I could see row after row of corn stretching off in every direction. Looking back the way we'd come, I saw the roofs of our house and the barn. In the distance ahead of us, I saw the grain silo of the McKinley place. The pond itself was a milky brown color, and was probably more mud than water.

My friends and I had played many a game of King of the Mountain on the hill, and I myself had been soaked in the pond's muddy shallows more than once upon being dethroned. We didn't play there much any more, though, not after what happened to Delroy McKinley last summer.

To me, the pond seemed lonely and bleak these days.

"I wish we could go swimming." Abbie still loved the spot. She liked throwing stones into the depths or launching paper sailing ships across the surface or watching tadpoles along the shoreline. She scooted down the hill and stood on the pond's bank. "It's hot enough, that's for sure."

"I wouldn't want to swim in that mudhole."

"You would too."

"Go ahead and take a dip if you want." I knew good and well she wouldn't. Abbie never swam in the pond, even before what happened to Delroy. "I'll stay right where I am, thank you very much. You enjoy yourself."

"Maybe I will."

She kicked off her shoes and dipped her toes in the water.

"Have fun," I said. "It'll just be you and Delroy."

"Shut up!" Abbie hopped back from the water as if she'd spotted a shark's fin slicing across the surface. "You ought not say that!"

"Well, it's true." I smiled wickedly. "They never did find his body."

"That's because he didn't drown. He ran away from home."

"If that's what you want to believe, that's fine. But I think he's down in the deep, dark water, sunk in the mud at the bottom so he don't float to the surface. But I bet if you go swimming he'll come up to give you a hug!"

I rolled my eyes back in my head and did my best stiff-legged, stiff-armed voodoo zombie impersonation, reaching out for my sister with spastic fingers.

Abbie shrieked.

Spiders might not have scared her, but ghosts were another story.

She scurried up the hill and pushed past me. She didn't even bother to pick up her shoes.

"You're a jerk, Seth!"

She crashed through the corn stalks and vanished. I had a good laugh at her expense, but it only lasted a few seconds. If Abbie broke our agreement and told on me, Mama and Daddy would be none too pleased with me for frightening my sister. I scrambled down the hill to grab her shoes, then climbed back up and hurried after her.

The leaves of the corn stalks slapped me in the face as I called for my sister. Somewhere up ahead, I heard Jerry Lee's high-pitched barking. It might have been easy for someone who didn't know any better to get lost among the cornstalks, but I would have known the way home with my eyes closed. When I emerged on the other side of the field, I found Abbie, standing in the back yard. My heart jumped in my chest.

The hired man was on his knees in front of her, and he held her hands in his own.

I rushed to her side.

"What's wrong?"

Abbie pulled her hands away from the hired man. "N-nothing," she said. Her face was flushed.

Cole stood up. He towered over the two of us.

"Something spooked her pretty bad." He fished a pack of cigarettes from his breast pocket. "I'd hate to think her big brother was trying to scare the poor little thing to death."

Ain't none of your business, I thought, but I didn't say a word.

"There's plenty of things to be scared of out in the world," Cole said. "Hell, I bet some of them would even scare the spit out of a big, strapping boy such as yourself. How about that, you ever been real scared, Seth?"

I ignored him and took Abbie's hand.

"Come on. We need to get cleaned up for supper."

"I bet you have." Cole sneered. "I bet you've been so scared you nearly wet your pants from time to time."

I pulled my sister along as I walked away from the hired man. I trembled like I'd been out in the cold. His words chased after me, nipped at my heels.

I *felt* his eyes watching me.

Watching Abbie.

方 方 方

We should have burned the rats.

Daddy didn't like us manning the burn barrel without him around, but we'd done it before, more than once.

Maybe if we had burned the dead rats right away, everything would have turned out differently.

That's a silly thing to think, of course. The rats didn't cause the troubles that beset our farm. They were just the first of the symptoms.

Symptoms, like with a disease.

A disease Cole Jensen brought down upon us.

We went to bed pretty early that night, because Daddy's hands were worrying him something fierce, and Mama, who was due to give birth to my baby brother or sister any day, wasn't feeling good at all. I shared a bedroom with Abbie. It might have been a nice place to rest my head. It was plenty big, and the second story window overlooked a good portion of the farm, including the barn and the new tool shed. But an imaginary line split the room in two. On one side was my stuff – my matchbox cars and comic books and Indian arrowhead collection. The other side was done up in pinks and flowers and paint-by-number portraits of ponies. The room could have been the size of a castle and it still wouldn't be big enough for my little sister and me. Abbie's side of the room seemed to grow larger with each passing day, while mine became more and more claustrophobic.

In a few months, I thought. *I'll be thirteen. That's too old to be sharing a room with my sister.*

I had hoped that when the baby was born, my folks might let me move out to the guest quarters in the tool shed. Mama didn't like the idea, but Daddy thought I was plenty old enough. It had been a long time since I'd had any real privacy, and I had big plans for fixing up the room. Now that Cole was living out in the shed, my dreams had been dashed. With my luck, I'd soon be sharing a crowded room with Abbie *and* the new baby's crib.

The hired man had been there for just one day, and I was already anxious for his departure.

I sat in bed, reading an issue of *Famous Monsters of Filmland.* Abbie lay on her belly on her own bed and played with a set of paper dolls. We both liked to stay up as late as we could, regardless of how tired we'd be the next day at school. Sleeping was for babies and old folks.

Outside, Jerry Lee barked. I didn't really pay attention at first, but the dog kept on yapping, like something was driving his poor little doggie brain into a frenzy.

"What's that mutt going on about?" I put my magazine aside. "Daddy's gonna wring his neck if he don't shut up."

"Maybe there's somebody out there," Abbie said. "Somebody who shouldn't be."

Yeah, I thought, *like Cole.*

Maybe Jerry Lee *was* barking at the hired man. After all, the dog didn't know him at all, and it was likely he sensed something strange about him. Dogs had a keen nose for such things.

Something crashed outside – a metallic thud and rattle.

I knew right away what it was.

The burn barrel.

I hopped out of bed. Every now and again, raccoons or possums got into the trash, and it was usually my job to run them off. If I didn't haul my behind out there and scare them away tonight, there'd be trash and dead rats strewn from one end of the farm to the other come morning. And I knew who'd get stuck with the chore of cleaning up the mess. Better to take care of it now rather than later.

Abbie started getting dressed, too, and she dragged the flashlight out from the top dresser drawer. One thing about my sister – she was plenty curious, even about the smallest things. There was no way she was going to let me got out there by myself.

The farm was dark and quiet, except for Jerry Lee's incessant barking. I was a little surprised Daddy hadn't heard the racket. Sometimes at night he took pain medicine for his hands, and the stuff near about knocked him out. That might be the only thing saving Jerry Lee's life.

Abbie carried the flashlight, and the glow bounced across the ground ahead of us. The barn rose out of the shadows like a great fortress.

A fortress full of rats.

The blinds were drawn over the window to the tool shed's guest room. The room was dark. Obviously, Cole could sleep like the dead, too.

Abbie flashed the light around the corner of the barn. Sure enough, the burn barrel lay on its side. It rocked gently back and forth. Trash spilled out of the mouth. My sister turned the light towards Jerry Lee. His eyes gleamed in the dark. He pulled at his chain as he barked at the overturned barrel.

"Hush!" I hissed at him. "Be quiet now!"

I approached the barrel and lifted it back upright, spilling a little more garbage onto the ground. Something twitched at my feet. Dozens of smallish forms crawled all around me. At first, I thought an entire family of possums had gotten into the trash and were now scurrying all around the barrel. But I saw the burlap sack spread out across the ground.

Saw the hole ripped in the cloth.

Abbie pressed up behind me. She aimed the flashlight's beam at the ground.

"Look, Seth! Look!"

Those rats had been dead as doornails when we threw them in the barrel. I would have put my hand on the Bible and sworn it. But they were alive now...and squirming and squealing and hissing in the dirt.

I backed away.

Slowly.

"What's wrong with them?" Abbie asked.

Some of the rats writhed and wriggled towards us, but they moved in herky-jerky spasms. Others just squirmed around in circles. Still others simply trembled and spasmed violently where they lay.

"They almost look like they're dancing," Abbie said.

But they weren't dancing, not really, and they weren't alive, either. The rats we'd tossed into the burn barrel had been ripped and torn and broken by Jerry Lee's attack. Blood still covered their fur. The hair and skin peeled away from the glistening flesh of a few of the rodents. At least one trailed a fleshy strand of its own guts. There was no way the rats should have been convulsing and scrabbling and shimmying before us.

They were dead.

And they were dancing.

Behind me, Jerry Lee barked.

"Abbie," I said, "quiet Jerry Lee down before he wakes up the entire county. I've got to get something from the barn."

"What are you gonna do?"

"Just keep the dog quiet, ok?"

Abbie nodded and rushed to Jerry Lee's side. She calmed him as best she could, but he still woofed and growled.

From the barn, I gathered a shovel and another cloth sack. I saw the red eyes of the other rats – the living rats – staring at me from the shapeless dark.

I hurried back to the burn barrel and laid the sack open on the ground. Using the shovel, I scooped up the shuddering rat carcasses and tossed them into the bag. As I bent down to shovel up one of the rats, the creature twisted and lurched at me. I dropped the shovel and staggered away, but the rat sank its fangs into the meat of my palm.

"Ahh!"

The dead rat clamped its teeth into my flesh. I flung my arm about wildly, trying to shake the rat free. My hand stung where the rat bit me…

But it was also cold.

Like ice.

Only colder.

For a second, I felt like I was sinking into icy water.

Finally, I flung the rat to the ground. Clutching my hand, I drew my foot back and kicked the rat. It squeaked and rolled across the ground.

My hand bled from several small puncture marks. The skin around the wound looked dry and gray. Several black veins ran across my skin, leading away from the bite. I felt like I'd stuck my hand against a piece of frozen pipe. As I watched, the dark markings faded and the color returned to my skin. All that remained was the bite marks.

What in the world…

Thankfully, I didn't think the bite was serious enough to need stitches. It was going to hurt like Hell over the next few days, though. I flexed my fingers. The memory of the sudden, strange coldness lingered in my nerves.

I snatched up the shovel and used the flat end to bash each and every one of the rats. Some of them stopped moving as soon as I smashed them. A few others needed three or four good whacks before they lay still. The one that bit me, I must have hit a dozen times or more, and when I was done there wasn't much left of it but a puddle. Then I went back and finished off the rats I'd already tossed in the bag before they got a chance to gnaw through the burlap. When I finished, a greasy stain covered the sack-cloth.

My hand throbbed. Blood dribbled down my fingers.

I tied the bag's opening into a knot.

Jerry Lee had stopped his barking altogether now that the rats were dead.

Really dead.

I looked at my sister.

"Why don't you go back inside. I'll be along directly."

"Where are you going?"

"I'm gonna bury this bag out in the field." I tested the weight of the sack. "I'm not sure how far just yet, but out somewhere we won't find it again, I hope."

"And then what are we gonna do?"

I looked out into the darkness of the field. The stalks hissed at me in the wind. The sound reminded me of whispered secrets.

"Then we'll try to forget what we saw."

I only wish we could have put the night behind us.

But, like I said, the rats were only the beginning.

方 方 方

On the bus ride to school, I asked Abbie to keep what she'd seen secret. She'd managed to get through breakfast without mentioning the rats, mainly because Mama was still in bed feeling poorly and Daddy was already working the farm. We had made ourselves cereal and toast, and we'd eaten in silence. I didn't know if she'd be able to make it through the entire day without telling her friends. I'll admit, I wanted to tell my buddies about the rats, too. I was sure I could spin one helluva yarn.

But something about the rats…

Something told me this was one of those secrets that needed to stay buried.

"It might be best if we keep our mouths shut about last night," I whispered. Abbie had her forehead pressed against the window, and she sighed as she watched the world pass by. For her, the ride to school every morning might as well have been a trip down death row. "We should keep this between us, I think, at least for a little while. Abbie? Are you listening to me?"

"I hear you." She scrunched up her face the way she did when she saw or smelled something disgusting. "I don't even like thinking about those rats. Why would I want to tell anyone?"

"Swear?"

I held out my hand, and Abbie wrapped her pinky around mine.

"Swear," she said.

For Abbie and me, a pinky swear was just as good as a blood oath. She could always go back on her word – either of us could – but to do so was unheard of when it came to me and my sister.

She'd let the story die. In time, she might even forget about it altogether.

My hand ached like you wouldn't believe. I'd bandaged it up as best I could. Blood had already seeped through the gauze. If somebody asked me how I'd hurt myself, I'd just tell them I slipped and cut my hand on my pocket knife.

Eventually, the bite would heal, and I doubted it would scar.

As long as the rats stayed dead, we'd be all right.

方 方 方

Some time after sunset, Jerry Lee started barking again. The memory of those rats, shuddering and jumping on the ground, biting me with their icy teeth, sent a shiver up my spine. Daddy was having a devil of a time with his rheumatism, and even though Mama had cooked up some oats to soothe his swollen knuckles, he was in a foul temperament.

"Seth," he said, "go out there and do something about that dog. His barking's getting on my last nerve."

I didn't often hear such an edge in my father's voice. Daddy wasn't a cruel man by any stretch of the imagination, but he wasn't one to trifle with, either, especially when the dreadful pain in his hands flared. I put my homework aside and stood.

"Come on, Abbie."

My little sister, who had finished her own homework and was busy coloring, put aside her crayons.

"Leave her be," Daddy said. "Can't you do this on your own?"

I looked down. "Yes, sir."

Abbie pouted, but returned to her coloring book. I didn't need her help, but I would have certainly felt more comfortable with her by my side. That's something I would have never admitted back then, but these days, I don't see any reason to deny it.

Daddy winced at the dog's yipping.

"Just hush him up. I don't care if you have to bring him inside with you."

That last drew a stern look out of my mother, who hated the idea of having animals in the house. Daddy didn't notice the look, though, and Mama decided not to argue.

The night air was still, and the only sound was that of Jerry Lee barking up a storm. I stomped down the steps and around the house to where we kept him leashed, but the dog wasn't there. His chain lay in a silvery pile on the ground. The clip on the business end of the leash was snapped open. That happened sometimes, usually when Jerry Lee tugged and pulled too hard. I still heard him barking, though, so I figured he hadn't gone far. I hollered and clapped for him. For a second, he stopped barking, and I halfway thought he might be heeding my call. But only a few seconds passed before he started yapping again – this time louder than before. Sighing, I followed the sound.

Jerry Lee stood guard outside the old shed – the one with the sagging roof and crumbling old walls. The door to the shed stood ajar, and the little dog vented his fury in the direction of the opening. The pitch of his snarling sounded different up close – less menacing and more frightened – and he didn't dare take another step towards the building. I walked right up and hooked my fingers around his collar. I gave him a quick jerk to quiet him. He yelped and looked up at me.

"What's gotten into you? You keep making such a ruckus and Daddy will haul your sorry hide to the pound."

Jerry Lee cocked his head to the side and regarded me with large eyes that seemed to say, "*What's the matter with you? Can't you tell something's wrong here?*" Then, he caught wind of something in the shed again, and despite the fact that I had ahold of him, he started barking again. He thrashed and jumped so violently, he almost pulled free of my hand, and nothing I did seemed to calm him.

More than likely, one of the lazy barn cats had managed to nudge the door to the old shed open and had crept inside. If not cats, then maybe—

Rats.

I thought of those dead rats…dancing…and I started to drag Jerry Lee away from the shed. As I looked up, I saw a shadow move beyond the open door. Whatever it was, it didn't look much like one of the cats to me.

"Who's there?" I asked. No one answered. I asked again – "Who's there?" – this time raising my voice to be heard over the dog's frenzied barking.

I knew I should just hurry back inside and tell Daddy what I'd seen. If there was a prowler about, Daddy would see to running him off. But I also knew that if I was just jumping at shadows – and shadows were, after all, the only thing I'd seen – my father would be none-too-pleased, considering his mood.

I stepped closer to the shed. *Just a peek*, I told myself, *before I jump to conclusions.* Bolstered by my company, Jerry Lee cautiously followed. A low growl settled in his throat.

I looked inside. Daddy threatened on a regular basis to tear the old shed down. We didn't use it any more, but my father must have had a soft spot for the old shed, like he believed it added a kind of weed-overgrown charm to the farm. Inside, deep pools of shadow gathered in the corners, spreading along the walls. Here and there, weak beams of moonlight shone through small holes in the rusty ceiling and rotting walls. Dust spun lazily in the damp light.

I didn't see any skulking prowler, though, so I stepped inside for a better look.

"Ugh!"

A veil of sticky webs swept across my face. I spat and frantically slapped the sticky strands away. Even after the webs were gone, I continued to brush at my face, and I imagined spiders crawling all over me.

Jerry Lee growled at the darkness.

"Come on, boy."

Suddenly, the shadows didn't look so empty. It seemed as though the shed had grown in the darkness, swelled inside to hold all the haints and goblins of the world. I wished I had brought the flashlight with me.

I heard a faint humming somewhere above. I looked up. The pale moonlight shimmered through a delicate canopy of webbing overhead. Here and there, small, dark objects were entangled in the web – almost like stars dotting the night sky, only if the sky was white and the stars were black as pitch. Flies, I realized and wasps and horseflies and snake doctors, all caught in the webs and long dead.

Only, they weren't dead at all.

Each and every one of the insects twitched and buzzed in the web, wings vibrating, legs quivering as they tried to free themselves. The entire blanket of webs trembled overhead, and I worried that the frantic spasms of the trapped insects might bring the whole thing down on top of me like a net.

One of the insects – a large horsefly – shook free and plummeted to the dirt floor. It lay on its back, wings buzzing, legs kicking frantically. Jerry Lee took a step towards the bug, lowering his head to take a sniff. I grabbed his collar again and pulled him back.

The horsefly was nothing more than a shell, an exoskeleton hollowed out of all the meat within by the spiders living in the webs. It was a dead thing – had probably been dead for weeks or longer – but it still moved as if alive. The horsefly managed to right itself, and it began crawling in crazy patterns upon the floor.

Something...foul...was happening on our farm, something bringing the dead back to life.

For the first time, I noticed all the buzzing and chirps and clicks, not just coming from the death's web above, but from all around. From the shadows along the left wall, a trio of desiccated crickets scurried. They, like the horsefly, were but empty shells. One of them was missing a leg. Another looked as if it had been crushed at some point. Across the room, I spotted a large, dead spider scurrying crab-like in the dirt, only half of its legs working like they should.

More insects fell from above.

Something buzzed past my ear.

Jerry Lee snapped his jaws at empty air as a dead fly swooped by.

I took a step back, pulling the dog along.

Another.

And I backed into the man who stood behind me.

Cole placed a firm hand on my shoulder to hold me still as he looked around the shed. His cold gaze lingered on the crawling insects, then he looked up at the web.

"They're dead!" I blurted. "They're dead but they're still alive."

Cole took a half-step, and crushed the twitching horsefly under his boot. The *crunch!* seemed as loud as a gunshot. Still, he held onto me, even as I held onto Jerry Lee. The dog snarled and growled, this time at Cole himself, and struggled against my grasp. The hired man paid the dog no mind. He squatted down in front of me, so he could look me in the eye.

"Don't let them touch you," he said.

I wanted to get out of the barn and away from the dead things, but Cole held me fast, his fingernails digging through my shirt and into my shoulder.

"Ow," I whined. "Let go!"

"Listen to me." Cole's gravelly voice was low. A halo of dead flies seemed to circle around him. "Some secrets are meant only for the dead. I'd hate for your mama or daddy to learn a hard lesson because you've been seeing spooks."

He gave me a quick shake.

"Some secrets are meant only for the *dead*," he said again. "Get me?"

I didn't answer. At least, I don't think I did. For all I know, I might have agreed with him, then recited the Gettysburg Address and the Pledge of Allegiance. The world around me seemed to be a chaotic, chittering mess, and my mind couldn't seem to get a lock on anything tangible.

Cole released me, and I stumbled from the shed. I didn't remember doing so, but I had scooped Jerry Lee up in my arms. I clutched him close, hugging him. He fidgeted and whined but I didn't let him go.

Cole didn't follow me, and I didn't dare look back to see what he was doing. I pictured him stomping and crushing all the dead insects in the barn, dancing a grim jig on their empty, fragile shells. And I imagined him smiling as he went about his work.

"Some secrets are meant only for the dead. Get me?"

His words and his sneer and the foulness of his breath haunted me.

My mother saw me carrying the dog into the house, and she pursed her lips in disapproval.

"I couldn't keep him quiet any other way."

I forgot all about my homework and carried the dog upstairs to my room. Abbie, excited to have Jerry Lee's company for the night, bounded upstairs after me, giggling all the way.

Her happiness left me cold.

I lay in my small bed and stared at the ceiling. On the other side of the room, Abbie laughed as she used a corner of her bed sheet to play tug-of-war with Jerry Lee. The dog growled playfully as he tried to pull the covers from her grip. Jerry Lee lived only in the here and now, and he had already forgotten what had happened in the old shed. I envied him.

Something tapped lightly against the window pane. A moth fluttered just outside, flying into the glass again and again in a futile attempt to reach the light within. After several attempts, the moth gave up and flew away.

I wondered if it had been alive or dead.

方 方 方

The next day, I couldn't pay attention in class, and Mrs. Sutton jumped on me for daydreaming more than once. She even threatened to send a letter home to my parents if I didn't shape up. It didn't help that I hadn't finished my homework the night before. When the final bell rang, I stepped out of school with the usual amount of homework…and orders to finish what I'd skipped the night before…and an assignment to write an essay about why paying attention in class is important.

None of that mattered, of course, not as long as I worried over the evil stirring back home.

Now more than ever, I was convinced that Cole had brought it with him.

"Some secrets are meant only for the dead."

Even if not for Cole's threat, I couldn't tell my father what I was thinking. I guess there comes a time in every boy's life when their fathers stop believing them, at least for a little while. Maybe he thought I always had my head in the clouds, that I spent too much time playing and making up stories, that I read too many comic books. It might have bothered me on the best of days, but now – when something awful was unfolding all around me – it ate away at my insides as if I had swallowed a belly-full of those dead insects.

"Why're you so quiet?" Abbie asked as we walked along the road. Our house was only a couple of miles from school, and while we could have ridden the bus, walking got us home more directly. "What's wrong with you?"

"Nothing."

She didn't argue, but she didn't believe me, either.

Daddy and Cole were working on the old tractor when we

got home. Unlike the rats and the bugs, the tractor didn't show any signs of coming back to life. Daddy's hands were still hurting. I could tell by the way he held them close, protecting them, not wanting to so much as brush them against anything. He watched over Cole's shoulder as the hired man took a wrench to the tractor's guts.

I didn't like my father working so closely with Cole. What's more, I hated the nagging idea that if it came down to believing me or Cole, Daddy would take the hired man's side in an instant.

I silently wished the tractor's engine would suddenly spring to life, clamp down on Cole's hands, and yank him into the engine and mulch him among the gears.

Cole stretched his back, wiped his brow, and stared at me. His mouth was set in a tight, toothless smirk. He stared me right in the eye, trying to cow me, daring me to look away. I forced myself to meet his gaze for as long as I could, but I only made it a few steps before turning my eyes towards my feet. I could feel his smile grow.

A rush of heat washed over my neck and face.

In that moment, I hated myself almost as much as I hated the hired man.

方 方 方

At supper that evening, I decided I could no longer keep my mouth shut. I don't rightly know what got into me. The questions just sort of slipped out.

"How much longer are we gonna need him working here?"

"What's that?" Daddy asked.

"Cole." I put my fork on he edge of my plate. I wasn't hungry any way. "How long is he going to be here?"

Mama glanced at Daddy, then looked at me. "Why?" she asked. "Don't you like him?"

I shrugged.

"There's nothing wrong with that man," Daddy said. "He's just trying to make a living same as the next. And he's already been a damn big help around here, especially considering the wage I pay. He's only been here a couple of days. Let's not run him off just yet."

"He's—"

My words fell short.

"The dead. Get me?"

What would I have said anyway? *"He's bringing the dead back to life just by being here."* I could envision Daddy's reaction to something like that, and it wasn't pretty.

"Seth thinks he's creepy," Abbie said, almost cheerfully. "Cole gives him the wiggins."

"Does not," I said.

But everyone around the table knew she was right.

"Well—" Mama clumsily rose from her seat. She kept one hand on her round belly, the other braced upon the edge of the table as she pushed herself up. "—it never hurts to help someone who's down on his luck. And like your father said, he's been very helpful."

"That's right." Daddy sat back. His chair creaked like straining bones. "But if it makes you feel any better, son, I don't imagine he'll stay with us more than a few more weeks. I'll be sorry to see him go, truth be told, but I can see it in his eyes. A man like that, he don't stay in one place for too long."

"Sounds like you envy him a bit." A smile played at Mama's lips.

"Maybe I do." Daddy smiled back at her. It was a forced effort, because he was still in dreadful pain. He started to reach out and take her hand, almost like he'd forgotten the gnarled claws his hands had become. He stopped himself let his hands fall to his lap. He winked at her. "Almost every man longs to be free every now and again."

"Well—" Mama's words were light and playful. "—you think about how cold it's going to be come winter before you go a-wandering." She rose from her chair and whispered something in Daddy's ear. Daddy smiled and laughed. Mama laughed, too, and pretty soon Abbie was giggling right along with them, even though she hadn't been let in on the joke.

I didn't laugh, though. I didn't think anything was funny. Cole couldn't leave our farm fast enough for my tastes.

And Daddy might have seen a restless soul in Cole's eyes, but I knew the truth. I'd known the truth since the moment I first laid eyes on the hired man.

He was running from something.

Daddy stood up from the table. "Seth, why don't you go ahead and bring the dog in for the night?"

"Why's that?" Mama asked. "I haven't heard a peep out of him."

"And I'd like to keep it that way, too." Daddy looked at me, almost pleadingly. "Please, son, just bring him in."

"Yes, sir."

I staggered to a stop as I stepped outside. My breath caught in tightening throat. Cole sat on the front steps, finishing his supper. He glanced back at me, nodded, then returned to sopping up gravy with a bit of cornbread. He didn't make way as I descended the steps, and my leg brushed his shoulder.

"Is it true what they said?" he asked.

"Huh?"

"Is it true? Do I scare you?"

We usually only keep the screen door closed in the early evening. From the front porch, Cole must have heard every word coming from inside. He fixed me with those cold, dead eyes of his.

"You scared of me?"

"No."

"Don't lie to me." He dropped his plate to the steps. The silverware clattered against the plate. "Because I ain't going to lie to you."

"What do you mean?"

He looked back at the front door to make sure no one else was listening. "What your daddy said, about me moving on soon? He's wrong. I ain't going nowhere, not for a long while."

He used his fingers to wipe grease from his lips, and nodded to himself as if entertaining a cruel notion.

"No," he said, "I like it here."

方 方 方

"There's somebody outside," Abbie said.

"Probably just Cole having a smoke."

"I don't think so."

She stood at the bedroom window, staring out into the yard. The curtains draped over her head and shoulders, and she looked like a sheet ghost, the way she just stood there, real still, staring.

I sat on the floor, my back propped against the side of the bed. Jerry Lee lay next to me, his head across my legs. I leafed through a big stack of horror comic books I'd bought for ten cents at the flea market. I usually enjoyed the eeriness of the stories. *House of Mystery* was my favorite, but I liked *Witching Hour* and *Dr. Graves* and *Screamfest*, too. But tonight I didn't take pleasure in the tales of murder or monsters or ghosts.

Or curses.

One of the stories was about a man who'd been cursed by an old gypsy woman. Everywhere he looked, the man saw awful, twisted monsters. His boss, his best friend, even the pretty girl he met at the park – they all looked like hideous monsters. The ghastly sights drove him mad until, while crossing a bridge, he looked over the edge and saw a tentacle-covered, many-eyed thing staring back at him from the waters below. He hurled himself over the side of the bridge and to his death below.

The idea nagged at me.

Maybe Cole was cursed, too; only his curse was that wherever he went, the dead grew restless. Maybe not all the dead; otherwise, every place he visited would be crawling with the zombies, like in *Night of the Living Dead*. Maybe only the unburied dead came to life when Cole was nearby. Maybe—

"What's he doing out there?" Abbie said.

I shivered like someone had just traipsed across my grave. I tossed the comics aside and went to the window. Jerry Lee growled softly. There have been times in my life when I knew deep down in my bones that I didn't want to see whatever it was I was about to look upon. This was probably the first of those times, but I went to the window just the same.

A boy – just a little older than me by the looks of him – wandered around our yard. He was skinny and pale – so pale that his skin seemed to glow in the moonlight, so skinny I could count his ribs. He was blonde-headed, and his hair was matted wetly to his scalp. He wore only a pair of cut-off jeans, and they were soaked, too, the denim dark and sodden, the long strings dangling from the hem and stuck to the boy's bare legs. He staggered across the yard like he'd been hitting a secret stash of home-brewed whiskey pretty hard.

"What's he looking for?" Abbie asked. "Who is he? Do we go to school with him?"

"I don't know. I can't see his face."

I had no sooner uttered the words than the boy shrugged around, and I got a good look at him.

Abbie moaned and turned her head. She still gripped the window sill. The blood drained from her fingertips she held on so tight.

For a second or two, I didn't quite understand what…who…I was looking at.

Then it hit me like a speedball to the gut.

Delroy McKinley.

He had drowned in the swimming hole last summer, but there he was, plain as day, shambling around behind my house. His wet hair hung in tendrils in front of his face, but I could tell—

"He's got no eyes," Abbie whispered.

Where his eyes should have been were only gaping, pulpy sockets. I imagined fish and water bugs nibbling away at Delroy's body down in the cold, muddy depths. I got the notion that he could somehow still see, at least well enough to know he wasn't where he was supposed to be.

"Where's he going?"

He's lost, I thought.

The boy shambled past the barn…past the new tool shed…

A flare of red caught my eye.

A figure stood in the shadows between the barn and the shed.

His face lost in the shadows except when he took a deep drag on his smoke. The cigarette cherry painted his face in stark crimsons and deep blacks. He looked, I thought, like the Devil might look if he were spying a lost soul that had wandered into his stomping ground. Only, in this case, he stood guard over the farm, not Hell.

Cole. Abbie hadn't noticed the hired man, but I saw him. I couldn't tell if he was watching the dead boy or gazing up at me.

"Abbie, get back to bed," I whispered.

"But what about—"

"Don't argue. Get back in bed."

For a split second, Abbie looked like she might pitch a fit. Her face reddened, and a veil of tears glistened in her eyes. But she must have realized I meant business, and instead of crying, she crawled into the bed and threw the covers over her head. Jerry

Lee hopped onto the bed and burrowed under the covers with her.

"We should wake Daddy," Abbie muttered. "Daddy would know what to do."

She might have been right. Part of me wanted to wake Daddy, too.

"Some secrets are meant only for the dead," he had said.

And I knew the hired man would kill me, Abbie, Mama, Daddy, and anyone else who threatened to expose his vile secret. I had seen it in his eyes. He was no stranger to death.

More importantly, he was no stranger to killing.

"Only for the dead." And he had smiled as he said it. *"Get me?"*

Cole pulled himself away from the shadows. He dragged a rusty shovel behind him – the same shovel I'd used to kill the rats the second time. The point of the spade scratched a trail through the earth and spit up a tiny dust cloud. The hired man stalked up behind Delroy, and I couldn't help but watch, my eyes growing large , a scream catching in my throat. The dead boy didn't see or hear Cole's approach. As the hired man raised the shovel, his face twisted into a grimace of disgust and rage.

He brought the shovel down, and Delroy's head came open like a pumpkin dashed against the pavement on the day after Halloween. The dead boy fell, and Cole stepped after him, raising the shovel again and bringing it down sharply. Delroy didn't scream, but he squirmed and kicked on the ground as Cole bashed at him with the shovel. He grasped blindly for his attacker, and Cole was careful not to let Delroy touch him. Flesh and bone gave way beneath the assault. Bits of pale skin and chunks of meaty tissue caked the shovel's head, but there was no blood left in the corpse. Only cold water spilled across the ground. Black-shelled insects that had been nesting in the boy's body scurried for safety. As Cole continued to strike the dead boy, he turned his gaze towards my window.

Get me? His eyes seemed to say.

At last, Delroy lay still.

Cole tossed the shovel aside and grabbed the dead boy by the ankles. He dragged the corpse across the yard and around the side of the barn. I figured Cole was dragging the body off into the fields somewhere.

Just like I had done with the rats.

"What is it?" Abbie asked. "What's happening?"

"Nothing," I lied. "It's over."

"The boy…"

"He's dead."

I should have said the boy was gone – not dead – but the truth sort of slipped out.

"What's going to happen to us?" Abbie asked.

This time, I found the wherewithal to lie.

"We're going to be fine. Just fine."

方 方 方

I dreamed about dead rats, only they weren't dancing.

They were eating me.

The rotting, broken creatures scurried and scrabbled and spasmed across my body, tunneling under my clothes, gnashing at me with needle-like teeth. Their filthy nails scraped at my flesh as they climbed up my legs, across my privates, over my belly – moving towards my face. They squealed and chattered…

And whispered.

The rats hissed through blood-soaked sneers, and their voices sounded like the hired man.

"*We're gonna eat you up, and there's nothing you can do about it. Get me?*"

Their touch was as cold as ice. I felt black veins spreading through my body like icy worms crawling beneath my skin.

I frantically brushed the rats away, but they clawed at my arms, snapped at my fingers. I tried to scream for help, but one of the dead rats leaped into my mouth, and I tasted the musk of its fur, the rush of my blood down my throat as the creature sank its fangs into my tongue.

I jumped up in bed, gasping.

And they were gone.

I could still taste the blood in the back of my throat, but the rats were nowhere to be seen.

Abbie slept quietly in the other bed. Beside her, Jerry Lee raised his head and looked at me.

I pulled my pillow close to my face so they couldn't hear me crying.

I knew I was going to have to stop Cole before something awful happened, and I got my chance the very next day.

I failed.

方 方 方

When we got home from school, I noticed right away that Daddy's pickup was gone.

"Something's wrong," I said.

"Maybe he just went to town for something," Abbie suggested.

"No. Something's wrong. I just know it."

I felt it deep in my gut, like a nest of ice cold eels wriggling in my belly.

I crossed the yard with my sister in tow. I don't even remember my feet touching the porch steps I climbed them so fast. As I pulled the screeching screen door open, I looked around the farm. I didn't see any sign of Cole, but I thought I detected a trace of cigarette smoke hanging in the air. The hired man was around somewhere – I just knew it, just like I knew that if something bad had happened, he was responsible.

"Mama?" I called.

The house was too quiet. Too warm. Sweat tickled my collar.

I yelled for my mother again as I roamed from room to room.

No response.

My heart slammed in my chest. A terrible image flashed through my mind – Cole Jensen tossing the mutilated bodies of my parents into the bed of the pickup, driving out to the middle of nowhere and dumping them in the weeds to rot. I squeezed my eyes shut, wished the idea out of my head.

It wasn't so unusual for my parents to be gone when we got home, but it wasn't an everyday occurrence, either. But nothing seemed out of place. I saw no sign of a struggle. If it hadn't been for Cole lurking around the farm, I might not have thought twice about it.

Abbie yelled, "Mama?" but no one answered.

I almost missed the slip of paper on the kitchen counter, but I breathed a little easier as soon as I saw the hastily written message.

"Gone to town." The handwriting belonged to Daddy. "Be back soon."

Almost an afterthought:

"Make yourselves supper."

I was shaking and sweating and out of breath. I steadied myself and read the note to Abbie. She smiled.

"See? Told you there was nothing to worry about."

"I guess. I wonder where they went."

"Maybe they're at the hospital!" Abbie beamed. "Maybe mama's having the baby! Maybe when they get back I'll be a big sister."

That might have been a possibility. Mama was due just about any day. But the note didn't say anything about the baby.

We grabbed our book bags and headed up to our rooms. It was a strange and exciting feeling, having the house to ourselves, even if just for a little while. Like we were growing up. When Mama and Daddy got home, everything would be different. We'd have a new member of our family. I couldn't even begin to imagine all the adjustments we'd need to make. Still, for a brief moment, I felt excited and happy.

Hopeful.

I smelled the cigarette smoke just as I opened the bedroom door.

I'm pretty sure my heart skipped a beat.

"Come on in," the hired man said.

He sat on the edge of my bed. One of Abbie's stuffed toys lay in his lap. He paged casually through one of my comics. His big, meaty fingers crinkled the cover.

"What are you doing in here?" I asked.

"Thought I'd make sure you two children were all right, seeing how your folks aren't around."

"We're fine." The eels swam frantically through my bowels again. I tried not to let my voice shake, for all the good it did me. "Now, get out."

Cole looked past me. Abbie stood in the hallway, her eyes wide.

"It's her room, too," Cole said. "How 'bout it, little darling? You want me to leave?"

Abbie looked at me, then Cole.

I took a half-step closer to the hired man, positioned myself between him and my sister. "Doesn't matter what she wants. I'm the man of the house right now, and I told you to get out of my room."

"That right?"

Cole stood. The bedsprings creaked as he rose. He crumpled the comic book and tossed it to the floor.

I'd be a liar if I said I wasn't about to wet my pants.

Cole moved towards me.

"So, you're the man of the house, huh?"

He threw his head back and laughed like a villain from one of my comic books.

"Ain't but one man here," he said. "You're just a little boy can't keep his mouth shut."

"What do you want?"

"What I wanted was a few weeks of peace, but I ain't gonna get that I figure, thanks to you. And I thought we had an understanding."

"What are you talking about?"

"I saw you, last night, watching me. I know it's just a matter of time before you go sniveling to your Daddy about the boogieman. You probably said something already."

"I didn't—"

I wanted to tell him that it wouldn't have mattered even if I had said something. Daddy wouldn't have believed me.

Cole drew his hand back and slapped me. I don't think a mule could have kicked any more forcefully. I spun on my heels, slammed into the wall. My head spun. Everything went fuzzy for a second or two.

"Seth!" Abbie cried.

"Oh, he's all right, little darling." Cole's voice was a growl. "I just needed to teach the little bastard a lesson is all."

The floor creaked as he lunged across the room and grabbed my sister. He buried his fingers in her hair, yanked her close.

Abbie squeaked.

I moved towards them, but Cole swung Abbie out of my reach, like he was playing a game of keep-away. Abbie clutched at his arm, scratched at him, but he refused to let her go. His knuckles cracked as he clenched his other hand into a fist. He punched me in the stomach so hard my feet came off the ground.

"Oof!"

I went to my knees. I couldn't breathe. Couldn't think straight.

"I warned you not to say anything." Cole's voice seemed ever deeper than before. "Didn't I?"

"I…I didn't." My stomach turned. My lunch threatened to come up. "I swear."

Cole pitched his cigarette butt to the floor, stomped it out. He threw Abbie towards her bed. She tumbled across the mattress, and her skull struck the wall. She cried out, grabbed the back of her head, and curled up into a little ball.

I could barely string words together as I struggled to catch my breath.

"My Daddy…"

"Your daddy ain't here to help you. He's too worried about your mama. Seems like some d-con somehow got into her lunch. I wonder how something awful like that might happen…"

"You…"

"You should have heard her moaning and wailing as your daddy dragged her out to the truck. Hope he made it to the hospital on time. Hope the baby's all right, too."

I've never felt so angry in all my days. My every muscle trembled. I screamed like a wild animal as I threw myself at the hired man.

Cole smashed my face with his elbow. Blood leapt from my nose. I staggered away and fell. The side of my head struck the hardwood floor.

Cole raised his foot.

I flinched and threw my arms up to protect my face.

He planted his boot across my throat. He pressed down, near about crushing my Adam's apple. I wheezed and clawed at his leg, tried to push him away.

"You should have just let me be, boy. You should have let me be and you should have kept your mouth shut. I bet your sister can keep secrets even better than you. How about it, girl?" He looked at Abbie. "Can you keep a secret?"

He barked out another laugh when she didn't answer.

"Don't you touch her." I forced out the words. "Don't—"

"You just don't know when to quit, do you?"

God help me, I wanted to give up.

It would have been so much easier to just let darkness drag me down. But I couldn't leave my sister to Cole's whim.

Tears and bloody snot ran down my face.

"Leave…her…alone."

"God damn, but you are a stupid little bastard." Cole pulled his foot away, and he bent down. His fingers clamped down on my neck like a vice. He pulled me to my feet. My legs felt like rubber. My arms flopped uselessly at my sides. "All you had to do was lay there and play possum and I'd be gone by the time you woke up. But all of a sudden you want to act like some kind of tough guy."

I flailed weakly.

"Well, tough guys don't scare me none. I've known a whole bunch of them, and you'll never guess how every one of them ended up."

He grabbed hold of the front of my shirt, yanked me close.

I spat in his face.

His lips peeled from his teeth.

Cole shoved me as hard as he could. I felt my legs pedaling beneath me, my arms pin wheeling, my back smashing into the bedroom window.

Glass shattered.

I pitched backwards over the window sill.

The world spun out of control. The sky filled with glittering shards of broken glass. For a second, I felt weightless.

And then I landed.

My brain bounced in my skull. My teeth sank into my tongue, and my mouth filled with blood. My bones popped and snapped.

I couldn't move.

I wanted to, but couldn't.

I knew I was hurt pretty bad, but didn't feel much. I thought that was probably a bad thing.

Time seemed to slow.

I'm not sure how long I lay there.

All around me, the world dimmed.

I heard only the rush of my blood in my ears, like ocean waves breaking upon the shore.

The rush of blood.

And Abbie's screams.

方 方 方

Somewhere in the darkness, Mama called to me.

I heard the roar of the truck's engine…

...The front door slamming...

...Daddy's voice – or was that Cole? – yelling...

...Something crashing over...shattering...

...Cole, cursing...

...Mama, calling to me...

Her voice roused me.

"Seth, baby, are you all right? Oh, sweet Jesus, Seth."

Pain rushed in now, like water filling an empty glass.

I coughed. Blood speckled my lips, ran down my chin. I opened my eyes.

Mama looked down at me. Her face was blurry. She was pale, sweaty.

I still lay on the ground, but my mother knelt in the dirt next to me. She squeezed my hand. I just barely felt my fingers in her own. Every nerve in my body cried out in pain. My bones felt as though they were scraping against one another in all the wrong places. Dozens of tiny cuts covered my body.

"Seth, baby."

"Mama." My voice was little more than a rattling breath.

"Try not to move, baby, not until we know how bad you're hurt."

"Mama..."

"Shh. Just be still."

"Cole...Abbie..."

I was surprised I could move at all, but I managed to lift my head. From where I lay, I could see the shattered window of my bedroom. I could see the front porch, too, and Daddy's truck, parked crookedly, in front of the house. A cloud of dust still drifted in the air, settling upon the truck.

Suddenly, the front door whipped open and cracked on its hinges. The frame splintered as Cole Jensen toppled out of the house, smashing through the screen door. The wire mesh covered him like a funeral shroud. The hired man spun like a drunken ballerina, tripped on the ruins of the screen door, crashed through the porch railing and Mama's rose bushes. He fell on his ass...hard... and started kicking in the dirt, pushing himself away from the house.

I struggled to push myself up on my elbows.

Cole was bleeding from a split lip. His right eye was swollen shut. The flesh of his cheek was puffy and purple.

Daddy plowed out of the house like a rampaging bull. The cry that erupted from his lips was the most unearthly, inhuman thing I have ever heard.

I hated the sound of it.

Cole scrabbled to his feet, just as Daddy tackled him, knocking the air out of him. Both the hired man and my father slammed into the ground.

I tried to get up. Pain lanced up my legs.

Mama staggered to her feet. Her stomach was still large and round. The rat poison Cole had slipped her hadn't hurt the baby.

"Stay here," she told me.

Like I had much choice.

Daddy and Cole rolled around in a billowing cloud of dust. Daddy kept right on screaming as he pounded his fists into Cole's face over and over again. Cole flailed and tried to wriggle away, but Daddy dragged him back into the fight. The hired man didn't look so big and bad any more; he looked weak and afraid.

Cole's hand slipped into his pocket and reappeared holding a switchblade. The knife flicked open.

"Daddy!" I yelled.

The blade darted towards Daddy's face. My father jerked away, and the point of the knife nicked his cheek. Cole clambered to his feet, and he waved the blade back and forth before him, warding Daddy off.

My father couldn't even rise to his full height. He stood more like some sort of half-beast than a man. He hunched over, holding his trembling hands close. His fingers looked like raw, red hamburger. Tears and blood ran in mixing rivulets down his reddened face.

Cole flashed the knife from left to right. He kicked sand in my Daddy's direction.

"My children!" Mama shrieked.

She came at Cole with her fingernails bared. He turned towards her, and she clawed at his face. Her nails tore gashes across his forehead, and if he hadn't flinched away, Cole might have lost an eye.

He brought his knee up into her stomach.

Hard.

Mama wheezed and crumpled.

Daddy lunged at the hired man, but Cole's blade lashed out,

slashing through my father's arm. Daddy staggered away. Blood flowed between his fingers as he clutched at the cut.

Mama bled, too.

Between her legs, her dress was a crimson ruin. She grabbed feebly at her stomach, trying to protect her unborn child.

Cole spat blood and teeth to the ground.

"You stupid, fucks." He wiped the knife upon his pants leg, leaving a crimson arc on the denim. "You think I'll just let this pass? I'll fucking kill every one of—"

His words caught in his throat.

He looked past me, and his mouth opened and closed in silence, like a fish out of water.

A shadow passed over me.

Several shadows.

A half dozen figures walked past me.

Little girls, every one of them, some younger than Abbie, a couple older than me. Their skin was pale, their eyes the color of spoiled milk. They didn't so much walk as shamble. Some of them wore tattered dresses, and the fabric hissed softly. Others were dressed in soiled jeans and ripped blouses. Others wore nothing at all. I noticed purple bruises around the necks of a couple of the girls.

Dead, each and every one of them.

The knife slipped from Cole's fingers and embedded point-first in the earth.

Fear flashed through his eyes.

I knew what he'd been running from.

Cole had a hunger – a hunger that left the dead bodies of girls in his wake. But he also had a curse that brought the unburied dead to life. The girls he'd killed, they'd been searching for him. And they'd finally caught up with—

Their prey.

Cole turned to run, but Daddy threw out his bloodied arm and caught him across the throat. Cole's feet went out from under him, and he slammed to the ground.

The dead girls fell upon him.

Cole screamed.

The girls clawed at him, their fingernails shredding his clothing and peeling away strips of flesh. They scratched at his throat, his face, his chest, and stomach…and lower still.

"Get them off!" Cole's voice was shrill. "Get them off!"

Like I said, there are plenty of awful things I've seen that I never wanted to witness. This, however, I watched with joy.

He kicked and spasmed and trembled.

The dead rat danced.

Wherever the girls touched him, black veins spiderwebbed through his flesh. His skin turned grey as the rivers of black crawled beneath his skin, intersecting, forming pools of darkness. His flesh dried, began to flake. The girls were sharing bits of their death with him, pulling him down into the cold depths of nothingness.

His screams became gurgles, then whimpers, then a long, rasping breath, dying on his withered lips.

When the girls were done with him, only the desiccated corpse of Cole Jensen remained. It was already beginning to flake in the breeze and blow apart like ash. Within minutes, nothing remained.

The hired man was gone.

The girls stepped back to observe their work. Their arms were covered in splashes of gore up to their elbows. Their fingers dripped blood. As the droplets fell, even they turned to dust.

Daddy moved past the girls to Mama's side. He fell next to her, lifted her head into his lap. Mama whimpered and moaned.

The dead girls looked us over.

I wanted to thank them, but I didn't have the strength.

Mama opened her eyes, looked back at the girls, and muttered something about angels.

A flash of movement on the porch caught my eye.

My little sister, wearing her tattered school clothes, staggered outside.

"Oh, Abbie," Mama whispered.

"Jesus." Daddy gaped at his daughter. His lower lip trembled. "Oh, Jesus, no."

One by one, the dead girls turned their backs on us and started walking away. They formed a neat, single file line. I figured the girl in the front was the first Cole had killed, the next his second. The last girl…

Was my sister.

Abbie didn't speak a word to any of us. She descended the

steps and quietly took her place with the other little dead girls. Her legs were wobbly, like those of a newborn calf. He skin was ashen, her eyes pale white.

A necklace of purple bruises surrounded her throat.

Mama called out for her. Daddy held my mother close and shushed her.

Tears obscured my vision. I blubbered and trembled.

I like to think I saw Abbie look back at us, just for a moment, before she vanished from sight. But I couldn't be sure.

Mama buried her face in Daddy's chest and sobbed. He hugged her tightly. His own tears were silent.

I painfully dragged myself towards them. The ground around Mama was soaked in blood so dark it was almost black.

"You need a doctor," I said.

I reckoned we all needed one.

She gazed up at my father.

"I think the baby's all right," she said. "It's still kicking."

方 方 方

"Take it out to the pond," Daddy said. "Take it out to the pond, Seth, and throw it in. I don't think it can drown, but if you weigh it down, we'll never see it again. You can do that, can't you?"

I said I could.

But I lied.

方 方 方

All those years, gone in the blink of an eye, and the only thing that remains are the memories.

I guess you can pretty much figure out we didn't live happily ever after.

Cole Jensen, dead as he was, saw to that.

Mama never recovered from what happened to Abbie and Becca. Becca. That's the name we gave my little sister. Mama lived the last two years of her life in the nervous hospital in Raleigh.

Daddy died another year after that. Cancer took him from me.

I was almost a man grown by that time, and I was alone. Even good old Jerry Lee was gone. I never saw the dog again after the day the hired man died. My guess is that Cole untied him from his post and the dog dashed off on one of his runs, never to return. Or maybe Cole killed him. I preferred to imagine Jerry Lee survived, though, and maybe he found his way to Abbie's side. I like the idea that he spent the rest of his days alongside my sister, keeping her and the other dead girls company.

The old house is gone now, burned to the ground not long after my eighteenth birthday. The fire took the barn and the sheds, too. I live in a decent apartment in the city. I work in marketing and make a good living. I still walk with a cane, even to this day, but I get around just fine.

I don't have any other family left, really. Cole took them from me. All that remains of my mama and daddy and sister are the memories.

But it's odd.

Family's fall apart and die. Childhood homes crumble to rot and dust. That's just the way of things, the cruelty of time. Even memories fade. But Cole managed to give me something to always hold onto – something that would last forever, I supposed.

I keep Becca in a shoe box in the closet.

And she's still kicking.

Granny Kisses

I buried my grandmother two weeks ago, but the yeast infection that killed her wouldn't stay dead.

From deep within the cemetery, it slithered – a sinister consciousness growing within the cancerous, curd-dribbling cootch culture. Like a slimy snail, it emerged from the mildewed recess of granny's gangrenous gash to crawl from the grave. It couldn't shake free of the dead woman's cadaverous camel-toe, so it dragged her carcass along like a grandmother-shaped dingleberry hanging from its puckering, starch-encrusted poopshoot.

My nana was a sex addict, and her preferred partners were aging devil worshippers. I'll never forget the night I accidentally caught her in the middle of one of her geriatric fuckfests. Seeing her sandwiched between two old men was bad enough, even if her dentures hadn't been dangling from the Viagra-fueled cock of one of her lovers, even if a 100-year-old guy sporting Robert Smith mascara and silver-plated nipple rings hadn't been banging away at her Ben-Gay lubricated honey hole…

But to hear the filth she caterwauled in the throes of passion – it turned my stomach.

"Give it to me!" she howled. "Give me that juicy jellied jizz whip!"

I always figured the lethal infection was the byproduct of the miasma of STDs in her bloodstream. When she was alive, she scratched a lot, reaching under her dress to tend her itching, inflamed privates. Sometimes, she'd withdraw her hands and suck meaty scabs from under her nails. And sometimes her breasts spontaneously lactated a viscous gravy and giblet-like milk, which – if she felt generous – she'd let one of the cats lick from her teats. There's really no way to know what manner of illness bred in the withered, prunish space between her legs.

And when I say prunish, I'm talking about the smell – a spoiled fruit odor – not to mention the sticky, black ichor – the asshole au jus – slathering her pitted, dimpled inner thighs and seeping like bubbling crude from her worn-out Victorian-era vag.

But I didn't realize how awful her yeasty visitor had become until I awoke to find it gumming my cock and ball sack with its lamprey-like lips with a sound like—

Slurp...Slurp...Slurp!

It was awful – covered in fuzzy tufts of fungal matter and dripping chunks of creamy goo that looked and smelled like cottage cheese harvested from the sweaty butt crack of a sasquatch. And it grew from my granny's corpse, which was sprawled belly-down across my legs, the veiny, bumpy mounds of her icy tits mushed against my shins, her head bent back at an odd angle and staring at me with milky eyes. Her jam-caked toes kicked at my face, her ragged, unclipped nails scratching my cheeks, an oily athlete's foot discharge dripping from between her piggies and onto my lips. Parasites the size of hermit crabs still wriggled in her mangy pubic mound.

Her butt bounced in rhythm to the infection's ministrations. The necrotic muscle spasms causing dollops of old, gray fecal matter to spit from her winking and stinking orifice. The colony of mushrooms around her crack puffed open, releasing a cloud of spores into the air. Her mucousy anal fissures seemed to breathe, and her bloated belly vented a stale beer stink. She farted and queefed and belched, a fetid flatulence erupting from her ass, nose, ears, and mouth. The fart-stench was awful, mixing with the potato salad reek of ear wax and thick tartar buildup from between false teeth that had never been flossed.

The stink paralyzed me.

I passed out as I felt something like fuzzy ramen noodles probing the itching, burning inner walls of my penis.

I awoke sometime later, and saw no sign of my granny or the yeast creature. I looked at my sore package and froze like a deer in dicklights.

It was swollen to three times its normal size, which wouldn't have been so bad, but it looked raw and red, like peeled bratwurst left in the sun. It was covered in pus-leaking lesions, and the head was splayed open like the petals of a spam flower. When I took a breath, something like a green-grey cotton ball puffed out of my penile canal.

I tried swabbing an alcohol-soaked Q-tip on my itching member, but as I did, a tiny tendril shot out, snatched the swab, and pulled it hungrily into my urethra.

My dick quivered, and the peephole suctioned open and closed, like a drooling mouth speaking with my nana's voice, gibbering phrases she's said in life.

"Always wear clean underwear!"

And

"If you can't say something nice, don't say a thing."

And

"Spread the seed!"

I couldn't take it any more, I shoved my dick into one of my granny's old spell books and slammed the cover shut.

Reaaaaggh!

My rod ruptured, blooming from the sides of the book like bloodied, boiled potted meat. Yellowed corruption oozed from this flaccid flapjack, from this man-meat manhole cover, but even that didn't stop the chittering voice.

"Go forth!" Granny's voice shrieked. "Go forth and spread the seed – the seed of the jellied jizz whip!"

In their October 2006 issue, UNZIPPED *magazine said: "You could call him the Stephen King of gay horror." Rick's most recent published work includes a thriller about a serial killer using a gay hookup website to find his victims called IM (Quest Books, May 2007); a tragic vampire love story set in 1950s Greenwich Village and modern-day Chicago called* IN THE BLOOD *(Quest Books, September 2007); and a paranormal page-turner about a psychic reluctantly caught up in the murders of two teenage girls in her small western Pennsylvania town called* DEADLY VISION *(Quest Books, January 2008). Other published novels include* A FACE WITHOUT A HEART *(a modern-day version of Oscar Wilde's* THE PICTURE OF DORIAN GRAY*),* PENANCE*, and* OBSESSED*. His horror short story collection,* TWISTED: TALES OF OBSESSION AND TERROR *was published in April 2006.*

Upcoming novels include a sexy thriller called HIGH RISK *about a bored housewife who chooses a very handsome – and psychotic – stranger to come on to (Amber Quill Press, February 2008); a reincarnation love story called* ORIENTATION *(Amber Quill Press, Spring 2008) that crosses boundary and sexual orientation lines; and* DEAD END STREET*, a young adult novel about five teenagers who form a Halloween Horror Club that takes place in a house that may or may not be haunted (Amber Quill Press, October 2008). His short fiction has appeared in more than 20 anthologies. Rick lives in Miami, FL with his partner.*

Visit him on the web at www.rickrreed.com.

RICK R. REED

Purfleet

PURFLEET PSYCHIATRIC HOSPITAL
INTAKE FORM

Patient name: Unknown
Address: Unknown
Date: September 26
Sex: Female

Entering complaint: Patient found outside Admitting in semi-stupor. Physical examination revealed trauma to the neck. Although her eyes respond to standard tests, patient unresponsive to aural or other stimuli. Vital signs normal. Patient was chilled from being exposed to low temps and rain.

Patient removed to observation area. Staff attempting to discover identity.

They wonder what goes on…inside. The scrabble and scree of my thoughts. I will not tell them. Cannot. I must silently bide my time. I must get away from them. From him.
It's a matter of survival.

Outside Observation Room 200A, two doctors converse. The first doctor is older, silver-gray hair, thick as a young man's, full beard and tiny rimless glasses, framed in titanium. White lab coat does what it can to mask a late middle-aged paunch. His slacks, though, are perfectly pressed linen, his shoes expensive, Italian, soft leather. His protégé, acolyte, is much younger. Red hair, green eyes, the same white coat, but this time, it hides nothing save for the contours of youth and fitness. A black skirt and flats lend her an aura of credibility.

"Any response at all?" The older doctor – let's call him "Seward" – asks the younger, whom we'll call "Murray."

"The reflexes are all there. She'll follow a light. When I clapped my hands behind her, she turned to look. But I've tried every kind of gambit to get her to talk to me, to even *look* at me, but she won't. It's like I'm not even there."

"Do you think it's a ruse?"

"I don't know. I guess I haven't had enough experience with that sort of thing to know. There are tell-tale signs?"

"Not if they're good. That's the problem."

Murray cocks her head and leans closer to the doctor. "This isn't right, though – talking about her putting on an act. The woman's obviously been traumatized." She flips through papers on a clipboard. 'Lacerations and contusions to the neck.' I managed to take a look at those. Someone tried to do some serious damage to her. It's like they were trying to…." She lowers her eyes. "Cut her." Murray's eyes look damp and she shivers; she hasn't yet acclimated herself to the violence Purfleet Psychiatric sees on a daily basis. She had grown up in a privileged suburb on Chicago's north shore, attended Vassar, then Harvard medical school. Somehow, her experience had never included running into women who looked as though someone had wanted to behead them. Her internship here at Purfleet was proving to be eye-opening, yet in her months of training, she had yet to run into a patient who aroused her sympathy and curiosity more than this one.

Seward rubs his beard and takes off his glasses, cleaning the lenses with the bottom of his lab coat. "Well, it doesn't take a doctor to piece together the fact that someone tried to do the poor woman some harm. It doesn't take a genius to figure out that most likely she was running from that same person when she showed up here."

Murray says, "Yeah, and maybe that person is nearby, watching and waiting for his chance. We have to be careful with this one." She turned to peer through the small glass window into the room where the woman sat on the floor, knees drawn up to chest, slightly rocking. Her neck was swathed with gauze and tape; her long mousy brown hair a tangled mess, thick and still damp, her frame was skeletal: ashen skin stretched over bone.

Good Lord, Murray wondered, what brought her here?

His rage and suspicions had been a long time coming. Ever since I got sick. He would never believe my explanations, even though he was a doctor himself. Maybe not a medical doctor, but educated enough to know that what I have, I can't help. And pawing at old-fashioned superstition would get us nowhere.

"I know what you are," he whispered to me earlier in the night, as I dozed on the front porch. The hammock rocked gently beneath me. The air was still, but every so often, a breeze blew up, from the north, chilling me. "I love you, but I know what you are. And I can't let that be. I just can't. For your sake – as well as mine."

I raised my eyes to his, took in the fire of his gaze, even though it was twilight and the only illumination was from a crescent moon and a few stars, up high. On the horizon, a bank of clouds crept stealthily across the pitch.

My husband is what one might call a zealot. He has this thing about…about…well, how can I even think it without sounding like a penny dreadful? Like something dreamed up by Bram Stoker?

It had been months, this watching me. Cold, clinical observation from a man whom I had once loved. And he had loved me. There had been a time, not so very long ago, when the two of us were in a cocoon of our own making, oblivious to little else save the wants and needs of each other.

And then he had made certain discoveries, become obsessed with things that might better be placed in the purview of gothic literature. His mind, I suppose, was filled with silly, cliché imagery: full yellow moons, silhouettes of bats splayed across its glowing surface, men in capes, glowing, feral eyes, pointed teeth. How could such an educated man be consumed by such malarkey?

After he began his studies (and God knows what else: he would disappear for entire long nights and come home exhausted, the tang of blood in his hair, on his person), it seemed he began to look at me in a different way. Notice the little things that my illness, of which he had always been aware, might signify in his mind. He began to interpret my symptoms differently. I know he did, even though he never said anything explicit. Just leading questions, such as: "Why don't you ever go out and get some sun? You're pale as a ghost."

But, as I said, he never did anything explicit. Until tonight. And where his fear ended, mine began. He was trembling, ever so slightly, as he stood above me, looking respectable in his academic tweeds and his shock of unkempt hair. But I could not mistake the hunger and passion in his eyes. And this was no want born of carnal desire. He wanted to do me harm. Serious harm. I trembled when I thought of it, already contemplating how I must, must get away from him. But it would have to be done craftily, with stealth. I knew words held little sway over his beliefs, but they were all I had.

"You're crazy, Abe. You're crazy. I told you…"

It was then I noticed the axe, leaning against his leg, like a malevolent servant, waiting to do his bidding.

Notes (Dr. Seward): Patient continues semi stuporous state. She will not engage with me or – apparently – anyone else on the staff. She has begun some movement, pacing the room we have confined her in, stopping every few minutes to gaze out the window. It seems as though there's something outside the walls of the asylum that she fears.

We have put in calls to the police, to other hospitals, to shelters, to see if any of them have reports of a missing woman, on the younger side of middle age. So far, we have gotten nowhere. The reports of the missing and the injured do not jibe with her thin frame, her mass of wiry hair, her silence. None, anyway, matching her frail description.

I stood, silently, cautiously backing away from him, pretending that I didn't see the axe at his feet. If anyone is insane, it is he, with his folklore and beliefs that have no place here in an age when science and reason have become the bedrock of most peoples' beliefs. I cannot bear light. Is that such a rare thing? Doesn't he understand that my too pale skin is from anemia and not from something out of a horror story?

I disappeared into our home, watching him out of the side of my eye, his cautious caress of the axe. I headed for the medical dictionary in the bookcase near the entry hall. My fingers run across the spines of many books, until it comes to the thick, hardbound tome for which I search. "Listen. Listen," I turned and told him, flipping frantically through the pages, searching for the impersonal medical description of my condition. I tried to keep the hysteria out of my voice, knowing instinctively that to be too shrill, too worried, too intent on getting away will be exactly what causes my demise.

"Here, look at this," I proffered the book of medical terms. I tapped at a place on the page. "Read this. This is what I have. I'm alive, Abe, alive."

I bit my lips to hold back the tears, bit so hard that I almost taste blood, felt the pulse of it just below the tender flesh of my lower lip.

He looked away; he was, I suspected, beyond rational explanations. He believes what he wants to believe and that's what's so terrifying. He's like a murderer who believes his killing is under the orders of God. It's unflappable.

But I must try. If he won't look at the book, I will read the description to him, watching as his hand never leaves the axe's oak handle.

"Listen, it says right here: 'Porphyria. A metabolic disorder caused by an extreme deficiency that inhabits the synthesis of heme, the more extreme form of which causes an extreme sensitivity to light." I slammed the book shut, knowing that, in his eyes, that my trying to find a logical, perfectly natural explanation for what's plaguing me is nothing more than a ruse.

A ruse to divert him from the fact that I must now prowl the night, searching for the blood of living things. Small animals, people who will not be missed: the disenfranchised. Food. Or so he thinks.

I swallowed and backed into the shadows.

Abe advanced, axe in hand, carrying it like a scourge.

Murray sits outside the new – and anonymous – patient's room. She has rounds to make, medications to dispense, other patients to calm, but can't seem to get this one out of her mind. She is in there now, waiting…for what? For the person who tried to wound her to return, someone whose strength cannot even be checked by the stringent security measures of this hospital? Or is she waiting for her chance? Waiting for that moment when a careless orderly leaves a door open, or his keys dangling within her reach? And why not, when all of us suspect she is not quite here, not quite with us? A story burns like a fever underneath her chilled brow. Will I, or anyone here, be able to unearth that story in time to save her? The insane, the catatonic, are elsewhere, one of them might reason, and beyond the craft and slyness of a so-called normal, thinking person. Perhaps it is that kind of mindset she counts on, and awaits.

Murray pulls at her red hair, tucking it behind her ears, and stands to peer into the room.

What she sees shocks her. What she sees pumps adrenaline into her system and incites her to movement, running down the hall, heart pounding and a thin line of sweat already beading on her forehead, trickling in a chilly line down her back. She must sound the alert. This night, she knows already, is a night unlike any others, and likely to be unlike even another that might be waiting for her in the future.

The swoop of the axe through the air made a kind of whistle. I heard it just a fraction of a second as he swung. It was almost too late. He almost won. But in the instant I heard the rush of air behind me, I ducked and it was this simple, instinctive gesture that saved me. The blade did find purchase, and the pain was indescribable, a bolt of hot white, as if I had been burned. And then the quick, heat of blood gushing from my neck, its crimson flow running down my neck.

But it wasn't the blow he intended to land, my movement took his aim off true and the connection of metal to skin and muscle was hurtful, yes, but not fatal. I stumbled for only a moment, and managed to push myself out of his reach before he could ready another swing. I reached back to touch the hot crimson of my blood, its sticky wetness setting off alarms, making me want to scream.

I heard him, his shout, tinged with despair and rage. "I don't want to have to do this!" He cried. "Don't you see, my dear? I'm doing this for you, though it pains me to have to."

His step behind me was heavy, drunken. Perhaps his delusions were enough to convince him of the righteousness of his actions. Perhaps, deep inside his heart and that esteemed intellect, he really did believe that killing me…that chopping off my head…was some sort of final solution. Grave and sure, but the only way to prevent me from continuing on as what he perceived as one of the living dead.

As an animal being pursued, I knew without thinking that I was now faced with the old saw: fight or flee. He was too powerful for me, too filled with the zeal of the devout to let any opponent, especially one of the undead, with whom he had recently become so engaged, thwart his purpose.

And so I ran, blindly, through the home the two of us had so lovingly once furnished, tripping over chairs, bumping into tables, hearing the crash and tinkle of broken ceramic and crystal, blindly heading for the back door.

Through the kitchen, his grasping hands behind me, his calls for me to stop, his promise, suddenly, not to harm me (a lie). The axe swung through the air, making purchase in the hardwood floor, punctuated by his groans of frustration. Pulling the blade from wood gave me a few more seconds. And that was all I needed to reach the back door.

From there, it was a quick descent down a couple of steps and into the twilight, where my condition (this disdain for light) made my eyes those of a cat, preternatural, able to see things through which Abe could only stumble. This was my advantage.

The rain had begun. It came down in sheets of silvery wet, making the ground soft and yielding underfoot. One slip, I knew, would be the end of me. He would be upon me with the conviction of the righteous, doing the horrible duty he felt so compelled to do. The duty that he now saw as his vocation; his gift to a world plagued by creatures of the night.

I heard him behind me, on the porch, his breath heavy, the sour smell of his sweat telescoped into the sweet, heavy night air, chilling rapidly with the downpour.

I ran…and ran…blindly on, knowing he was stumbling behind me, getting further and further from me. The yard behind our home led into woods, and it was there I hoped to elude his grasp, to find comfort in deep shadows, and obstacles of fir, maple, and oak.

The night was filled with shadows, creatures who ran from me in terror, and I made my way blindly, as if guided by a supernatural hand, toward the walls of the hospital, just down the road from us.

A mental hospital. An insane asylum – if asylums can ever be insane and still call themselves an asylum.

Thunder cracked, and lightning illuminated my path with a flash of blue. I hurried to the hospital's front doors, knowing that this would be one of the last places my dear husband would choose to look for me, because, he would reason, such a place would be his ally.

Such a place would never be a shelter for one of my kind. It was almost as good as a solarium.

"Slow down. Slow down." Seward stares at Murray, whose face wears a sheen of sweat, whose eyes are wild. He sits at his desk, trying to project a calm exterior, to induce her to return to normal breathing, to quell the fire in her panicked eyes. It is a technique he has learned over the years, dealing with hysteria, dealing with patients who were clinically manic. Sometimes it worked: a kind of osmosis, his kindness, his gentleness, his calm, would seep into them like liquid into their pores, and they would slow down, relax.

But Murray wasn't a patient. She was a young intern, fiercely bright, and her panic had him worried. He feared that the osmosis would be turned around, so that her panic transformed his calm exterior to one that would match her own obvious anxiety.

"She's gone!" Murray takes in a deep breath, two, twisting a lock of her hair, letting it go, twisting it again. "I was sitting outside her room. She was there when I sat down! And now she's gone."

"Murray…Murray. That doesn't make sense. The windows are barred. And besides, we're four stories up. There's no way she could have escaped. Did you leave for a minute? Bathroom break? Maybe to get something to eat? Perhaps she managed to snag a key off an orderly's belt…"

"I told you: I didn't go anywhere."

"No one would blame you, Dr. Murray. You were never assigned to stand guard."

Murray speaks slowly, as though talking to someone slow, brain damaged. "She…is…gone."

"That's impossible. It just could not happen." He didn't want to treat her like a patient, but interns put in long, sleepless hours. Perhaps when Murray looked inside the room, the patient had hidden herself somewhere, under the bed, behind a desk. Given her state, it wouldn't be so surprising. She had to still be in the room.

"Listen, Murray, this is what we're going to do: we're going to go back and see if our dear patient managed to hide herself from you. Okay?"

Reluctantly, Murray followed Dr. Seward down the green tiled hallway, knowing that his assertions, reasonable as they were, were wrong. The patient was not hiding under a bed. She had not glanced into the room and somehow missed her. The patient, inexplicable as it was, had vanished.

As I waited outside the hospital's emergency entrance, calm returned…a coolness, an iciness that I knew would get me through this. I was certain he was probably still tramping through the woods, calling my name, beseeching me, lying to me and telling me that all would be all right if only I would come back. I could hear his calm, measured cadence.

He had been wrong. Had handled this one situation incorrectly, and it must have been killing him with frustration. I knew I was not the first he had dispatched, and I knew I would most likely not be the last. It was probably repugnant to him that his mission had grown to include the wife he had once loved, but again, his certainty, I'm sure, was enough to quell any doubts.

They are coming for me now, white-coated orderlies hurrying to the rescue of a silent, wild-eyed wraith standing in a storm.

Drs. Murray and Seward paced the small, sparsely finished room. Dr. Seward had already peered under the bed, looked behind a small wardrobe, even though a child would not have been unable to conceal herself behind it. Both had stared out the window, feeling around its frame, looking for some breach that might have allowed their patient to escape into the night. But the window was framed in steel, and its crosshatch of bars would never admit the body of a full-grown woman.

So how had she escaped?

"I don't see how this is possible. She couldn't have walked through a wall."

Murray shook her head. "I saw her in this very room when I sat down outside. I didn't leave."

"You must have. A bathroom break? It would only take a few seconds for an orderly to unlock the door, on purpose or inadvertently, and set her free. It's happened – rarely – but it's happened. Maybe we should talk with John and Elmer, see what they have to say."

"They'll have nothing to say. I didn't leave. Not for a second. And I haven't seen either John or Elmer in the last hour."

As if on cue, John, the senior orderly working that night, appeared from around the corner. Dr. Seward, in spite of Murray's protests to the contrary, was about to ask the older man, if he might have left the room unlocked. But the question, poised on his lips, stopped before it emerged, because John had something to say, something that belied that he had any knowledge of the new patient's whereabouts.

"There's someone here, sir, ma'am. Someone who says he knows who the patient is. We might just have an answer to the riddle. I left him..." John stopped as a man appeared from around the same corner. He was an older gentleman, with a shock of unkempt silver hair, wearing a pair of rain-splattered tweeds, muddy shoes, and a brown wool sport coat gone almost threadbare. The lenses of his wire-rimmed spectacles were smeared with water.

"I was talking to the orderly here," the man was having trouble drawing words. "And he tells me you have a woman here who might be my wife, who has gone missing." He stopped to remove his glasses and clear them with the bottom of a white Oxford cloth shirt that had become untucked from his pants. "From what he has told me, she fits the description of a new patient you took in tonight."

Dr. Murray went toward the man. "Who are you?"

"My name is Abraham Van Helsing. My wife, clearly, has lost her mind. If she's here, I need you to remand her into my care immediately."

Both doctors turned to look into the room behind them, where the door still hung open. Neither knew what to say.

Darkness surrounds me. The rain has slowed to a soft hiss. The lights of the hospital have vanished as I made my way down the highway. Up ahead is our town, not large, but big enough to shelter those without homes, those who have left behind anyone who could possibly care.

I must feed before the sun comes up. It will be easy, quick, merciful. It always is. What won't be so easy is, after I have found a place to rest out the burning light of day, to find a place where I can escape the man who knows me better than anyone.

Moving Toward the Light

1

There is only darkness. She blinks, trying to focus, but the black presses in: a warm presence, engulfing, suffocating. She reaches out, wondering if she is floating in a vast, starless sky…and her hands connect with wood. Reaches up…and her hands connect with wood. Hard wood, she realizes now, supports her back. She takes in a great quivering breath, wondering how much air is left for her. This is too unreal, she tells herself and once more reaches around herself, fingers groping like subterranean insects, sensing only by touch.

The box in which she has been trapped is little bigger than she is. At best, there is only a few inches on either side of her, above her. Before the panic sets in, she touches the holes drilled in the top of the box.

But even with the assurance of an air supply, she is terrified. Bile rises up to lodge and burn in the back of her throat. Although she trembles with cold, her body is covered with a slick veneer of sweat. She swears she hears blood pounding, constricting her temples. Her chest feels tight, as if too great an intake of air might cause her heart to burst.

And then the panic takes over, the adrenaline pumping through her like an electric current and she is slamming herself from side to side, lunging upwards, clawing the box's top with her fingernails. Clawing and clawing until she can feel hot points of pain at her cuticles and the warmth of blood there.

She's screaming, but she might as well be gagged. Her shrill cries carom off the box's interior, bouncing around inside. Her hot breath is sour, leaving a bad taste.

"Please!" she shrieks. "Please, you have to let me out! I can't stand this!" She kicks until her breath is ragged, until it's coming so fast she

begins to hyperventilate and it's not just the box that's closing in on her, but her own lungs.

And then, and then (and this is the part where everything goes cold), she hears a key being fitted into a padlock above her. The soft clicking of the key as it turns suddenly becomes the only sound. No more cries. No more pounding heart. No more blood rushing in her ears.

Just a key being turned in a lock and then the rush of cold air as the box is slowly opened.

She scrunches up her eyes and wills her body to disappear into the wood.

No…

She will not look at him. Will not. Cannot. Look.

But her eyelids flutter anyway.

A dark hand draws closer, above her, closer, until nothing exists but that hand pressing down on her face.

Miranda awakened sweating, the sheets twisted in a ball next to her. The striped ticking of the mattress, with its topography of stains, looked dull in the gray light pouring in from the bedroom window.

Miranda sat up and ran a hand through her spiky red hair, another trembling hand across her cold, sweat-slicked face. Her temples throbbed, her throat was dry.

Outside, the el train rumbled by, carrying commuters south, to their jobs in the Loop: downtown Chicago.

She recalled the date: just a couple days before Christmas and the scattering images of her nightmare and the simple chronology make her tremble. Miranda reached out to the milk crate beside the mattress and shook a Marlboro out of the pack, lighting it with trembling fingers.

It had been four years.

Miranda stood and walked to the window. Outside, Lawrence Avenue was already bustling – the cars like insects, busy and hurrying, the buses roaring and throwing plumes of dark exhaust into a cloud-choked sky.

Four years ago. Miranda had made the papers then, so had Jimmy, War Zone and Little T, a girl she never knew, a runaway called Julie Soldano. They had all been kidnapped by a sicko called Dwight Morris. Kidnapped and imprisoned in his basement on the west side. The dream was already growing murky, but not the memory: how she had been kept, like the rest of them, in a coffin-shaped box crafted of plywood. It had been Dwight Morris's intention to rid the world of street kids, mere children who kept his passion for them alive. By eliminating them with the cleansing tool of fire, he must have thought he could rid himself of his own personal demons.

Whatever hell Dwight Morris now rested in, she hoped, was filled with demons.

He had succeeded in taking away one of her best friends back then, Carlos Garcia, a fifteen-year-old hustler, too effeminate to be anything but an object of ridicule among his peers and a utilitarian tool by men much older than himself. Carlos' blood had stained the interior of Dwight's pickup truck.

The worst though, was that Dwight Morris had taken Jimmy away. Jimmy Fels, with his sandy hair, and tough guy swagger, thirteen years old and already far too wise for his own good.

Miranda didn't want to think about this. But the cigarette burned in an ashtray as she stared out the window, remembering. She saw him standing down there on Lawrence, ripped jeans and Metallica T-shirt, a cigarette dangling from his little boy lips, eyes scanning the traffic for a potential john, one who would give him the money to buy a little food, maybe a bottle of wine if he was lucky.

And then he would come home to her, where they had all once lived, an abandoned apartment building, soulless, eyeless with boarded up windows of plywood. They would lie together on an old mattress with the stuffing seeping out, huddled down among blankets, old coats, newspapers...anything to keep the Chicago chill at bay. Snuggle down and plan their futures, which did not include selling their bodies to get by, did not include the dangers of the Uptown streets which they knew so well.

But Jimmy was gone and Miranda drew in a shuddering breath at the thought of him, the clear picture which remained in her mind. She would not cry. She picked up her cigarette and dragged on it, sucking in the smoke, wanting it to fill her lungs not with tar and nicotine, but oblivion.

It had been four years ago today that it had come down. A priest, Richard Grebb, had saved them. He was a tortured man Miranda had never known, but she could recall his tear-stained face as he huddled with her and the other kids outside Dwight Morris's house, as the structure went up in flames, with him inside.

Jimmy, too…

Oh God, why did it have to happen?

For a while, she had been a celebrity, a survivor of this twisted atrocity, a scene so sick and twisted it played itself out over and over, raining down on houses and apartments across the country.

Miranda had been recognized on the streets for months. The johns came from as far away as Joliet, Kenosha, Kankakee, just so they could fuck her, the famous one, scarred by brutality and perversion. In fucking her, they could touch fame.

And the only way Miranda could escape any of this was through alcohol. She had been drinking on a daily basis since she was twelve and after all the shit came down, the drinking intensified, until Miranda did little more than drink, drinking in the morning, drinking in the afternoon, and drinking until she passed out at night. More than once, she would awaken to find blood between her legs and all her money gone.

But that was then. Miranda was nineteen now. When the drinking got so bad it landed her in Cook County hospital, near death, she decided to seek help. *Six months*, she thought, *six months without a drink.*

And still, like a demon, it pursued her. She awakened each day wanting it and fell asleep each night, trying to recall the taste of the fortified wine she preferred, longing for the warmth it once filled her with.

Outside, the sky spat snow – icy rain that tapped on the cracked window of her room. Around her there were no signs of the holiday. Her room consisted of nothing more than a mattress, crate, a card table and two folding chairs. Her clothes were heaped in a corner.

She was due to start her shift at McDonalds in an hour.

Miranda sat on the bed, lowered her head almost to her knees and wept. This was never how it was supposed to be. Wept more for the loss of Jimmy, who, through the years, had always seemed to her a kind of salvation. Together, she knew, the two of them could have broken the cycle of poverty in which they were trapped.

But alone…

Miranda wiped the tears and the snot on the back of the long sleeved T-shirt she had worn to bed, wandered once more to the window.

A yellow neon sign taunted her. Just across the street. So simple, so convenient.

What in hell was she thinking when she had rented this room right across the street from a liquor store?

TJ's, the hot pink neon read. Lights blinked around the big sign. The store's windows were obscured by hand lettered signs offering this week's specials. Christmas cheer going by names like Johnnie Walker, Red Dog beer, Zima, Finlandia, Cisco.

Cisco…she had once conducted a passionate love affair with the fruity, fortified wine. Hell, she would blow a guy and drink his come in exchange for a bottle of the stuff.

It seemed then that everything in the city paused as one thought rang out in Miranda's sleep-clouded mind: just one drink won't hurt. Just one to get me through this day. *Jesus Christ, think of the hell I've gone through.* Not to mention this drab existence that now passes for a life, but the horror of four years ago: a horror no one, and most people, should never experience. She imagined herself unscrewing the cap, the sweet smell wafting up, making her mouth wet, and her heart race with the mere anticipation of it. She imagined lifting the bottle to her lips, the burst of sweetness and the slight burning in the back of her throat, sweet oblivion.

Just what she needed.

Miranda dressed quickly, pulling on jeans and a sweat shirt, a pair of sneakers. She shrugged into her coat, a navy pea coat she wouldn't have been caught dead in four years ago, with sleeves that reached down to her fingertips.

Fuck McDonalds. Fuck AA. Fuck the whole grimy gray world in which she found herself trapped, not so very different from the box in which she was imprisoned four years ago.

Today she would honor Jimmy's memory by blotting it out.

Miranda headed toward her door, thinking of nothing, but anticipating, anticipating…

方 方 方

Miranda sat alone, murky light of dusk seeping into her room, making of the scattered, battered furniture monstrous shapes in the shadows. Warmth filled her and a haze had settled around her brain, like a mist surrounding the soft pink tissue.

It had been so long and the feelings were just right, perfect for this day, this anniversary of death and despair.

Miranda thought of nothing. The empty bottle of Cisco lay on the floor, near the mattress, its magic transferred, working to create an almost electric buzz in her body.

A siren wailed by and Miranda stood on shaky legs to look outside. Night encroached on the scene below, transforming the darkness into electric color. Headlights glowed. Bar and store signs blinked, hummed in electric neon color.

Wind rattled the storm window and the flakes of snow, dying as they met the ground all day long were now finding refuge on the backs of cars and the trash and dead leaves in the gutter, the approach of night lengthening their life spans.

Miranda again shrugged into her coat and left her room. Outside, the cold hit her all at once, cutting through her with the precision of a surgeon. Just west of Lawrence was a bar she knew would serve her. In her pocket, she had five or six dollars, enough to buy a couple drafts, enough to keep the buzz humming.

She began making her way west of Lawrence, to Broadway Liquors and Tap, imagining the look of surprise on Keith, the shaved head, tattooed and pierced bartender who had once been her friend, as she entered.

It would be a homecoming of sorts, Miranda thought and grinned, her teeth coming together too hard. Perhaps there were other things Miranda could trade for alcohol, other ways to barter with the bartender. Miranda knew these ways well.

A few more steps and she was passing through the smoked glass door into Broadway Liquors and Tap. The thump of the jukebox, playing the Rolling Stones' "Beast of Burden", the smoke-choked air and the smell of stale beer and tobacco all seemed to her like old friends.

She couldn't wait for her first drink. She found an empty stool among the swiveling faces that turned to stare at her as she selected a seat, sat herself down and with a righteous grin, searched in vain for Keith.

A woman with bleached blonde hair and fat ass put down the glass she was drying and wandered over to Miranda, none too fast.

Her eyes, rimmed in pale blue shadow, regarded Miranda coolly. "What is it you want, honey?"

"Where's Keith? Off tonight?"

"Honey, Keith hasn't worked her for at least a couple months."

"Oh?"

"Yeah, he got fired for selling to minors."

"Shit." Miranda lit a cigarette and directed a plume of smoke toward the black painted tin ceiling. "Bad break."

The blonde nodded. "Yeah, a guy could lose his license over shit like that."

Miranda began to know this visit, this homecoming, might not be as warm and receptive as she had anticipated.

"So what can I get you, sweetie? A coke?" The blonde's eyes were tired; she knew what was coming.

"How about a draft?" Miranda nodded toward the taps.

"Got some I.D.?" The woman's face already betrayed that she knew Miranda was too young.

Miranda wondered why she was bothering to play the scenario out. But if she didn't try…. "I left it at home."

The blonde smiled. "Well, then you better go home and get it, sweetheart."

"Oh come on, don't be a bitch. It's cold out. I'll bring it in next time. Promise."

The woman rubbed her forehead. "Next time, when you bring in your I.D., honey, I'll buy you a drink."

Miranda slid from the stool, eyeing the brass beer tap, suddenly wanting the beer more than she had ever wanted anything. "Oh, fuck you."

The blonde hissed. "Get out of her, you little whore. Right now."

Miranda stood, then gripped the bar to stop the room from spinning. "Look, I'm sorry," she pleaded. "Just one drink and I'll be out of your hair."

"Door's right over there."

"I hate you," Miranda hissed.

"Stop, honey, you're breakin' my heart."

Miranda searched the room for a man, one who would save her.

But no one was paying any attention.

No one save for a middle aged guy, good looking really, with salt and pepper hair and a big mustache. He wore a black leather biker jacket, tight, faded jeans and combat boots. He stared at Miranda through a haze of cigar smoke. When their eyes met, he smiled.

She sidled up to him. "Hi. I'm Miranda."

"Tom." The man offered his hand, upon the back of which a tattooed cougar stretched out. Miranda grasped the hand and held it, staring into his eyes.

How easy, she thought, I fall back into routine.

And then the blonde was behind her. "I thought I told you to go."

Miranda, without letting go of Tom's hand, turned to glare at the woman. "I'm just visiting my friend Tom here."

"Fine, no skin off my ass. But if your friend Tom here tries to buy you a drink, you're both out."

"Fuck it." Miranda whispered, turned and hurried out the door.

Snow whirled around her and once again, she was drawn back to the time four years ago when all the shit came down. Miranda passed an alley where a rusted out metal drum shot flames into the sky.

Miranda checked her pocket, making sure the few dollars she had were still there and started toward the liquor store. The hell with Broadway Liquors and Tap: she would buy a bottle and have her own party, remembering Jimmy until she too passed into at least a temporary oblivion.

"Hey! Wait up!"

Miranda stopped. She didn't turn, but closed her eyes and lifted her face to the sky, letting the wet kisses of snow cover her face. It didn't take much imagination to know to whom the footfalls behind her belonged.

A breathless person stood behind her. Miranda took a deep breath, opened her eyes and turned around.

Of course, it was Tom, the man from the bar. He stood shivering in front of her, a nervous grin causing his grizzled features to crinkle. She had seen the look before and wondered how much he would offer her.

"I saw what happened back there."

"Yeah? Well, she was right to refuse me. I'm not twenty-one yet."

"Fuck her. You wanna go someplace with me and have a drink?"

"Where did you have in mind?"

"I just live a few blocks down, on Winthrop." He grinned. "Got plenty to drink. We could have us a little party."

"A little party…" Miranda echoed. It was just what she needed, what she needed to get through this miserable day. A way to forget. Tomorrow would no longer be the anniversary. And, even though her depressing, hopeless life would remain unchanged, at least things could go back to normal. "That sounds like just what the doctor ordered."

"Or the bartender."

The two laughed. Tom slid his arm around her and they crossed the street, heading east, toward Winthrop. What the hell, Miranda thought, what she had already had to drink whirling around inside her, maybe I can even make a few bucks tonight.

2

Tom lived three blocks south, in a graystone three flat, just like so many others in this neighborhood – all over the city, really. When they got to his front door, a piece of plywood over where the glass should have been, marred by gang graffiti, Tom turned to her. He hadn't said much along the three or four block walk, which was fine with Miranda, but now it seemed as though he had something to say to her.

"Um, listen, babe, I've already got a few buddies over. I hope that's okay."

Miranda knew where this was going. She had been the pass around party pack girl at other gatherings of this sort. She didn't mind; not tonight anyway. It was a chance to make enough to pay the rent, which was coming due in a week's time. But she wanted to make sure Tom understood that her favors did not come for free.

"That's cool." Miranda dug in her pocket for a Marlboro and lit it, expelling the smoke at Tom's expectant face. "I just want you to understand that I'm not here for just a good time."

"Oh?"

"Yeah," she said and put on what she thought was her most alluring smile. "I'm here to make some money."

Tom snickered. "No problem. We expected that. Twenty per guy enough?"

"Make it fifty and I'm there. How many are there?"

"There's five."

Miranda calculated quickly. $250 for a night's work. Not bad. She wondered what she was doing working at Mickey Dee's. "I can live with that. Just so they can all cough up fifty."

"Won't be a problem. C'mon: it's cold out here."

Miranda followed him into a marble vestibule that had definitely seen better days. The floor was littered with garbage; the mail receptacles had been burglarized many times before, the brass smashed and dented, names scratched off and re-written a dozen times. A couple of the mailboxes hung open, their doors hanging down like metallic tongues.

She followed him upstairs. Inside, it smelled like old urine and the despairing culinary attempts of countless residents. It was what Miranda was used to; her own hallway smelled the same.

On the third floor, Tom fished his keys from his pocket and approached the door to the left. Miranda heard the thumping bass of a stereo and male voices. When Tom fitted his key into the lock, the voices stopped.

3

Miranda entered the room behind Tom and for just a moment, froze, wondering what she was doing here. Perhaps the wine was beginning to wear off; perhaps her common sense had rushed back in to taunt her. Turning a trick was one thing. But taking on a whole apartmentful of guys was foolhardy.

Tom stepped aside and she saw them.

"Hey guys, got us a little party favor here."

And suddenly all Miranda felt was sick. She was surprised at her own abrupt about face. But the thumping bass of the music, some industrial club dance mix shit that Miranda hated: all the screaming and repetitive backbeat. The volume was so high it hurt her ears.

Just below the ceiling hung a layer of thick, blue/gray smoke. Tobacco and marijuana. The coffee table was littered with candles, whose wax dripped into the marred dark wood surface, dirty magazines opened to pictures of spread-eagled women, a small mirror dusted with white powder, a razor blade next to it, aluminum foil packets, a crack pipe next to them. This was a serious party.

Four guys lolled around the room. Two were on the couch, their eyes bright with interest at her arrival. Miranda wanted to shrink back into the walls, into the grimy, colorless plaster, disappear. She wanted to just turn and run, but an absurd sense of decorum prevented that. It would be too strange. No money had been exchanged yet; she could just talk her way out of it.

The two men on the couch leaned forward. "Hey babe," one of them slurred, "How's it goin'?"

"Good." Miranda blurted out, her gaze everywhere but on the men. But the intensity of their stares brought her eyes back. The man who had spoken to her wore nothing but a pair of ripped and faded jeans. A fat, hairy belly bulged over the top; he had breasts like a woman, that hung down, crowned with large, dark nipples. His face was grizzled, like Tom's, with a three or four day old growth of beard, graying. His head was shaved and he had hung a big crystal on a chain from one ear. His companion on the couch was black, and surprisingly well-dressed when compared with the rest of the group: dark, baggy slacks, a black banded collar shirt open to reveal a thick rope of gold chain around his neck. He had a pencil thin mustache above his full lips and his dark eyes were set close together. He nodded at her, but said nothing.

She felt Tom's hand on her back, moving slowly up and down and Miranda did her best not to recoil from the touch, but it reminded her of bugs crawling along her back. *Don't shiver. Don't shiver.*

The two other men in the room lounged on the floor, big legs spread out before them. It was hard to make out their features in the light thrown off by the flickering candles, but Miranda could see one was very fat with dark hair and a Pancho Villa mustache, probably Hispanic. The other was his opposite: light, thinning, shoulder length hair, a beard and an almost skeletal body. Both men wore nothing but jeans.

She couldn't do this. None of the men were even remotely appealing.

"What did you say your name was, honey?" Tom whispered in her ear; she could smell the alcohol on his breath. The heat of his whisper caused her to shrug her shoulders.

"I didn't." She turned to look at him, seeing the surprise in his face. "Listen: I don't think I'm into this tonight."

"Oh, no!" Tom shouted, startling her. He turned to the group. "Girlfriend here says she's not in the mood to party."

Everything happened so fast then. Miranda turned toward the door and then they were all upon her, pulling her back. She started to scream, but a hand landed hard enough on her mouth to stifle the scream and at the same time, split her lip. She tasted the copper of her blood and panic rose up like electricity, jolting her. There were hands on her legs, her arms. In moments, she was aloft and being spirited deeper into the room.

"No," she tried to whisper through the sweaty hand at her mouth.

One of them opened the bedroom door. She heard the creak. *This isn't happening*, she told herself.

She was flung on the bed. She felt like a doll, landing amid dirty sheets, the springs squeaking beneath her. Laughter all around her.

"Listen guys, how 'bout I just blow—"

A punch landed on her jaw, causing her teeth to slam together in a sickening crunch.

What was the term they used in the movies? Montage? That was how the rest of the night went for her: bits and flashes of horrible things happening, so fast, so fast…The entire encounter spinning dizzyingly out of control, like a car crash, no time to prevent the horror.

Even if her screams could be heard above the driving bass beat, which she doubted, one of the guys was thoughtful enough to slap a piece of duct tape over her mouth. To the back of the duct tape one of them had affixed a small, red ball which Miranda had no choice but to take into her mouth.

One of them, the black one she thought, although certainty had deserted her, stood above the bed and pissed on her. Strong, aromatic stuff, wetting her clothes, her hair, the stench of it rising up to assail her.

Hands groping, scratching, tugging…until she was naked. Fingers probing, prodding, entering her cunt, her ass, forcing themselves deeper and deeper, until her eyes watered and her face twisted up in a grimace. Fingers twisting her nipples so hard she wondered if they would be ripped from her body, arching her back to try and buck out the pain.

They mounted her, one after the other, sometimes two and three at a time, flipping her body around like a rag doll, laughing and hitting her, punches landing squarely, if she attempted to make any movement to thwart them. At one point, there were two of them inside her cunt and one up her ass. Miranda held down the bile that rose up to burn the back of her throat, sure that to let it go would mean death by suffocation.

Warm blood trickled down her thighs to pool between them, causing more laughter.

Over and over again. Come landing on her face, her chest, to liquefy and roll, in fat beads like beetles, crawly over her skin.

Something shoved up inside her, cold and metallic. Miranda was beyond caring: she lay limp, unable to do anything to prevent the onslaught.

A fist landed on her face once more and with it, a sickening crunch. Had her jaw broken? Fat hairy thighs lowered themselves on her face and the crack of a hairy ass positioning itself just above her nose. Shit rained down on her face.

Hands around her throat, cutting off air.

Merciful, Miranda thought, merciful…just before everything went black. Just before all the air disappeared.

4

Miranda was alone. She didn't know where she was or where all the pain had gone to. She stood uncertainly, sure her legs would fail her, but they felt fine. She looked down at herself and found, surprisingly, everything intact. There were no scratches, no bruises, no scorches where they had burned her with cigarettes.

It seemed everything had healed in one miraculous moment.

She looked around her and gasped. There were no walls, no floor beneath her, no ceiling above her. All she saw was dim gray light and a mist rolling around her ankles.

A dark bird, its wings making a great shadow above her, chilling, swooped by. Then another and another, until the air above her was filled with the sound of beating wings, their blackness blotting out the dim, feeble light until Miranda found herself in darkness so deep it was palpable.

And then she felt herself being lifted, felt claws digging into her flesh. Her feet left the ground as she was taken up into this huge moving shadow, the sound of beating wings her only company.

Their beaks digging into her flesh didn't hurt. Surprisingly, there was only a comforting warmth being among all these black, avian creatures, as if she were being swooped up and enfolded in their care and protection.

And then, dimly at first: a tiny pinprick of light. As the birds moved toward it, it grew larger, larger, at first a round ball, a tiny pewter sun, growing, growing until the white light before her became blinding, until she had to close her eyes, certain that vision would be scorched out of them by the brightness and heat.

And then it all stopped: the beating wings, the company of thousands of crows.

Miranda was alone. She stood in the bright light, feeling as if she were a deep part of it, its warmth enfolding her in its bosom. She lifted her hand to her face and saw that it was glowing; she had been transformed into a creature of light. With her other hand, she reached a finger out to touch herself and saw that the finger went easily through the other palm of her hand.

Weird, yet delightful at the same time. She twirled and found that her feet connected with nothing solid. She could move up into dizzying heights and plunge downward, never connecting with anything solid.

Where was she? Where had she been? Miranda could remember so little. Even the memory of what had happened only minutes before had deserted her. All that existed now was the present.

And the present was just that: a delightful present. She had never felt warmer or more secure.

She never wanted to leave.

And then she heard him. A voice calling so dimly at first as to be nothing more than a drone, growing louder.

She knew who it was and didn't wonder how it was possible. It was just another delightful gift, needing no explanation.

Turning: he was beside her. Jimmy. Nothing had changed about him: he was still thirteen years old, still wearing the same ripped jeans and black T-shirt, emblazoned with the logo of yet another heavy metal band. But: he too was bathed in the heat of the white light that surrounded him.

There were no words. But Miranda knew he was delighted to see her and she knew as well, how happy he was to be reunited with her. When she embraced him, they became one and she merged into the skinny, adolescent body without even trying. The warmth here was a comfort she had never known.

A chill, a slight coldness came from somewhere within him and he was moving back away from her. A small voice, Jimmy's, whispered deep within her brain.

Too soon. Too soon. Everything's gonna be all right.

5

Her eyelids fluttered, at first taking in nothing. And then, bits and pieces. A bed, its mattress stiff beneath her and the feel of something rubbery beneath the linen. Her eyes opened and details became difficult to take in; everything blurred. Finally, a little clearer and she could make out two metal contraptions at either side of her making of this bed in which she lay a crib. A metallic voice in the air: "Dr. Timmons, Room 354. Stat."

Above her, a plastic bag of clear liquid hung from a metal post. Miranda traced the clear tube down until she saw it had entered her arm. The IV was dripping sustenance into her.

So she was in a hospital. She was not dead.

Miranda attempted to move her head and with this tiny movement, pain came. The heat and deep bruised feeling of it cascaded through her, making a dim nausea rise up in her gut. She wanted to vomit.

In spite of the pain, she turned her head more, until she faced a window, a great square rectangle of blinding yellow light.

A crow flew by, its wingspan impossibly large.

Miranda closed her eyes to shut out the light. Closed them and fell back into oblivion.

6

Driving bass beat filled the car.

"What is this shit, man?" Carl, large, lanky, black, drew in on the one hitter, held it with a snort and watched the road.

"It's Moby. You like?" Brian-Mark took the little brass pipe from his friend and clamped it between his teeth. Without taking his eyes from the road, he fired up the disposable and brought it to the marijuana within the one hitter, taking his eyes from the road for just a second to watch the little point of orange light grow as he inhaled, watch as it disappeared.

He tapped the one hitter against the ashtray to expel the tiny ball of ash.

Carl and Brian-Mark were on Lake Shore Drive, heading south. Brian-Mark was Carl, except in white: the same lanky body, the same aquiline nose. But where Carl's hair was black, nappy, Brian-Mark's was long, stringy and blond, so blond it was almost white.

Brian-Mark added to the cloud of pot smoke already hanging in the car. "I picked up this cassette down at Tower."

"You mean you stole it." Carl barked out a short laugh.

Brian-Mark joined him and grunted, "Five finger discount, man. Five, fuckin' finger…best value in town."

The two men laughed and took the curve. Across from them, the lights of the city's towers rose up, impossibly beautiful, hard to believe it was man-made.

They were heading south to the Eisenhower Expressway, which would then take them west, to their destination: Cicero. Cicero, where they could load up on crack rocks for distribution to a large and hungry clientele on Chicago's northside: Uptown, where the crack would offer a temporary respite from the poverty and the grime.

Brian-Mark: "You think that bitch is dead yet?"

Carl replied, "If she ain't, that girl is one strong motherfucker."

The two men collapsed once more into giggles, remembering the young girl with the red hair, a skinny young thing, who, just hours before, had become for them the ultimate party favor: a lump of yielding flesh to mold into their own version of erotic nightmare.

"Man, you think we were too hard on the piece?"

"Only if she still breathing," Carl said. "We don't need no accusing fingers to point us out."

"Shit, that bitch knows she better not fuckin' say anything.

There's plenty more where that came from. Fuckin' put her light out before she gets a chance to say much."

"Damn right." Carl watched as Brian-Mark slid across two lanes to make his right that would lead them through the Loop and onto the Eisenhower. The car, an old yellow Electra 225, maneuvered through the lanes of traffic. Its rear view mirror reflected the tall buildings of the Loop as they pair headed west, away from the city.

The men drove on in silence. The road was slick beneath them, the thrumming of the tires inaudible over the music.

Brian-Mark glanced in the rearview mirror before attempting a lane change to the left, where the lane was clear and he knew he could gun the car up to eighty, ninety miles per hour.

They would be in Cicero in no time.

As he looked in the mirror, though, something black whooshed across, reflected in the glass. Brian-Mark gripped the steering wheel. "Fuck! Did you see that?"

"What you talkin' about, man?"

"Look in the backseat. Christ, I think some kind of bird got in the fuckin' car."

Carl swerved his head around to examine the dark – and empty – backseat. "Shit, man, how many of these fuckin' things you done?" He held up the brass bat.

"Shit. I don't hallucinate from that, for Christ's sake."

"Well, there ain't nothin' back there."

Brian-Mark winced as he felt something sharp pinch the nape of his neck. "Damn! What did you do?"

"What the fuck are you talkin' about?"

"You pinched my fuckin' neck, right?"

"Oh yeah, sure." Carl stared out the window.

Brian-Mark wondered if he was going crazy. He kept his eyes focused on the ribbon of black asphalt before him, gripping the steering wheel too hard, leaning into it.

"Man, you as tense as a motherfucker. Relax."

Brian-Mark tried to relax, tried to settle back into his seat, but it was as if someone had rammed a column of steel up his spine. He took a cautious glance back in the mirror again.

The face of a young boy smiled back at him from the glass.

Brian-Mark said nothing this time. He looked again.

The same face, except this time, the boy stuck out his tongue.

"Damn!"

Carl turned to look and saw what Brian-Mark had seen. "What the fuck?"

Brian-Mark felt a cold hand on his neck, gripping. He yanked the steering wheel hard to the right and heard the blaring of horns. The car was all over the expressway. At one point, a Nissan Sentra glanced off the front bumper and sent them into a tailspin.

Both men shrieked as they saw a semi bearing down on them, its horn sounding like the scream of a dragon. Brian-Mark applied the brakes, throwing his back into the seat behind him for leverage as he bore down on the pedal.

The grill of the truck grew impossibly large in seconds as the truck made impact. Brian-Mark, as his final act, gripped the steering wheel so hard it bent in his hands.

The truck slammed into the car, sweeping it underneath the cab. The roof of the Electra was shaved off and two heads, one white and one black, flew into the midnight sky and landed hard on the road, barely avoided by a station wagon carrying a group of teenagers on their way home from a Christmas party.

A large crow swooped out of the darkness, as if it was made from it and pecked an eye out of the decapitated head of each man.

7

Miranda turned in her bed, her nightmare causing her to whimper.

And then smile.

Her eyes fluttered open for a second and there was Jimmy. She reached up to touch his face, but couldn't quite reach. He moved back from Miranda, his grin never leaving, his gaze never leaving hers. Even though he was partially obscured by the IV and the pole from which it hung, Miranda could see he held up two fingers.

She smiled again and went back to sleep.

8

He had been fat all his life. No wonder. He came from a whole family of fat people. His parents, back in West Virginia, and his two sisters grew up in front of the television. To break the monotony of canned laughter, screaming car chases and gun fire, his mother always had treats. Every night. One night it would be powdered sugar donuts out of a box, another night plastic bowls heaped high with ice cream. If his dad got ambitious, he would run over to the Burger King and they would all scarf down Whoppers and fries while seeing what Jack and Chrissie were up to on "Three's Company."

And now, as Luis Soto sat in front of his own TV (a 36-inch Mitsubishi), his eyes bulged along with his cheeks as "Tales From the Crypt" spewed out another tale of gore, violence and revenge.

He loved "Tales from the Crypt" the best. It was the only reason he paid extra for HBO. As he watched, stuffing his mouth with barbecued potato chips, a Voodoo priestess cast a spell on a young man who had cuckolded his Master, taking his wife while the Master was off overseeing work in the fields of the banana plantation on which they lived.

It sure was some scary shit, Luis thought, washing down a mouthful of potato chips with Mountain Dew.

The voodoo priestess had made a likeness of the handsome young man who was a frequent visitor to the plantation owner wife's bed. She held it up and Luis shook his head.

Couldn't these fucking TV people get anything right? The fuckin' doll looked nothing like the dude who couldn't get enough pussy. For one thing, the doll had bulges in all the wrong places. Instead of massive pecs and biceps, the doll had a big beer gut and monstrous thighs (just like his own). Instead of blond hair, the doll's hair was a mass of black strings (just like his own) and the dude in the story didn't have a mustache, but the doll did.

And so did Luis.

Wait a minute. Luis barked out a short laugh and groped in the bag for more chips. Empty. The doll looked a lot like him.

The priestess held the doll up high, staring up at it from the light of a hundred flickering candles. After whispering some unintelligible curse, she placed the doll back down on the rough-hewn wooden table that was the centerpiece of her shack. The camera moved in for a close-up and damn! If the doll wasn't a spitting image of Luis, he didn't know his own reflection in the mirror.

The whole thing was kind of spooky. Luis closed his eyes and looked again. Sure the action was a cliché, something he had seen before on "Tales from the Crypt," but this was just too weird.

The doll looked the same. Shit, he'd have to write to the producers and see if he couldn't buy a replica from them. The thing would look so cool hanging on his living room wall.

Suddenly there was a crash in the kitchen and what sounded like…what?…the fluttering of wings. Damn, Luis thought, getting up from his chair. What was it now?

He'd been on edge ever since a couple nights ago, when he had gotten together with Tom, Carl, Brian-Mark and Dave to do that little red-haired street trash whore. They'd been too rough and Luis feared the girl might die.

He shrugged as he headed out the kitchen. He told himself again: they had no ties to the girl and who gave a fuck about a piece of trash like her anyway? No one had been around when they had left her lying near a dumpster behind a high-rise on Kenmore.

But still, what the fuck was that noise? Luis kept casting glances back at the TV as he moved to the back of the apartment. He didn't want to miss anything.

The kitchen was still. Luis flipped on the light and the only thing moving were two or three cockroaches skittering away from some grease near the stove.

No windows open, no door left ajar. But wait, what was that on the floor near the door? Luis moved closer to get a better look, unable to believe that what he had thought he had seen was really there.

He stood over the small mess on the linoleum. "What the fuck?" he wondered, staring down at the white smears across the grimy floor. It looked like bird shit.

Luis shrugged. He could worry about it later. No way it could be bird shit. Besides, he didn't want to miss any more of "Tales." He snagged a bag of Fritos on his way into the living room.

As he settled down in his chair and removed the clip from the Fritos, he stopped with his hand in mid-air and dropped the corn chip he held.

That voodoo priestess was black before, wasn't she? And she was a priestess, not a priest, right?

It was the same outfit: the same long, flowing robe decorated with jungle flowers and birds, the same turban, fashioned from a rough black material.

But the priestess had changed from a woman to a young boy. Wisps of dirty blond hair fell out of the tunic.

He was chanting and holding a big pin aloft. He stopped chanting and with it, the drumming that had accompanied his voice stopped too.

He held the pin up and plunged it into the little doll's forehead.

Luis screamed as a sharp pain bloomed into existence behind his right eye. He dropped the corn chips to the floor, reaching up to claw at the eye, to try and somehow remove the burning torture from back there.

His hand came away bloody. "No," he whimpered.

And then the voodoo kid took another pin out, this one bigger than the last, topped with a dangling black feather and brought it down, right into where the doll's heart would be.

And Luis groaned, not having the strength, with the sudden awful constricting pain in his chest and the numbness in his arm, to scream.

Luis collapsed in front of the TV, one spasming hand reaching out to knock over the glass of Mountain Dew on the TV tray to his left.

Luis' eyes stared sightlessly up at the ceiling as the laugh of the Crypt Keeper carried him to death, as the laugh dissolved into the cawing of a crow.

9

Miranda emerged from murky nightmares: the cawing of a crow and demonic laughter. Her room had the strange faint light of dawn: everything gray, the light absorbing color, rather than illuminating.

Jimmy Fels floated above her bed, glowing. She wanted to cry out. She wanted to take her battered body up to meet and merge with him.

He held three fingers up.

Miranda drifted back into a dreamless slumber.

10

What a fuckin' life, he thought, as he stumbled west on Catalpa, toward the shithole he called home. Dave Ellis' whole body was singing with alcohol: the feet that carried him felt numb, almost as if he were drifting along on a cushion of air; the rest of his limbs felt the same. It was late enough so that the streets of Uptown were quiet for once: no squealing tires, no sirens, no horns blaring, no pneumatic wheezes as busses stopped to pick up and discharge passengers. The street lights above him dissolved into an amber sodium vapor haze when he lifted his bloodshot eyes to gaze up at them.

He was in no hurry to get home. All that awaited him was his fat, hairy wife (where had the young girl he had once fucked senseless gone? when had she been replaced by this greasy, corpulent shrew? what a lousy fuckin' trick to play on a man!). Barb would be asleep, mouth open to spew out the most disgusting noises, borne up into the darkened air on a stinky cloud of garlic and cigarettes.

It was no wonder he had to cheat on her. It was no wonder he got together with his buddies every so often to have a little party, where they used and abused some whore who always got just what she deserved…what she was looking for.

Dave Ellis felt sorry for no woman. That hole between their legs just took and took and took. No wonder men died before women in general. They stole the life force from men, sucking it out with their cunts, their assholes, their mouths. It was all a big, fuckin' conspiracy. He was sure they giggled about it when they were alone together.

He didn't give a flying fuck if things got even more out of hand with that redhead the other night. Couldn't care less that right now if she could be lying in a morgue down at Cook County.

She got what she deserved. Payback time for all her sisters stole from men.

Dave stumbled up the walk of the courtyard building, taking a right that almost sent him wobbling into the bushes. It was just past 4 a.m. and he was glad he wouldn't have to put up with Barb's accusations, questions, recriminations. Glad he could just drop into bed, catch a few Zs and be off again in the morning, before

Barb got up for work. By the time she got down to her secretarial job in the Loop, he would already have had his first couple of beers. The bitch was good for something: keeping him in smokes and beer. He had to have some reason for keeping her around. It sure wasn't for pussy.

He attempted to fit his key in the lock and on the third try, succeeded. Stumbling up the stairs, he longed for the time when he wouldn't have to take another step, when he could just drop his clothes on the bedroom floor (for Barb to pick up later) and collapse on the mattress next to her. And should she say anything to him about the lateness of his return, why, a good hard backhand to her mouth would silence her.

It had worked in the past.

Inside, the apartment smelled like grease. Barb's cigarette smoke still hung in a cloud near the living room ceiling.

Dave went into the bathroom, puked in the toilet, splashed cold water on his face and glanced at himself in the mirror. Except for the red-shot eyes, he still looked pretty good for a dude pushing forty. The shaved head and the big crystal earring gave him a roguish look and the three-day-old beard he maintained kept him looking tough. Even if he had put a few pounds on, he still looked damned good. That fuckin' Barb…what was wrong with her? You'd think she'd still be begging for his dick. Weren't many guys around who were real men like he was.

Dave stripped out of his clothes in the bathroom and padded naked into the bedroom. Damn, it's dark in here, darker than usual. Bitch must have closed the blinds good and tight tonight.

He stumbled over something that gave him pause, something that felt made of feathers. Fuck it. He was too tired to turn the light on.

When he lay down, the room spun only a little. He was used to it. Besides, he had a new preoccupation – one that was totally unexpected.

His dick was rock hard. What was this? He grinned and reached down to stroke himself. Perhaps he should just mount the old girl once more for old times' sake, shoot a load up inside her so she could grin all the way to work next morning.

But Barb beat him to the punch. He felt her hand on his dick, stroking it up and down. She had even had the good sense to put some spit on her hand, so the up and down motion was slippery and felt oh so good.

Dave groaned. He reached out to touch his wife and she pushed him away. "Wait," she whispered. Fuck, it didn't even sound like Barb, sounded younger somehow. Hell, Dave could get into a little fantasy action and he was too wasted to even think of becoming aggressive. Just lay back and enjoy.

Barb's shape, feeling somehow lighter, rose up in the blackness to straddle him. Again, Dave reached out to touch her and had his hand gently replaced on his chest. "Wait," she whispered again.

And then Dave really moaned. Fuck! What had gotten into her? He could tell from her positioning and finally, the feel of it, that she was sinking down on him not with her pussy, but with her ass.

Barb had never done anything like this before and as the velvet tissue surrounded him, gripping him tightly, Dave closed his eyes, enraptured.

Barb began moving up and down, slowly at first then quickening her tempo. Damn, this felt good. Almost too good. It was almost as if someone new had crawled into his bed. Barb had never let him fuck her up the ass before. What had gotten into her? A dark cloud moved across his alcohol-addled brain as he wondered if his question should not be what had gotten into her, but who.

Fuck it, this felt too good. Dave raised his hips upward to meet her downward thrust. Life was full of wonderful little surprises.

And then everything changed. The grip on his dick grew tighter, which felt good at first, but the pressure steadily increased until it was so hard, Dave was afraid his dick would explode. Already he could feel some blood vessels had popped: there was an additional wetness inside her he was sure was blood and a burning sensation deep within his urethra.

The gripping grew tighter and Dave screamed. It wasn't just pressure now: razor sharp teeth were cutting into him, penetrating deeper, deeper, shooting white hot spikes of pain throughout his whole body. Blood gushed; it poured down over his thighs.

"Christ!" he croaked, as he felt the sharp teeth penetrate so completely he was sure that in just a second, his dick would be torn from his body.

He reached up to grab Barb and suddenly stopped, the shock

taking away, for just an instant, the pain. The body above him was smooth, hard. There was no flab, there were no tits, only two tiny little nipples on a hard, silky chest. His hand dropped down to brush across an erect penis.

Just before he passed out, he felt the thing above him move away, taking his penis with him. The thing was laughing and the laughter merged into the cawing of a bird.

11

Miranda lay in bed, listless, tracing a hairline crack on the ceiling. In the hall: busy chattering. Visiting hours had just begun and patients' friends and families swarmed the halls, along with the nurses, doctors and orderlies who made this resting place for the ill and dying their home.

She felt better. The pain was now little more than a dull throb and she was staying awake for longer and longer periods. Even had the strength to eat something.

A crow landed on her window ledge; its caw causing her to turn her head just in time to see it take flight.

And a small voice whispered in her ear, "Four."

12

It was Saturday night. Tom Bauer was so hopped up on coke, he virtually tingled. The stuff hummed and throbbed in his veins. He cruised the streets of Uptown in his '67 orange Mustang, looking for prey, searching for the one with whom he could share his boundless energy, his bottomless well of depravity. Christmas Eve and the streets were as alive as he felt: crowded with last-minute holiday shoppers, revelers making the most of the holiday, knowing that tomorrow there would be no mindless jobs for them. The storefronts and bars seemed more brightly lit than usual, the neon augmented by flashing colored Christmas lights, Santas and Snowmen backlit to glow.

It had been three days since he and his buddies had shared the sweet little henna-haired wench. Tom laughed as he thought of what they had done to the girl, violated every orifice with panache (the bowling trophy they had used on her was a stroke of genius

– he would have to thank Carl for that, if he ever saw the dude again; he hadn't been around lately) and left her with a necklace of black, blue and yellow, enough, he hoped, to end any fears he had of discovery. If the chick wasn't dead, she should at least be sensible enough to know that if she ever did talk, there would be hell to pay. Hell.

But the bitch wasn't enough to satisfy him. Tom reached down to turn the radio up. Melissa Etheridge was singing, appropriately enough, "Your Little Secret" and Tom thought about his own secret. His buddies would have been amazed, since he played the part of the stud with so much conviction.

But the truth of the matter was the girl from three night's past left him feeling empty and unsatisfied. And the truth Tom could only admit to himself was that the reason for his unquenched longing was that she didn't have the right equipment. Okay, she wasn't a boy.

Which was what Tom wanted. And alone like this was the only time he allowed himself the opportunity to satisfy the lust he had for smooth young bodies, flat chests and cocks that rose up out of whispers of pubic hair.

And Uptown was the place to look for that, even if it was his home turf. This city was big enough for one to disappear into anonymity whenever one wished and that was just what Tom was after tonight or – more precisely – what gave him the safety to go after what he wanted.

Snow spit down, the tiny flakes dancing in the dark air, illuminated now and then by the yellow glare of a street light. Tom had seen several boys standing in storefront doorways, their poses defiant come-ons, cigarettes dangling from underage lips. But none of them had been exactly what he sought. It was still early enough in the evening (10:10 read the little, stick-on digital clock gracing his dash) to not cave in to desperation. He was still buzzed enough to believe he could find just what he wanted: the perfect Christmas present for himself.

Hell, no one else was going to buy him any gifts. All Tom had to look forward to tomorrow morning was an empty studio apartment and an enormous weariness as the coke wore off and the sleepless night took its toll.

Fuck it.

No time now for such depressing fare. He was on the hunt. Tom lit a cigarette and at the light, hooked his pinkie fingernail (which he had grown long and curving for just such a purpose) into a small brown vial and brought out a hefty little mound of another kind of snow. Before the light changed, he had snorted it down, already anticipating the delicious bitter drip at the back of his throat which would give him the energy in the not-too-distant future to revel and rave the night away with his Christmas present to himself.

And just like the appearance of the angel to the shepherds in the field, Tom saw his own angel, standing just ahead.

The boy must have been only about thirteen. There was a casual defiance in the way he leaned against the storefront doorway, pelvis thrust out just enough to attract the interest of the cars cruising by more slowly than the others. He wore a faded jean jacket, Metallica T-shirt, pegged jeans and Reebok pumps. His ripped T-shirt deliberately exposed a nipple and a flash of smooth white stomach. The top of the T-shirt was cut away to reveal a gold rope chain, glinting in the glow of the streetlight above him.

Perfect. Tom maneuvered the car into the far right lane, the one closest to the boy, while at the same time, managed to rummage around in the box of cassettes on the passenger side floor. He pulled out Metallica's *Black* and popped it in, cranking the volume.

Tom stopped in front of the boy. He leaned over to roll down the window. As if the boy were trained to respond to the rolled down window, he sauntered over to the car.

Tom was all smiles. "How you doin' tonight, kid?"

"Good." The boy shrugged. "Could be better."

"Yeah?" Tom's eyes brightened. "How so?"

"I need a little spending money. My ma's sick and I need to get somethin' to eat."

Tom flicked his cigarette out the window. "I'll give you something to eat." He snickered.

The boy didn't respond.

"Let's cut the shit." Tom leaned closer, lowering his voice. "You wouldn't be standin' out here in this fuckin' cold dressed like that if you weren't sellin.'"

The boy began to back away from the car.

"Just fuckin' wait! Get back here."

The boy moved closer, lowering his head to look into the dark interior. Christ, the face of an angel. Skin so pure, so white, it could have been fashioned from light. There was no way Tom Bauer was letting this one go.

"Look. I ain't a cop, I ain't a pervert. I just need to get close to you. I got money, I got a gram of coke and back at my place, lots of beers. You wanna party? I'll make it worth your while."

The boy paused, as if considering the offer. Tom thought he needed to do that to hang on to his self respect. He waited. And then the boy did exactly what he expected: opened the door and slid in.

"Atta boy." Tom squeezed the boy's leg, threw the car into drive and merged into traffic.

"Be there in five. You like the tunes?"

Once they were in traffic, Tom asked the boy, "So you gotta name?"

"Jimmy," the boy said. "Jimmy Fels."

The name sounded vaguely familiar to Tom, but he couldn't get a handle on where he had heard it before. No matter. The kid was one fine piece. He and Jimmy were going to have themselves a time.

"Pleased to meet you, Jimmy. You live around here?"

"I've always lived around here."

They drove on in silence. Stopped at a light at the corner of Lawrence and Broadway, Jimmy turned to the guy and said, "Listen: I been thinkin' about this and I don't know if I got the time for what you got planned."

Tom closed his eyes to try and shut out the disappointment. Sure he could attempt to force the kid home with him, but memories of the other night intruded and he didn't know if he was ready for another scene like that. He sighed, "Suit yourself." Tom waited for the boy to exit the car.

Life was full of disappointments. Why the fuck should Christmas Eve be any different?

The boy turned to him, his face alight with a smile. "I've gotta a little time, though."

Tom perked up. "Yeah?"

"Maybe we could go down to the park at the end of the street and fool around a little there. It's pretty safe. I done it lots of times."

Tom knew the cruisy lakefront park only too well. He pondered for a moment, then caved. The boy was too pretty to not take something, no matter how little. Perhaps after a while, he could find another boy to come home and do the party scene with him.

They found a spot under a tree, near Montrose, the south end of the park, where it wasn't as cruisy and they wouldn't be bothered by so much traffic. The harbor was just in front of them and beyond that, the skyline of Chicago rose up, its lights twinkling.

Tom let his hand wander to Jimmy's thigh and then up until he was rubbing the soft, worn denim covering the boy's crotch.

Jimmy removed Tom's hand.

Tom rolled his eyes. "You gotta problem?"

"Pay first."

"Jesus." Tom reached into the inside pocket of his leather jacket and took out his wallet. Before he knew what was happening, the kid had snatched the wallet and almost simultaneously, was opening his door.

He was halfway out the door before Tom grabbed hold of his pants.

"You little prick! Get back in here!"

Tom's delight at finding the boy vanished as rage took over. Why couldn't things ever go right for him? Why did he always have to be the poor soul who never got a break? This time, he decided, things would be different.

The rage clouded his brain, like a swarm of angry bees: black, buzzing, blotting out reason. He yanked Jimmy back into the car, slamming him into the seat. His hands wrapped around the boy's throat, just as they had wrapped around the girl's the other night and he began to squeeze, his thumbs digging into the soft flesh just beneath the boy's Adam's apple.

The boy gagged and choked, squirming, left arm flailing out to pound on Tom's back over and over. It felt like nothing and Tom increased the pressure. The boy tugged at himself, lower and lower on his leg, until Tom wondered what the hell he was doing.

He didn't have to wonder long. The glint of the switchblade in the boy's hand solved the mystery pretty quickly. There was a click as the boy exposed the blade.

Tom jumped back for an instant, the silver knife glinting in the wan light of the moon, hanging low over the lake.

The instant was enough. The boy rose up and plunged the knife into Tom's throat. His eyes widened and a gurgling noise spewed out of him, along with blood, which pumped across the steering wheel to stain the front window of his car.

And then everything went dark, the only sound in the car the beating of Tom's heart as it slowed and finally stopped.

And then he was watching himself. As if he were looking at a movie, he saw his own body slumped back against the vinyl interior of the car, his blood, coagulating in the darkness, looking like chocolate syrup, oozing down to stain the front of his shirt.

A great wind howled across the lake. The cold scooped him up, higher and higher until the roof of the Mustang was nothing more than a tiny rectangular shape, until it faded into darkness. Tom felt himself carried across the water, staring down at the silver ribbon the moon's reflection made. A dark bird moved across his vision, casting a black shadow over the opalescence lying atop the water.

And then he was plunging downward, faster and faster, as if the churning waters were rising up to meet him. He slammed into the water, its surface hard as concrete and everything went black.

When he awakened, it was to darkness. So dark around him, all he could do was reach out to see if the darkness had boundaries.

It did. Just above his face, his hands connected with a rough wooden surface, upon which he pushed to no avail. He reached out to his sides, but could barely extend his arms because the same rough surface encased him on either side. As he squirmed, the same wood supported his back beneath him.

And then he felt the crawly sensation of tiny legs, thousands of them, moving across his body. Tom squirmed, trying to get them off, but there was nowhere for them to go, nowhere for him to go. And then they were biting: tiny stings on his legs, his arms. They marched across his face, moving up his nose, into his screaming mouth.

When had he started screaming?

When would this end?

13

Miranda awakened ravenous. She felt miraculously better. All the pain was gone, vanished, healed while she slept, dreaming of Jimmy, ascending into the sky, until the silver light of the moon absorbed him.

And as he rose, he had called something out to her. What was it he had said? *All, all gone, Miranda. You're free.*

Miranda pressed the call button. One of these nurses ought to be able to bring her something to eat.

Stung

The invitation to Cigar and his wife's summer home was a godsend. It let Amelia know she was one of the "chosen few," destined to rise to the top at the factory. "I always knew I was meant for something big," she told Mother not long after her boss's invitation arrived in the mail.

"Yeah, like those panties you wear." Helen snickered and then sang, "Not too big, not too small, just the size for a cannon ball."

"Oh Mother, honestly!"

"I just hope and pray you won't have to show up in a bathing suit at this shindig. I don't know how the society up at the lake would react to such a sight."

"You know, it's a wonder I have an ounce of self-confidence with you for a mother."

"And it's a wonder I still have my sanity with you for a daughter."

"I question the sanity part," Amelia said, disgusted. She went into her bedroom to look through her summer clothes, hoping she could find some ensembles that would prove both festive and fun. "And slenderizing…and slenderizing," she whispered to herself.

Saturday arrived clear, with a lemon drop sun in a blue sky. Amelia yawned, stretched and threw off her sheets. The night before she had slathered herself in QT and now saw she was a healthy shade of orange. "Gawd," she whimpered, "I look like a great big carrot."

Helen barged into the room. Amelia squealed and tried to pull the sheet up. "Honest to God," Helen said, "Playing with yourself again? No wonder you never got married. Probably couldn't find a man to fill the demanding shoes of Mr. Thumb and his four sons."

"Jesus, Mother, you're sick."

"Well, I didn't come in here for browbeating…" Helen sighed. "Or to watch *you* masturbate."

"Mother!"

"I came in here to tell you you better get that fat ass out of bed so we can get on the road. Lake Erie is three hours away. And I know you don't want to miss lunch."

方 方 方

Amelia was exhausted by the time they arrived at Cigar's summer home. She and Mother had bickered the entire way, over such things as the size of Amelia's thighs and whether her new haircut looked better than her old. Amelia wondered herself if going in for a new "do" the night before she wanted to make a good impression had been such a wise idea. But Mother's contention that she looked like the "White Owl" in the old cigar commercials had been too much. Amelia wanted to burn her with the cigarette lighter.

But the sight of the glass and cedar home rising above the gleaming bluish waters of Lake Erie restored her. She put the car in park and sat back. "Mother, we have arrived."

方 方 方

The day had been a tiring one, but Amelia couldn't complain, as she relaxed with a tall glass of lemonade in an Adirondack chair. The four hours they had been there had been action-packed. After Amelia and Mother had been introduced to the ten or so other guests, Cigar led them on a virtual smorgasbord of summertime activities: swimming (Mother had made unkind cracks about killer whales when Amelia showed up in her one-piece black and white Catalina swimsuit), boating, hiking…the group even played a game of badminton and Amelia and Helen defeated two of the more athletic men in the group.

But exhaustion had brought on hunger. Amelia wiped away a line of drool with her Spice Girls beach towel as she anticipated the lunch Mrs. Hughes was inside preparing.

方 方 方

Amelia felt bloated. She had eaten three hamburgers, a bratwurst, about a pound of potato salad and a large bowl of Cool Ranch Doritos. She washed everything down with several tumblers of cherry vanilla Coke. When Mrs. Hughes brought out freshly baked apple pie, Helen snickered and said, "You wouldn't. Not after all you've already had."

"Shut up, Mother," Amelia whispered, then squealed to Mrs. Hughes, "OOO! That looks yummy! Give me a big piece."

Everyone had stared at her, gaping, but Amelia had eyes only for the pie.

Helen was so embarrassed she passed on dessert.

And now Amelia was sorry. Her stomach felt expanded, turgid with food. She needed to have a bowel movement but knew that Chipper Hughes, Cigar's brother, was taking a shower. He had been kidded earlier about his long, hot showers.

Amelia gazed longingly at the copse of pine trees behind the Hughes' summer home, thinking the soft needles would be ideal to squat in, culottes firmly around one's ankles, engineering the course of the chocolate choo–choo train. Amelia cleared her throat and when Mrs. Hughes' mother, Evelyn, looked up, said, "I think I'm going to take a little after-lunch constitutional. Don't let anyone have any fun without me!"

Amelia hoisted herself from the chair and, in spite of a fiercely churning and growling stomach, made her way into the trees.

Sunlight slanted down through the tall firs, illuminating Amelia's sunburned thighs as she squatted. She had looked around carefully before lowering her floral print culottes and now relief coursed through her as she emptied her bowels. The smell was unappetizing and Amelia was grateful; she didn't need anything to cause her to be hungry again. A few flies buzzed lazily around the mess she was making and Amelia felt benevolent, knowing that her lunch was making it possible for other creatures to have theirs.

When the wasp climbed inside her anus, Amelia giggled, thinking it was one of those pesky flies. She wiggled around, fanning her hand near her ass cheeks. "Here's the smorgasbord, little fella," Amelia sang out, indicating the pile in the pine needles.

When the wasp stung her, deep inside her rectum, Amelia shrieked so loud all commotion ceased. Birds stopped singing. Woodpeckers stopped pecking. Insects stopped humming. Amelia fell over, writhing in pain, drawing her knees up to her chest in agony. Good Lord, she thought, why is it always me?

Amelia lay on the bed of pine needles for a half hour, waiting for the burning inside her to stop. She hoped the damn insect hadn't ruined her day. Slowly, she got up to a sitting position and pulled her culottes back up. She looked around: the sky was still blue; there was a breeze off the lake, and the birds had resumed their chorus.

Amelia thought she had better be getting back: Cigar had promised them a game of Jarts and she didn't want to miss an opportunity to wound Helen with one of the spiked toys.

方 方 方

It was four hours before Amelia felt the full effect of the wasp's wrath. Just enough time for Amelia to down dinner: a 16-oz. T-Bone slathered in A1 and Worcestershire sauces, two baked potatoes, overflowing with sour cream, chopped green onion, grated cheddar and crumbled bacon, several Parker house rolls with butter, baked beans, tossed salad (Amelia's concession to health) and a large piece of German chocolate cake for dessert (topped off with a healthy spray of whipped cream and a cherry). Prior to dinner, Amelia had eaten a pound of shrimp cocktail all by herself. Appetizers and dinner had been accompanied by at least four apricot stone sours.

And now the wasp's sting had caused Amelia's rectum to swell.

Swell shut.

Amelia sat in the Hughes' bathroom, the picture of despair. Outside, she heard everyone laughing, ice clinking in glasses, the whoosh of the croquet mallet and the crack as it made impact. A soft breeze rustled the lavender priscillas in the window as the day wound down into dusk. The Hughes had lit Citronella candles. It could have been a perfect day.

She pushed again, bracing the balls of her feet on the bathroom floor. Grunted, groaned, rocked back and forth. It was like trying to force a rump roast through a pastry tube. Worse, because there was no opening at all.

Amelia began to cry. Her stomach was once again rock hard and she noticed angry red lines, indicating infection, had manifested themselves on her legs. She had to do something.

Taking the Hughes' bathroom plunger, she turned it upside down then stood on unsteady legs. God, she thought, the things I get myself into. She opened the medicine cabinet and found what she was looking for: a large tube of KY jelly. In spite of her predicament, she snorted as she picked up the KY, wondering what the Hughes used it for.

Holding back a gag, she greased the plunger handle liberally with KY, then put a generous dollop on her index and middle finger and stuck the lubricant in her anus as far as she could. Taking a deep breath, Amelia stuck the plunger's rubber cup to the floor, then stared at it, feeling a cold line of sweat at her brow. "I can't do it," she whispered, looking at the slimy handle sticking up. But she was seized then with an intense cramp. "I must." She positioned herself over the plunger. Taking hold of it with one hand, she slid down on it.

Amelia bit her lip. It wasn't long before she met resistance. It felt painful in there, tender. "Damn it," she said, "I'm gonna solve this. Savagely, she sat down as hard as she could on the plunger.

Something ripped inside and Amelia couldn't hold back the scream. She caromed off the plunger as if she had been burned. Her rectum was throbbing. She hobbled to the toilet, sat down and pushed. What followed was a loud flatulent noise, followed by a rush of blood, pus and feces so great it filled the bowl.

She closed her eyes. "Thank you, Jesus. Thank you for sparing me once again."

方 方 方

Amelia knew Cigar's younger brother, Chipper, had eyes for her the moment she set forth in the Hughes' yard. She saw the way he looked her over when she arrived (Helen had said: "He's just aghast at those orange floral print culottes…who wears culottes anymore?"), and had winked at her several times during the day (Helen: "It's a nervous tic, Amelia. The man has a problem."). Later, when they were having a midnight snack of strawberries and whipped cream, Amelia made a show of devouring her strawberries, first sucking the whipped cream off the strawberry, then licking and biting it. She was sure he got the message.

Now, as she prepared for bed, she was nervous with anticipation. She had reached a decision: she would go to Chipper that night and join him in bed. Amelia was 47 years old and realized if she wanted a man like Chipper Hughes, she would have to go after him. She looked at herself in the bedroom mirror, glad she had bought the pink baby doll pajamas.

"Your thighs look like tree trunks in those things," Helen said from her bed.

Amelia turned and glared at her mother. "What do you know?"

"I know I wouldn't want to be getting between them."

"Well, I didn't hear anyone issue an invitation so why don't you just keep your mouth shut." Amelia picked up a powder puff and dusted her cleavage with Ambush talcum.

Helen began coughing. "God! I've smelled better at the fish market!"

"Oh, Mother…"

"What are you getting so dolled up for, anyway? We're just going to sleep."

"Speak for yourself, Mum." Amelia applied pink lipstick and blotted it with a Kleenex. "Some of us are going visiting." Amelia picked up an eyebrow pencil.

"What in the Sam Hell are you talking about?"

"I think I know a fella who'll be real chipper to see me…if you get my drift."

Helen sat up. "You wouldn't. Please Amelia, don't embarrass me like this. Not when the Hughes have been so nice."

"Oh, no one's going to be embarrassed. That man's been lusting after me since I got here." Amelia snorted. "What a horndog!"

Helen slumped back down on her pillows and muttered, "Hopeless."

方 方 方

Chipper's room was dark. Silver moonlight glinted off his bald head. She tiptoed over to the bed, barely able to suppress a giggle and slid in beside him. Amelia was delighted to find he was naked under the sheet…and ready. Must be dreaming of me, Amelia thought, giving his manhood a squeeze. She slid out of the baby dolls and turned to kiss him.

Just then, the door squeaked open. Amelia saw a female figure pause in the doorway, looking down the hall, then enter. Amelia stiffened as the woman approached, stiffened more as she realized it was Mrs. Hughes', Cigar's wife. Near the bed, she dropped her robe.

Amelia stopped breathing.

Mrs. Hughes pulled down the sheet and tried to slide in beside Amelia. When she realized there was someone else in the bed, she let out a startled cry and switched on the bedside lamp.

Amelia sat up, and when Mrs. Hughes started screaming, Amelia screamed right back. Chipper woke up and screamed, too.

Suddenly, it stopped. Chipper looked over at Amelia. "Who the hell are you?"

Mrs. Hughes snapped, "Oh, she's one of the girls who work for Cigar down at the plant. Every year he has to slum and have one of them up here." Mrs. Hughes looked furious as she stooped to pick up her robe. She fished around in her pocket and brought out a cigarette. "What the fuck are you doing in here, anyway?"

Amelia stared, wide-eyed, at the woman. "Uh…gee…I don't know. I must have been sleepwalking." Amelia hopped out of bed, clutched her baby dolls to her front and ran from the room.

Outside her door, she stopped. Her heart was pounding and she was having trouble catching her breath. What just happened? Poor Cigar, Amelia thought, struggling back into her pajamas. His wife, his brother…what would he think if he knew? Amelia looked at the closed doorway to Cigar's room and made a decision: what was good for the goose was good for the gander.

Taking a breath, she opened the door.

Then slammed it shut again.

It seemed that Cigar was already occupied…sexually speaking. But who was it beneath him? Amelia decided enough had gone on for one day and she would return to her room, where things were safe. Amelia snickered. What would Mother say when she told her all about this?

But Mother wasn't talking. She was gone.

Amelia went down to the bathroom, thinking she'd find her there. But the door yawned open. She returned. As she passed Cigar's room, she heard squeaking mattress springs and moaning reach a crescendo. She couldn't help but stop and listen. Feeling herself growing excited, Amelia reached down and found herself wet. She slid the elastic of her pajama bottoms aside and stroked herself, fingering her clitoris.

Suddenly the door of Cigar's room flew open.

"Jesus Christ. Playing with yourself again?"

Amelia gasped. "Mother!"

David Thomas Lord is the author of the bestselling vampire novel BOUND IN BLOOD, *a Lambda Literary Award finalist. In 2006, he released the sequel,* BOUND IN FLESH, *and the novella, "The Secrets of the Fey", both nominees for the Lambda and the Spectrum Awards. He is currently working on his first non-horror novel. He is not the member of any organization. He has nothing tattooed but his memory, nothing pierced but his heart.*

DAVID THOMAS LORD

The White Room

A white man squatted in a white room under a white light by a white table. He was dressed – white shirt, white pants, white socks, white shoes – none too cleanly, quite disheveled. His hair had, no doubt, been once light, now white. And to his skin. So very white. Clownlike without comedy, deathlike without release.

He held small white cards in his small white hands. Neither as large as index cards, nor as small as business cards, but no matter. They were not imprinted on either side. He shuffled them, a card sharp inside. And dealt them. He would win.

This time.

He alternated the placing of the cards, back and forth, to his invisible adversary and to himself. Back and forth. One here, one there. Two and two more. Three, four, five. And yet somehow, each time, he did not know how, he did not ever deal the same amount to both. There was cheating in this white room. Someone was cheating. Again, some cheating. Each time, every hand. His opponent could not be trusted. Whether he dealt or no. But equal count or no, the game must proceed. The game must always proceed. He picked up his hand.

"Lavante," he whispered. He did not speak louder. He could, but he did not.

"Crispaine," he heard in reply. A challenge. A demand?

It could not be crispaine, he knew. Too much cheating here. But to challenge it? Yet? He would wait. Yes, wait him out.

"Tarfrin." And he laid the card down. Two could play this game.

He reached over and lifted the white plastic fork from the white damask napkin. Soiled, they both, from too much use and too little cleansing. He dug the white fork into the white flesh of the poached, dry chicken breast, skirting the cold mashed potatoes as he did. He would show his competitor. He did not care. His nerves were of steel.

"Arblant!"

He nearly choked on the proclamation he heard. Arblant so soon?

He wept.

When he awakened, he wished he had a mirror. Someplace to keep his dreams. He rose from his white pallet and went to the white porcelain sink, took his white toothbrush and applied the white paste. He brushed his white teeth. Thinking to himself: today I will do something different; try the exotic.

Milk!

How often do you get a thing like that? Milk. If only he could dare.

The table, he saw, still held the cards. But alone. Dinner from last night was missing. A castle of cards. A teepee of cards. Some abode or another, but constructed of his cards. His cards!

He knocked them to the white floor with one swipe of his white hand.

"Don't think I don't know what you're doing," he whispered. He could speak louder, but did not. He spoke into the soap. Pure – almost one hundred percent – and white.

He removed his white pyjamas without display. He picked up his white, terrycloth washcloth and his white bath towel. He jerked-back the white, plastic shower curtain and stepped into the white tiled stall. He turned the white tap widdershins and let the water warm him. He raised a white lather on his white form and in his white hair. It took little time for the water to turn cool, for the pleasure to turn to discomfort. For the white towel – thin and stiff – to absorb the chill droplets from his thin and shaking, white frame.

He was cold in the stark, white room. Images of snow banks and igloos drifted through his mind. What would have been igloos and snow banks, if he had known of snow banks and igloos. He removed white underpants from a white cupboard and stepped into them, one white leg at a time. He sat upon a white chair and pulled on white socks, not completely clean, but long and warm. He drew on a white undershirt, slipped on a white tunic, pulled up white pants. Smelled eggs.

Egg whites, scrambled with white corn cooled on one white plate. Crustless bread, quite white, on another. A white cup, filled five-eighths up with tepid milk, completed his breakfast. At the white table, under the white light.

He spread his woven, white blanket on the wooden floor, painted white.

"Breakfast was good today!" He whispered to no one. "But for the weary, white corn. I cannot abide weary, white corn. And the watery egg whites. And the bread that was cold and the milk that was not." His whispering wound down.

He arranged himself on that white throw. Then rearranged himself. Then arranged himself again. "Come," he whispered without need. "Look what I have for us today. This will be the best fun!"

The white man drew his white fists from the saggy, shapeless, white pockets of his shapeless, saggy pants. He unfurled his fingers to reveal white cubes. And his eyes shone. Bright white.

"See? See what I have here? We can play a game with these, you and I. A fun game," he whispered. Though he need not. He demonstrated his new acquisition to his unseen playmate. About one-eighth cubic inch apiece.

"The game is called 'Nat,' and we shall take turns. To see who is the better. Look," he whispered, unnecessarily. "They each have six sides. Although this one may have seven, I am not certain."

He instructed his unseen friend in the playing of Nat. Demonstrated the shaking of the white nats in his white fists. Tossing the white nats from his white palms to the white blanket. Counting the combined score of the white pips on the white nats.

"I shall take the first turn, but just in demonstration," he insisted, in whisper not needed. The score should not count if the nats should fall badly. He should not be penalized for teaching the game. Should he?

He tossed his white nats with considerable flourish. It was his game after all.

"Aha! What luck! A winner on my very first try!" A whispered, white huzzah.

He adopted a white conciliatory tone. He could afford it. Think of it, a lanta on his very first try. How often does that happen? Back and forth the game went, each round going to the white man. This was his game, no doubt. Forget cards. It was Nat from now on.

He ate lunch alone.

It was going to be this way for as long as he insisted that the playing of cards was over. He looked up from his lunch, cream cheese on crustless white bread, to see a white cathedral of white cards, a white synagogue of cards, a mosque of white cards. Some sort of building of worship of cards. He threw a marshmallow at it.

He wished he had a telescope, so he could better understand his companion.

He spent the time, from lunch to supper, in silence, white silence. He would not be, oh no, the first to falter. He would not give in. You simply could not use the luncheon cup to shake-up the nats. It is not just the cheating of it; it is the noise as well. Who wants to hear all of that? It was not right: the shaking; the clacking; the clicking; the sound. If anyone deserved an apology…

He considered it all afternoon. He considered it while he sucked the white cream cheese from between his white teeth. While he fixed his white hair with his white, latex comb. While he picked white lint from his white tunic shirt. Bored, he turned to his white book.

It was time he finished it, he reasoned. Books should be savored, to be sure. But how many years could one go without finishing? Surely, it was time.

He opened the white cover and turned the white pages until he located his white bookmark. He reread the last few paragraphs – white letters on a white page – to refresh his memory of the tale.

"Oh, yes. Here we are," he said in an unneeded whisper, more an attempt to attract attention to the quiet than any reason other. "These writers! How do they do it? Invent these outrageous tales?" He began to read, in whisper, aloud. As an act of contrition? Forgiveness?

"Mary and John waded into the warm, blue tropical sea…"

"*Blue?* I wish they would stop indulging themselves in words invented! 'Blue,' indeed! 'Mary' and 'John.' Who can comprehend this mickle-mackle?

"She parted her pink lips and pressed them against his coppery flesh." He hurled the white book across the white room. It met with a white wall and fell to the white, wooden floor.

Never had he been so incensed! So mocked! Who was this author? What was he up to? This jimbo-jambo of silly words. This idea of assigning "names" to the characters. And if that was not enough, giving one of them ridiculous body parts. As if parts would bulge bulbous and sway like that. Or others retreat entirely to be replaced by a deep, damp well. Of course it is inventive, but to what end? What about the reader?

"Have I no rights? Am I no one?" His whisper shook him. And he looked about the room. The one of his own making.

At the white walls and white ceiling and white floor. At the white furnishings: white table and white chair; white sink and white shower stall. White cupboard, white pillow, white blanket. White clothing and white food.

White toothpaste and white soap.

White lights and white bulbs that are always on.

White meals that no one prepares on white plates that none wash.

The white cards with no designs and the white nats with no pips.

A white life with no relief.

A white knife in a white hand.

White blade, white wrist.

Red blood.

The Great White Ape

Hutchins was a big man. Huge, really, for an Englishman. He stood at the dock peering left and right and left again, as if somehow he'd know on sight which member of this indistinguishable throng was his new employer.

It was March the third. Victoria was queen. Women dressed like ladies all, and men like gentlemen. And gentlemen dressed and comported themselves as such. At all times.

Hutchins was quite blond. That Saxon influence. Indeed, he looked very much the conqueror, standing there like a pillar of muscle on the damp and dismal wharf. He alone was dressed in khakis. Good enough. But, damnitall, he *looked* as if he were going on safari. Tall boots with his pants legs stuffed into them. Thick, wide leather belt. Col. Byrne-Jones wondered if that wasn't a sidearm he was carrying on it. And damnitall, he believed so! Every inch of the little colonel, decorated in India, cried out: That will not do, sir!

But the most egregious affront – to the colonel and, to his mind, to Her Majesty's Empire – was that damned open-neck shirt! Where in the blue blazes was the chap's tie? He had hairs peeking out! In the presence of women and children! Damnitall, that will not do! And yet, the colonel could not but remain riveted to the figure of the former sergeant-at-arms. For all his commonness of dress, this was a damn fine specimen of a man.

Colonel Leslie Byrne-Jones, Ret., was not himself tall. Not even average, truth be told. Good family and all, but nonetheless, a small man. Barely a meter and a half. His chin and hairline receded in mirrored proportion. His skin was permanently mottled from all those years Her Majesty's servant in India, from all those safaris to the Dark Continent. His nose, mottled as well from Bombay gin. Small of stature, of foot and hand. Short of eyesight and of breath. Cursed with eczema and halitosis. Arthritis, bursitis, colitis. English upper class, in short.

He approached the big, blond man.

"Hutchins?"

The colonel should have known, should have expected. Hutchins recoiled as from the French pox.

"Sir?"

"I am Col. Byrne-Jones."

Hutchins should have known. Should have expected.

"My pleasure, sir," the young giant recouped, extending his hand in good grace. Too *damned* good for a former enlisted man.

"Those boots make you look tall, Hutchins."

"Call me 'Hutch,' sir," the young man offered.

"I will do nothing of the sort," the colonel snapped. Then, thinking better of it, added, "Unless you will agree to call me 'Leslie.'"

Hutchins knew he could not. "Good of you, sir."

"You're damned tall, aren't you, Hutch? I mean to say, even without the boots."

"We've all been tall in my family, sir," Hutchins lied, hoping for an air of noncommittal modesty.

"Just *how* tall?" the martinet prodded. His tone had descended quickly in a taut spiral from conversational to interrogational.

Hutchins could find no good reason to lie. Hutchins could find no good *way* to lie successfully. He towered over the colonel.

"Six foot, sir." And instantly aware of his implied deceit, amended, "Plus seven and one-half inches, sir."

Col. Byrne-Jones quaked into laughter. "Six foot, seven and one-half inches? Are you quite certain you're an Englishman?"

"Quite, sir," was all the embarrassed man could reply.

Henry Hutchins had been caught at a lack of words. As only ever a moderate soldier, he lacked even more. Hutch was big and easy-going, certainly, but he lacked schooling, and worse, ambition. And that meant he attracted neither enough attention to make proper enemies or enough admiration to make true friends. He stood, looking in no particular direction, focusing on no particular thing, waiting for the colonel to make the next move. Someone always made the next move.

"Ready then, are we?" the colonel asked finally.

"All's aboard, sir," Hutch replied.

"We're off then."

And they were.

The adventurer, Colonel Byrne-Jones, enthralled the schoolboy in Hutchins all throughout the damp, nasty voyage across the English Channel from Portsmouth past Brest. He told him of the Pygmy, their culture, their abilities and nuances. "Got to learn them, Hutch, if you're going to deal with them. I learned; learned their ways. Never looked back. They've made me millions of pounds, my lad. Millions." The colonel drank more than just a little and stretched the truth more than just a bit. Nevertheless, he was a lodestone for one who required direction.

Byrne-Jones insisted they avoid the other passengers aboard whenever possible. Privacy issue. There were a few aboard, less than a dozen, to be sure. But still, a few. And who knew who was listening and to what? The one couple, German-sounding in name, had a grim, ugly daughter and a fat, effete son. The diamond was their game, or so they said. Hutchins said they were probably Dutch, but the colonel dismissed that.

"I like the Dutch," the colonel said. "Chocolate, tulips, and… those other things. Harmless, really. But the Germans? Bastards to a man!"

Hutchins wouldn't rise to the bait. "Tell me more about the pygmies, Colonel."

Byrne-Jones strode to the rails. He looked out upon the dark, roiling Atlantic. Like most small men, he thought he knew when he was being played. And like all small men, he resented all tall men's suggestions.

"Nonetheless," he said in answer to his own unvoiced thought. "The pygmy is the smallest man alive. His skin is nut brown, even darker than the Indian. He never lives in one place. He's a wanderer. Like the Arab." Then he looked directly into Hutchins' eyes. "Or the leprechaun!"

Byrne-Jones read the look Hutchins returned.

"What, Sergeant-at-arms, don't you know of the leprechaun? Short of stature? Robed in leaves? Dark-skinned? Superstitious?"

"Sir, I…," Hutchins started.

"Nasty, *vile*, UNTRUSTWORTHY?"

"Sir!"

The colonel came to himself. He relieved his waistcoat of a dainty handkerchief and turned his back to wipe his brow. All was silent but for the complaining of the gulls and straining of the ship's timbers against the waves and its sheets against the wind. And that silence strained against the men.

"It is growing hotter already, isn't it, Hutchins?"

Skirting the Bay of Biscay, they stopped for supplies in Portugal. They followed the coast back to Spain, and lost sight of Cadiz as they approached the African continent.

Hutchins had begun the practice of taking his early morning exercise stripped to the waist on the stern deck. His rugged frame glistened with perspiration. More and more so with every sea mile south to the tropics and the Equator. The heat and activity sloughed off the bare moments of fat stored from the British Isles, putting Hutchins at the best shape of his, or anyone's, life.

Byrne-Jones seemed confident that the reedy missionary lady, Miss Sarah Pratt, had noticed. He was equally convinced that the mollusk-like reverend, Dr. Oliver Tate, had himself cast a sluggish eye that way. And he did not wish to encourage interest. Oh, no.

The colonel ordered Hutchins to exercise in his dark blue woolen bathing suit from that point on. He'd have no half-naked aide on deck. There were Christian women aboard. And thereafter, Hutchins was covered as much as the modest suit would allow. Byrne-Jones never stopped to realize the arousing effect tight knit wool drawn taut across prime maleness might have in close quarters.

Hutchins continued to wear his woolens by day, however ineffectively. His massive muscles distorted the shape so that the arms and legs rode up and revealed even more of him. Now even the half-conscious cabin boy was paying attention. The colonel finally realized his error. But go back on an order? Never!

They traveled southward toward the Equator. Any thought of cold, damp England evaporated from their thoughts. For even in the face of the salty ocean breeze, the coast of Africa exuded its heat. And with the Atlas Mountains squeezing from the one side and the Canary Islands from the other, Hutch relinquished the civilization he knew and received the Sahara.

The ship docked at Dakar in Senegal for foodstuffs and post, and sailed right out again. This ship was sailing all the way to

South Africa. Even so, it was still a long way to Banana Creek and the mouth of the Congo.

As the days wore on, ennui infected passenger and crew alike. All but Hutchins. They were taken with his seemingly endless ability to find delight in the least of things: whether winning at whist or guessing the contents of a shellfish pie. He was enchanted by each sunrise, every sunset, all breezes and any salty mist. By textures, scents and sounds – new or recalled. Hutchins' fascination with all things, grand or mundane, was the talk of the ship – and possibly its sustenance. Despite the colonel's obvious attempt to keep him apart, Hutchins was already everyone's darling.

They passed Senegambia, the so-called "Grain Coast," which Byrne-Jones called "the great hump of Africa." He lectured that they were, at this point, closer to South America than they were to either England or to South Africa. Most did not believe him. Hutchins didn't care, it was a wondrous narrative.

They sailed down the six hundred kilometers of Liberian coast to the constant blustering of the little colonel. That unfortunate American president, Lincoln. For almost two days he and his freed slaves were constantly railed against. "You have to work the black man, not work with the black man," Byrne-Jones preached to all who strayed within the scope of his harangue.

The ship steamed easterly past the Ivory, the Gold and the Slave coasts. Byrne-Jones continued his discourses; Hutchins, his exercises. One rancorous, the other artless. A strange pair trusting each other into the dark heart of the Congo. They were fast approaching the Equator, and although the merciless heat kept most to themselves and their own thoughts, none found sleep.

"Why did you come?" Byrne-Jones asked Hutchins in the dead of one night.

The silver-blue moonlight streamed in through the porthole and shone directly on the big, naked young man. The colonel could not help but notice that Hutchins' large and well-favored body was almost completely covered with fair blond hairs.

"Beg your pardon, I thought you were asleep, sir. I was hoping to find a cool breeze. If you'll excuse me, I'll go put on a robe."

"It's not necessary, Hutchins. No foul. I'm not offended, like most, by the sight of the human body." He paused, momentarily, with the realization that they had gone back to their original habit of address. "But, neither am I aroused by it. No harm there, either. When you've been to the Congo as many times as I've been, Hutchins, well, nakedness just doesn't seem quite as sinful as the ministers would have you believe."

"Thank you, sir."

"But again, Hutchins, why? What brought you here? It wasn't for this deplorable heat and appalling humidity. There will be terrible inconveniences and deprivations. Moreover, there's dread and danger that you've yet to hear of. Nor, I dare say, dream of."

"I don't quite know, sir. The adventure, I guess."

Byrne-Jones leaned over in bed, scratched a lucifer against grit, and lit a small lamp on the night table. Its oily scent mingled with and overwhelmed their own. "Doesn't bother you, does it? The light, I mean?"

"Sir? No, sir."

His guileless face, uncreased by care or concern, lit up like a wondering child's, "There will be adventure, won't there, sir?"

"Adventure alright, don't you worry about that. Enough adventure to last the rest of your days." He had to turn away, creaking in his bed, from this beautiful child in man's form. "Still, is that all you long for, Hutchins? A story to tell your girl when you return home? A yarn for the family?"

"I have no family, sir. No girl, either. Just me."

Hutchins was telling Byrne-Jones nothing he didn't know.

"Well then," Byrne-Jones harrumphed in true colonial style, "we shall endeavor to gain for you a grand adventure, and treasure to boot!"

The next morning, the colonel pointed out the sights as the ship brought them through the muddy, jade-colored Gulf of Guinea. Behind the island of Ferdinand-Po, Hutchins watched as the majestic Mt. Cameroon seemed to crawl into the sea. By the time they reached the Bight of Biafra and passed between Prince and St. Thomas Islands and Mt. Batta, the colonel confided in Hutchins.

"See over there? If we were to go due east from that point, we'd be headed directly for the Kiko!"

"The Kiko, sir?"

"That's where we're going, man! The Kiko pygmy tribe! The Kiko have the secrets to all the hidden treasures from kingdoms long gone. You cannot imagine what it's like to be covered in those riches! Gold, son! Emeralds, aquamarine, and sapphires. Diamonds!

"They are the oldest tribe in all of Africa. They claim they were here before Christ was born. Before Moses freed the captive Hebrews. Even before the first pharaohs. The Kiko insist that their ancestors were the actual Adam and Eve!"

The usually radiant face of Henry Hutchins clouded over. And in those clouds was the suggestion of a storm. "I do not appreciate being made a fool, Colonel."

"A fool, you say?" The colonel's exuberance rolled over and died. As did the small affection he'd developed for his young assistant.

"Sir," Hutchins continued in the indignance favored by the young and inexperienced. "I accepted, on faith, when you said that the pygmy was not a little Negro, as is the popular description. I withheld my disbelief when you stated that he had auburn hair and blue eyes. But now, sir? No, sir! I will not accept that these little people of yours are the relations of my Lord Christ and Savior. No, sir!"

Hutchins stormed back into their cabin where he remained throughout the day and night, even to forgoing his luncheon and dinner.

Hutchins absented himself from the crossing of the Equator, when many of the men aboard shaved their heads in superstition. He missed the coastline of Gaboon and never responded to the haunting cry of the coastal apes, as compelling as a siren's song. He never witnessed the hot and hazy golden afternoon burn into the blazing vermilion of the African sunset, wrinkle into a mysterious prune twilight, and darken toward its charred, black night.

Hutchins awakened the next dawn with his blood coursing rapidly through his veins. His temples throbbed in jungle rhythm; he was drenched in Equatorial sweat. He dragged himself from his bunk to beg reassurance from his reflection in the mirror. And was horrified by what he discovered.

Hutchins had never in his adult life before allowed a full day's growth of beard. What would people say of an unkempt man in his station? He was no eccentric aristocrat. No libertine artiste, no primitive beast. He was a soldier. And a soldier was clean-shaven.

Hutchins filled the washbowl from the matching pitcher and

stropped his razor. He took wet brush to soap and lathered his whiskers. He shaved back to pure baby-fine skin, back to the day before cruelty shattered devotion.

He talced himself fresh and dressed in his khakis. He would go find the colonel, who hadn't slept in his bunk, and tell him that all was forgiven. Time to forget. He closed the stateroom door behind him and walked out onto the deck. And saw it.

The Congo.

It stole away his breath. It blurred his every sense in overstimulation. It was grander and more primitive than he could ever have imagined. Yes, pygmies lived here, he agreed for the first time. And those other large animals from the Kensington Zoo. Great apes and armored crocodiles and huge hippos.

Hutchins could just imagine the colonel's tiny brown people with their little weapons. The witch doctors with their jujus and smoky fires. The huts and the hunts and the horror. It was here. It was real.

It was then that Hutchins finally asked of himself, *"Why did I come?"*

"Hutchins!"

This was not the voice of a man who required forgiveness.

"Hutchins, look! The Congo! That's the Congo River!"

Col. Byrne-Jones must have slept somewhere. This was a man too fresh for an unrested dawn. Clean-shaven, pomaded and talced, decked out in fine expedition gear. There was no doubting that this was an officer of the British Empire. Retired.

He hurried on short legs with long strides. It warmed Hutchins' heart to view him as an overgrown puppy. All boundless energy in baby steps. He tried to grab Hutchins' shoulder when he capered up to him, yet had to settle for just above his elbow.

"There, see where the water seems to change color? That's Banana Creek!"

"Banana Creek, sir?" Hutchins replied, glad of the return of their verbal games.

"They'll let us off at Sogo near the coast. We'll make arrangements for our trip upriver from there."

"We're here then, sir. The Congo. This is it."

Byrne-Jones studied the big, handsome soldier a moment before answering. "No, Hutchins, this is not the Congo for men like us. This is Colonial Congo. For the merchants and vicars and bureaucrats. The real Congo, our Congo, is far upriver. Up to the Ubangi!"

He tried to listen to the colonel's instructions, but heard only the constant buzzing of the mosquitoes and gnats and flies, the incessant lapping of the shallow waves against the steamer, the persistent muttering of the palm leaves quaking in the salted, humid breeze.

The colonel said something about the gear and the luggage.

But Hutchins heard only chants and drums.

Something about the dinghy transport.

But Hutchins heard solely the cry of parrots and the chittering of monkeys.

About accommodations.

But all Hutchins could really hear was the conversation between his heart and soul. Between his boyhood and his manhood. Civilization and chaos. And their persistent arguments that insisted he was doomed.

It was less than an hour before they were off the gradually decreasing steamship and closing in on the fast-invading shore. Less than an hour of crisp handshakes marred by sweaty palm, less than an hour of prim kisses on stony lip and cheek. Less than an hour of fatherly hugs and motherly encouragements that fell on inert torso and dormant ears.

Hutchins felt well-trapped. There had been people all around him, yet he'd never felt so alone.

"Hutchins!"

He turned to finally see the colonel. But it was not the colonel. His colonel lived on a Victorian wharf back in Portsmouth with hundreds of Her Majesty's subjects all perfectly dressed around him. Or on a proper steamship of the British merchant fleet, cognac in the one hand, pipe in the other, telling fabulous stories of imaginary places.

Not this man. This hunter!

Sogo swelled up ahead of him. This was no seaport; this was not even a village. This was a sweltering slum of sapling timbers and drying palm leaves. Of filthy black natives and filthier black children clotting the streets. Of naked black men, reeking of the jungle, and shameless black women, swaying their exposed breasts with every languid step.

"Hallo, Brabant!" the colonel called. And Hutchins turned to see the slick, white man on the levee.

"Byrne-Jones, welcome back!" answered Monsieur Louis Brabant, a Belgian entrepreneur cast adrift of his family, upstanding bankers and investors all.

Hutchins disliked him at first sight. Brabant was of average height and weight, but there ended his normal aspect. His pomaded hair was jet black, perfectly straight and brushed back from his theatrical widow's peak. And it hung limp in excess of his collar. His face was gaunt. And while clean-shaven, his dark and heavy beard shadowed the lower half of his face quite blue. His *frightening* face, Hutchins concluded.

Brabant's nose was excessively long and sharp. To Hutchins' eyes, it looked more like an icicle or a beak. And it ran down his frightening face in a vertical line from his domed forehead nearly to his top lip. Had not his thin, black eyebrows met at the bridge, Hutchins would have found it impossible to tell where the Belgian's forehead ended.

And the bones of his brow and cheekbones were so prominent as to cast his dark brown eyes into a deep, hooded pit. Still, it wasn't just the darkness encircling their host's eyes or the yellowish tinge of their whites that was so unsettling. It was the constant shifting paired with the torpid lingering that utterly defined Brabant's gaze. First, Hutchins hoped he'd just settle upon one place to stare, and then he prayed he wouldn't. But his unique way of watching was less disturbing than the Belgian's posture.

Louis Brabant stood with his neck protruding horizontally from his torso. His weak shoulders were slung back in counterbalance, and he carried his wrists parallel to the ground. Louis Brabant looked like a vulture and smelled like a Turkish whore.

"But, Leslie," Brabant inquired in his sibilant, nasal sing-song as he welcomed Byrne-Jones to shore, "who have we here with you?"

"Monsieur Louis Brabant, may I introduce my new aide-de-camp, Mr. Henry Hutchins."

Brabant turned his already outstretched hand up ninety degrees from the horizontal. Hutchins was loath to take it, but courtesy allowed no escape.

His large, tanned hand engulfed the Belgian's smaller one, so pale as to seem dead gray. So malleable as to suggest ripe fish. So adhering as to suppose the sodomite.

"You're a hairy one," Brabant broached in his unctuous lilt as he brushed the back of Hutchins' wrist with his left hand. And then added, too softly, too solemnly, too secretly, "I'm quite hairy myself."

Hutchins thought to say, *is that so, sir?* Then thought better of making any response other than the removal of his hand. He turned instead to his employer and said, "I'll see about the gear, sir. Where shall I have it brought?"

"Never mind about that, Hutchins," the colonel replied. Then, Brabant turned and commanded something in a native dialect. Probably Bantu, thought Hutchins, I must learn.

Several native men came out of a long structure built near the wharf. It had regular doorway and window openings, all set in native style. But instead of glass windows and a wooden door, it had fabric draperies that they pushed aside to exit.

The men appeared to be between twenty and forty years of age, their molasses-colored skin and strong-looking, ropey muscles in direct contrast to their master. They all wore pantaloon-type breeches that only came to just below their knees. These were belted at the waist with what appeared to be braided jute. The younger ones were shirtless, while the elders wore a collarless, open-necked blouse that resembled a nightshirt, but for the fact that it only fell as far as the hips.

"I've instructed them to store your gear in the guest hut, Leslie, if it's all right with you. You'll grace me with your company through tonight's dinner and the morning's breakfast, won't you?"

"Louis, I'd be delighted! The trek upriver will keep until tomorrow, surely."

Brabant threaded his arms through the colonel's and Hutchins' and guided them toward his home. He called out something – in Kongo, not Bantu – over his shoulder and the native men took additional crates off the wharf.

"I've had some extra things brought from England and Portugal for the occasion," Brabant explained. "I don't get many visitors, Mr. Hutchins. So when I expect some, I treat myself to a banquet." With an additional wink and squeeze, he added, "But you know...I don't just do it for my guests!"

They entered Brabant's hut.

Far from being a native dwelling, this was a Congo manor house.

"My!" was all Hutchins could manage.

"Does that mean you like it then, Mr. Hutchins?" the vulture asked.

"This is extraordinary, sir. I'm amazed!"

Byrne-Jones entered the conversation. "Did it all himself, Hutchins. Our Monsieur Brabant is quite the engineer."

"Leslie, you flatter me!"

"Nothing of the sort! Look over here, Hutchins…" Byrne-Jones began to describe the dwelling to his assistant.

He told Hutchins how Brabant had the land cleared, except for certain trees he had stripped of their branches and bark, leaving the denuded trunks as the column supports for the equatorial mansion. Next, he had the natives cut down palm stalks, which were lashed together with raffia and vines and these walls were upended into trenches between the trunks. When the corners were lashed together, he had a standing, but roofless dwelling.

"It wasn't roofless for long," Brabant called out from what seemed to be a bar room. He brought three large glasses of gin-and-tonic water to his guests and kidded, "It's just for the quinine, you know. Please continue, Leslie. It's a pleasure to hear someone else describe it."

"Very well, Louis, if you insist. The roof, Hutchins…"

The colonel recounted the way that Brabant used local grasses and palm leaves to thatch the roof in the same way it is still done in the rural parts of the British Isles. The sun and the rains had weathered the exterior to the same color as bamboo, but one could still see the remains of the original dark green on the interior ceiling.

"Don't forget, Leslie, that before the thatching was done, we had to saw the openings for the doors and windows and frame them," Brabant interjected.

"About the windows and doors, sir," Hutchins countered, the gin finally overcoming his reticence about their host. "What are all those coverings?"

"Glad you asked, Hutchins." Brabant moved over to a window to demonstrate.

"Here's a gauze covering which acts like mosquito netting. It allows a little air in and light, but keeps out most of the bugs and heat. Then, there's this heavier fabric," which he slipped off of its peg for the demonstration. "That keeps out more bugs and keeps the place cooler, but it also shuts out the breeze.

"Then, for the rainy season, we add an interior and exterior shutter of palm fronds. They're tough and slick, and manage to keep most of the rain out."

"And what about your furniture?" Hutchins asked.

"Some of it was brought with me when I first arrived, naturally. My bedstead, a couple of camp chairs, a few mirrors. But the rest were made right here. Come, I'll give you the tour. You come, too, Leslie."

"But I've seen it all before," he objected from behind the bar, laboring over refills.

"Well, for your company then."

Brabant brought them to the "dining room," a four-meter by five-meter section of the hall walled in mosquito netting. The table was about two meters wide and three meters long and made of ebony boards suspended on large sawhorses. Each side had its own, smaller, ebony bench on smaller horses. Two thrones of rattan and bentwood striplings marked the head and foot of the table.

The "living room" was a large rectangle at one end of the great hall. Its oriental overabundance would have suited a pasha or a Bedouin prince. Overstuffed and oversized pillows provided the only seating and Indian carpets were laid over rattan mats. Brabant had installed four palm frond fans into the bamboo walls. They were manipulated by a belt-and-pulley system that connected to revamped bicycles on the ground. Four sloe-eyed Negro boys peddled and when the wheel spun, the belt moved. When the belt moved, the fan spun.

The other end of the hall was for Brabant's sleeping quarters and study. In one half, he had his cherry wood bedroom set. The other half held his desk and drafting table, his bookcases and file cabinets.

"It's very impressive, sir," Hutchins concluded.

"One drawback, though."

"And what is that, sir?"

"Well, I hadn't planned well enough for company. You see,

Hutchins, you arrived on the same ship as my new supplies. Ordinarily, I'd have given you both the guest quarters. But, what with my new crates and those of yours, there's only room now for one cot in the guesthouse. I'm afraid one of you will have to bunk in here."

Hutchins was annoyed, but not surprised. Divide and conquer, they say.

"I'll repair to the guest house, as usual, Louis," the colonel responded.

"I won't hear of it, sir. Kind of you, but it's my duty to look after the provisions, and I have every intention," Hutchins jumped in.

"Well, Hutchins, I won't argue with such a strong remonstration. I'll lie on the pillows like an old caliph!"

"Thank you, sir. You gentlemen will excuse me then."

"Hutchins?" Brabant stopped him. "Dinner is at eight. Don't be tardy. It will be your last good meal for many weeks."

"No, sir. Eight o'clock it is," Hutchins answered as he headed for the doorway.

"And Hutchins?" Brabant delayed him again.

"Sir?" he responded without turning.

"Moglo will show you to the shower. It will be your last of those, too." Brabant stepped behind the bar for yet another refill.

Hutchins walked the twenty feet behind the main house to the guest cottage. This, depressingly, was little more than a hut. The same stripling walls, the same palm frond and grass ceiling, but a hut nonetheless.

The small, sawed-out window was not as amicably dressed, the dirt floor only occasionally covered with rattan. No fan, no overstuffed pillows, barely a serviceable mosquito net. Mostly their gear and piled-up crates. Plus a small mirror and a basin-and-pitcher set on a small sideboard.

Hutchins undressed and put on a robe. Moglo had pointed out the shower to him on the way to the guest hut. Another palm frond and stripling affair, it consisted of four screens positioned a foot off the ground with an opening at one end for an entrance. There was a ladder on the outside that led to a water tower. A bamboo viaduct led from it to an open weave basket that acted, surprisingly well, as a spray spout.

When Hutchins arrived at the shower stall, Byrne-Jones was just leaving.

"There's a basket of soaps hanging just inside, Hutchins. I used the lavender, but left the basil for you. They say it keeps the mosquitoes away."

The shower had done little to sober the colonel.

"Good of you, sir."

"We'll see you at eight, then?"

"Eight, sir."

Hutchins entered the shower to see Moglo some feet above him on the ladder. He held a cord that would, so he mimed, regulate the sluice for his shower. Hutchins removed his robe, hung it on a peg and stood under the basket.

The water drizzled, rather than sprayed down, warmed by the equatorial sun. Moglo pointed to the soap basket and mimed its application. Hutchins followed this unwarranted instruction.

He soaped his fine blond hair and raised a lather on his chest and belly. He soaped what he could reach on his upper and lower back, on his buttocks and legs. He turned his back to Moglo and cleaned his private parts, allegro non tropo.

It was then he first noticed the guard tower on the compound. Not so much the tower itself, but the small sharp light reflected off it. The glint of binoculars?

Moglo released a second round of water. Hutchins rinsed the soap from his shampooed head and body. The spray ceased abruptly. Hutchins turned to ask the native for more. His eyes, he mimed. He couldn't see.

When Moglo finally obliged, Hutchins turned back to face the guard tower. Clean and damp and shiny, he couldn't find the small, reflected light again. He chalked it up to an imagined invasion against his modesty, but hurried into his robe and went back to the guest hut to change for dinner.

Dinner. In Sogo, at the mouth of the Congo. Who'd have imagined?

By the time Hutchins entered the manor house, the colonel and Mr. Brabant were already well into the newly imported sherry.

"Hutchins! You're in!" A disembodied voice called toward the main doorway.

"Hallo, sirs. Sorry to be late," Hutchins called toward the gloom of the living room.

Brabant walked into the dining hall to greet his guest. Hutchins couldn't believe the sight of Brabant. But for an indigo wrap with a geometric white design, he was quite naked.

"Not at all, my good man. Join us in a sherry."

It took all of Hutchins' nerve to decline. "Just some water, sir, if it's no bother. Really dreadfully hot here."

"I do apologize, but nothing I can do about it. Am I right, Leslie? Nothing to be done?"

From the darkened living room Byrne-Jones called, "Quite right. Nothing to be done, Hutchins. Nothing."

Brabant poured another sherry for himself and the colonel both and handed a third to Hutchins, egregiously ignoring his request. He escorted Hutchins back into the living room and led him to a pile of pillows.

"Make yourself at home, Hutchins," the Belgian offered. "I have a gift for you. Here!"

"Really, sir, this is quite unnecessary," Hutchins objected as he tried to maneuver into an acceptable position upon the pillows.

"Nothing of the sort. I won't hear a protest. It's a small thing really," he sniggered. Some joke, it seemed, between the colonel and himself.

He put a paper-wrapped parcel into Hutchins' hands. Hands already drenched with sweat. Droplets fell upon the wrapping.

"I do apologize, sir. I can't seem to get control of myself in this heat."

"Not so much the heat, Hutchins, but the humidity," Brabant offered. "But this is the exact remedy. Open it!"

Hutchins unwrapped the package. Inside was a folded piece of material. Bright red with a black native pattern stamped repetitively upon it. It was about a meter wide and possibly two long.

"It's cloth, sir," Hutchins contributed, knowing full well what kind of present it was, and its intended use.

"Of course it's cloth, Hutchins!" The colonel stood uneasily from his pillows, from the gloom. He was wrapped in a similar cloth. Dull olive imprinted with orange leaves.

Byrne-Jones was as hairless as a boy. His chest had fallen into pendulous breasts, protruding into oversized, colorless nipples.

His belly swelled from under his rib cage and spilled over his hips and waist. His arms were thin and what was visible of his legs, from shins on down, were bowed and bandy. And not a hair to be seen on his torso or his extremities. Brabant was quite the opposite.

Here was a hairy beast. His hair ran down his nape onto a terribly hairy back. The back hairs continued to his waist, where, mercifully, Hutchins thought, one was spared the sight of them until they reemerged from under his wrap upon the hairiest calves and shins and feet in the known world.

His belly was completely covered in the same wiry coils of thick, oily hairs. His small chest, sunken and underdeveloped, was obliterated by the dense growth. Indeed, it seemed to Hutchins that its wool, rather than its flesh, defined the mass of the Belgian's body.

Hutchins was caught between anxiety and repulsion by the men in their native sarongs, and shuddered to recall the mention of nasty practices revealed by seasoned soldiers in whispers and hushed tones. He shook his head to clear it and gulped down the sherry to dull it again.

"Come, Hutchins, let's get on with it!" the colonel coaxed with only a slight slur.

"With what, sir?" Hutchins felt the need to ask.

"Get yourself changed for dinner. Let's not leave it to get cold!"

Brabant sidled between the colonel and his aide. "Leslie, never mind. If Hutchins is uncomfortable…"

"Nonsense!" the colonel thundered. "Hutchins! You will change and now! You will not embarrass me in front of our host. A man I've know and trusted for these many years. The man's given you a gift, damnitall."

Hutchins was blushing quite brightly by then. He could only stammer, "Colonel, I…"

But Brabant intervened, "Perhaps you'd feel more comfortable retiring to the bedroom to change? There's a dressing screen in there. You won't be disturbed."

Trapped. And no way out. Hutchins could think of no way to refuse either the gift or the offer of privacy. He thanked his host and retired into the large bedroom. A good soldier.

Hutchins changed quickly, hoping to give his host no solicitous reason to come in upon him in his undress. He had intended to leave on his underdrawers, but discovered that he'd already sweated through them. And the wet spots they'd leave on his hated gift would mark him as childish and suspicious. Hutchins removed them and wrapped himself in the fabric.

The material was long enough to wrap around his waist almost twice. It was thin cotton and clung to his thighs and buttocks and privates. It was worse than being naked. He rewrapped the thing, just slightly looser, hoping for a more camouflaged effect. But then it wouldn't stay on.

The third attempt was the best. By wrapping the material once and gathering the remainder and tucking that in, Hutchins found that he could hide his privates within the material's folds.

When he entered the living room, the disapproval on the older men's faces was apparent.

"That's not the way that goes at all, Hutchins," the even-drunker Colonel contended.

"No matter, Leslie," Brabant placated, "He's done a fine job for a first try." Then abruptly switching subjects said, "Shall we dine, gentlemen?"

Brabant led his guests into the dining hall. One end of the table was set at three places with the best European crystal and china and silver and lace. One black servant was lighting the final candelabra, while a small black boy plied the single pedal-run fan.

"Byrne-Jones, you're here to my right," Brabant instructed, "and you, Hutchins, will sit at my left."

The meal was like no other to which Hutchins had been exposed. Certainly none to which he'd been invited.

He could barely count the forks – each with its different, distinguishing shape – much less discern their uses. Knives, much the same. An army of crystal stemware stood as if in full battle array. A small crystal bowl held a clear steaming liquid and a slice of lemon. Soup? He doubted it.

Hutchins played follow-the-leader throughout most of dinner. The steaming cloth and lemon-scented water, as it turned out, were to refresh his face and hands. The tiny knife and shell-shaped spoon were for the avocado. Yellowish-green in color, buttery in texture, it was like a salad, for it was grassy tasting. Pleasant on the tongue, but not at the back of the throat, Hutchins decided.

Prawns, they said, were next.

They were shrimp, all right. But enormous. Still had their heads. Chilled and delicious, except for the fat-sucking part.

The soup came next, with the third bottle of wine. Hutchins guard was dropping as his epicurean education was mounting. But still, he thought, he was keeping his head better than his host or his employer. It was served in a medium-sized tortoise shell. Chowder of local turtle and native corn with hot peppers. Hutchins drank nearly an entire bottle of a crisp Spanish viura without the sting ever truly leaving his tongue. But, in contrast, the rest of him felt strangely cooler.

His conversation also bloomed about then.

"How long have you been in the Congo, Mr. Brabant?"

"It will be eleven years this rainy season. But it's Louis, Henry. For heaven's sake, not so formal!"

"Eleven years! That's extraordinary! How often do you get back to Belgium?" Hutchins asked fully expecting a nice, middle class reply.

"Never."

"But then, your family, they come to see you here?"

"Never," he repeated.

"You must miss them terribly."

"Not a fucking one of them!" his host snarled. Hutchins had never heard this word outside of a barracks. And never from someone with any sort of education or breeding.

He retreated into a monosyllabic kind of silence through the following courses, emptying his wine goblet far too often.

He said nothing through the green salad. He nodded through the smoky, grilled salmon. A "yes" or "no" was all he could manage through the moist and fatty roast duck. The baked sweet potatoes and fried plantains warmed him into a "please" and "thank you" for additional wine. The crisp roast suckling pig with its accompanying Chateauneuf-du-Pape brought him back into conversation. The older men had patiently waited, never giving the slightest indication that he hadn't been fully participating.

The water buffalo cheese, warm and runny on crisp unleavened bread, was perfectly matched by an ancient port, just uncasked and swelling like rubies on the tongue. The flambé of ripe banana served with dark Swiss chocolate and strong native coffee finished the meal. The magnum of Perrier-Jouet finished Hutchins.

Hutchins awakened in the dark of the night. The moon was high and the light of it streamed in through the open window and over the cot he lay upon. The too-large moon joined forces with the suffocating heat, the drowning humidity, and the constant clamor of the jungle night to remind him of where he was.

He looked down at himself and saw that he was still wearing the native cloth from the dinner party. But, it was no longer fastened left-over-right with the bulk before him. The right side was now crossed over the left, then folded back and forth and left untucked.

Hutchins shot bolt upright in his cot. *This kilt has been opened and replaced. Did they think I wouldn't notice?*

He stood naked from his bed.

The silver-blue light of the moon settled upon him. Each platinum-to-dun colored hair on his body picked up and held that light. In the darkness of the hut, of the African night, Hutchins glowed. He tried to recall as much of dinner as he could. The meal, the conversation. And whether anything improper had happened. But no.

How could I even think this about the colonel? Or Mr. Brabant? They have been nothing but kind to me.

Hutchins hunkered back down into his cot. He pulled the material over him like a blanket. Again, he slept.

And the shadow crept back from beyond the packing cases, and out of the hut.

At dawn, Hutchins awoke and sensed something different about him. He'd slept naked before, sure, but this time was different. He was more aware of his body, and for the first time, he smelled it.

He lifted his arms. One then the other. He smelled of clayey earth and of sea salt and of vinegar. He smelled of butchered animals, fried plants and copious amounts of wine. He reeked.

And he reveled in it.

I am an animal, he thought. I can hunt. I can kill. I can survive.

For the first time in his adult life, Hutchins didn't shower, didn't shave. He adapted to the sense of his whole self. A very large, very muscular, very hairy man.

He dressed and went to the main house, where breakfast had been prepared.

"Mr. Hutchins, how are you feeling this morning?" Brabant, ever gracious, called out.

"Never better, sir," Hutchins answered and meant it.

"We were worried about you after dinner, Hutchins. Sure you're up to this?" Brabant wondered.

"Sir," he said as he grabbed him in a cheery, adolescent head lock, "I've never felt better!" Neither man mentioned his smell.

Hutchins consumed half a dozen eggs and rashers of bacon. Eight muffins made of ground local corn. Three pitchers of water-buffalo milk. He ate like a fifteen-year-old boy.

"Good, Hutchins! Keep it up! You'll be ready for Baruru," the Belgian delighted.

"Baruru, sir?"

There are some things that, once yielded, cannot be reinstated.

"Surely, the colonel has told you of the Baruru?" the snake-oil salesman in the Belgian asked. He was intent upon becoming an active player in this game.

"No, sir. We're going to meet the Kiko, a pygmy tribe. Near the Herb River and the Ubangi."

Byrne-Jones entered from his shower and joined them at the breakfast table. "Have I missed anything?"

"Our host was starting to tell me of the Baruru," Hutchins explained. Brabant cowered obviously. But for whose sake?

"Poppycock! Baruru, indeed!" the colonel harrumphed, a darkening scowl stealing across his face.

"Colonel? What is Baruru?" Hutchins wanted to know.

"Baruru, my good Mister Hutchins," the apparently inebriated Belgian answered, "is the great white ape!"

Hutchins khakis became stained and sodden at his armpit and chest. Between his shoulder blades and at his waist. His thick socks went wet and his undergarments saturated.

The Great White Ape.

"What, sir, is this great white ape?"

"A fairytale, man. Nothing but a fairytale!" Byrne-Jones insisted, "Perhaps I should have told you the story, but I didn't want to dishearten you with a lot of superstitious rot!"

The more he denied, the more Hutchins believed. *What was this strange thing? Why, again, did he come?*

Hutchins poured himself thick native coffee.

"Tell me the story, sir. If you place no faith in it, then neither shall I."

The colonel glowed in obvious victory, then lectured between bites and wipes.

"The Kiko tribe is an ancient one, as I've told you, Hutchins. They have a great many ancient beliefs. I've already told you that they think of themselves as the first people on earth."

"Sir, please…"

"No need, Hutchins," the colonel acquiesced. "I've told you that they believe this, not that I do!"

"Yes, sir. Thank you, sir."

The colonel slavered a muffin with water-buffalo butter, popped it into his mouth and washed it down with the rich and steaming African coffee.

"Once each year, depending on the moon or some such thing, the men of the Kiko tribe…"

"The warriors!" Brabant interjected, roiling the waters. A player, indeed.

"The *men*," the colonel persisted, "go out on a sabbatical. Or a retreat, you might say."

Byrne-Jones threw his right elbow over the armrest and crossed his left ankle over his knee, ignoring his host. He was signaling the need for attention. And attention he received.

"I presume that they have done this since time immemorial, in order to impress their women with their virility. They spend days sharpening spears and knives, retying bows and nets. All the while the women chant and prepare the last of the food for their brave men."

Hutchins was drawn in like an eager boy at bedtime. "What then, Colonel? What of the ape?"

"Hutchins. It's all masquerade, a charade! They go into the jungle for a fortnight, living off small animals and roots and berries. Then they teach the adolescents about manhood and survival. These boys return to the pygmy village as new men. No longer children, you see?"

"Sir, no, I'm afraid I don't. What of Baruru, the ape?"

"Damnitall, Hutchins!" Byrne-Jones shouted. This was no longer a good-natured lecture; he was beginning to rant as he did on the ship. "They return to the women and children saying that they've caught and killed a great white ape. This is what signifies them as warriors, as men of the tribe!"

"Are you saying that there is no ape, sir?"

Byrne-Jones vaulted from his breakfast in obvious annoyance. Hutchins suspected that the displeasure was with him. Brabant knew it was not, but once started, the game must be played.

"Hutchins," the colonel began as he slowly circled the table, "how could they kill and devour the same goddamn ape year after year?"

"Are you calling this a sham, sir?" Hutchins saw into it at last.

"Exactly! A sham, Hutchins! And while we're speaking of fraud, when have you ever heard of an albino ape?"

"Well, sir, and please bear with me, there are white rhinos, that I know. And polar bears. They're white too, aren't they, sir?"

"Hutchins," the tone of exasperation creeping back into his voice, "we're not speaking of rhinos. Or bears. Are we?"

Hutchins was crestfallen. He started the morning, barely over an hour ago, imagining himself master of the jungle. Now, he was just a slow-learning schoolboy being chided by his master. He felt his face burn.

"Check on the gear and the entourage, Hutchins. We really must be going now," the colonel commanded. And all the time thinking to himself, I never really lied, never really told him that there *was* no great white ape.

The leave-taking was an odd affair. The drunken, defiant expatriate hid his tearful face behind a palm frond fan. In kind, the colonel veiled his hateful look under a mask of bonhomie. And their good-natured ex-soldier buried his fearful appearance beneath a show of competence for all onlookers. This was the prelude to the jungle, and in the jungle nothing was as it appeared. The seductive beauty of feather or petal, fin or pelt, was, as a matter of course, a trap. All enchantment was entrapment. No femme but fatale. Hutchins needed to watch his step, but the mere act of watching would captivate and ensnare. Treachery was everywhere about him. Each sight, every sound and scent. Whatever he touched, saw or tasted would deceive him. Betray him. Destroy him.

Waving and weeping, Brabant slowly shrank from sight as the steamer chugged further and further from the quay. Hutchins found in himself a queer emotion: he would miss the strange and unctuous Belgian and his lonely outpost, a combination priory and fortress. He could not explain to himself his desire to jump ship, swim back and wrap himself in a native loincloth – all as an unconscious protection from his expectations.

He jumped when Byrne-Jones put a comforting hand on his shoulder.

"Very well then," was their entire conversation. And each went his own way on the decidedly small vessel.

It was but a few hours from Soyo to Matadi on the steamer; almost due east. Here the Livingstone Falls made river travel impossible. Brabant negotiated for a small group of natives to see them safely up the Congo and farther up the Ubangi. The first leg would be the hardest.

Hutchins and the colonel spent overnight in Matadi, gathering supplies for the journey and relishing what would be their last decent dinner until they returned to Matadi, and to Soyo, and eventually, to Her Majesty's England. Byrne-Jones presented Hutchins with quinine and arsenic, both of which he recommended in daily doses to prevent malaria.

The following morning, at sunrise, they headed out, on foot, along the Stanley Road for the two hundred and fifty miles to Stanleyville. The road followed the course of the Congo River called the Livingstone Falls. Hutchins could feel the land rising above him as they passed, day by day, the cataracts of the rapids. And as the road climbed with each steep ascent in the river, Hutchins felt the overwhelming unbearableness of the Congo pressing down upon him.

The mosquitoes and gnats and dragonflies launched full armadas against the colonel and his entourage. He and his blond assistant received the worst of it, while his black retainers seemed almost immune to the assault. The only insect the native men seemed to fear was the tsetse fly, all the while feeding off local grubs and caterpillars.

Their march lasted nearly a week. Day by day, exactly the same. Breakfast of local coffee and fruits. Break camp. March. The colonel's monologue was broken only by rare rejoinder or incessant sting. After forty miles or so, the colonel would order the men to make camp. Dinner was always the same. The natives netted and dredged up the local fish and mixed them with freshly-dug tubers to make a filling, albeit tasteless, stew. After eating, the natives would chant and drum around the fire. The colonel reviewed his charts. The idle Hutchins found only one way to avoid thinking of his surroundings. Sleep.

Or try to sleep.

It pleased Hutchins, initially, that he had his own tent and didn't have to share. But even on this well-worn road, the jungle was just steps away, and the night made that point so well. The birds and monkeys and nocturnal animals screeched and slaughtered all the night. Their clamor haunted Hutchins, and the stinging insects made sure that he was awake to hear it.

They finally reached Stanleyville and the Stanley Pool, a virtual lake formed by the swelling of the Congo River. Directly in the center was the island called Bamu. The very name of it restarted the fear. Bamu. A mysterious island formed in the center of a lake that was no lake. Baruru. The great ape that did not exist.

"More than fifty feet deep, Hutchins."

"Is it inhabited, sir?"

"They say it harbors more than two hundred varieties of fish."

Hutchins turned to face his employer. "The island?"

"The Pool, Hutchins! Stanley Pool! Fish on an island, indeed!" he muttered as he made his way down the lane and into Stanleyville.

Hutchins just stood and stared at Bamu for hours. Until it disappeared. It was as if the fog from the humid river rose to clutch the thick darkness of the African night. The tendrils of mist stretched out over the pool and curled like tentacles grasping the banks. Bamu was no more. No shining star or waning moon could retrieve her. Hutchins felt terribly alone and hurried gratefully toward the lighted, occupied town.

He found Colonel Byrne-Jones at a seedy hotel bar at the river's edge. For the first time, Hutchins was leery of an ill-lit, noisy room occupied just by men. Every size and shape. Each nation and dress. Old and young. Agitated and ugly. Mercenaries. Here, they secured the services of a small, stout steamer, captained by another Belgian.

Captain Pierre "Cappy" Adam was a strong young man, and everything that his countryman, Brabant, was not. True, his hair and eyes were as dark as Brabant's, but his nature was genuine and manly. A sailor, to be sure, but military just the same.

Everything about Cappy was robust, from his laugh to his appetites. He took an instant liking to Hutchins, even if he seemed a bit uneasy with the colonel himself. And both Englishmen reciprocated his feelings.

Hutchins and Cappy became fast friends during the long journey up the Congo. They ate together and laughed together. They talked and exercised together. They stripped and wrestled on the deck to the amusement of the African crew, and swam naked in the river to their dismay. And the closer the two young men became, the greater the distance they put between themselves and Byrne-Jones.

They stopped at Bolobo to take on fresh water and supplies and at Yumbi to drop mail and medicine. Hutchins was astounded that his new friend, barely older than himself, was not only the captain of his ship, but master of his surroundings.

"Come with us," Hutchins said to Cappy one languid, starry night. The steamer chugged along at barely two knots on the placid sheet of the Congo surface. They were approaching the Equator, laying side-by-side on the poop deck, staring into eternity.

"To the pygmy?" laughed Cappy, stripped to the waist and barefoot as always.

Hutchins, properly dressed for the colonel's sake, rolled over onto his stomach and urged, "Why not? There's adventure there. And riches!"

"For the likes of your Colonel, not for me."

"Why not?" Hutchins asked, a childish pout creeping into his voice.

Cappy sat up and pulled the bill of his ever-present cap tauter over his forehead. He stood and went to the rails. Hutchins wondered, but did not follow.

"My life's on this steamer, Hutch, working for my living. Not roaming the jungles stealing the treasures of tiny people!"

"Stealing?"

Hutchins did rise and go to the rail near his friend.

"Hutch," Cappy began, desperately hoping that the younger man would see things his way. "The people you're about to meet are not much more than a meter tall! You know what that means, Hutch? About half your size. They only come up to your navel!"

Cappy emphasized his point with a stab at Hutch's stomach.

"I know that, Cappy. The colonel explained that to me."

Cappy came in close, grabbing Hutch's collar in his hands. He had to look up into his taller friend's eyes. He could see that this wouldn't be easy.

"You're not the first of Byrne-Jones's assistants in the Congo."

"What of it?" Hutchins could not imagine where this was going. Not for the life of him.

"Did you know that he never uses the same assistant twice?"

"Why should he?" This was growing no clearer for Hutchins. "He makes them wealthy. They retire to the country, or go into business or something. What of it?"

"Doesn't it strike you as odd? Byrne-Jones returns year after year, and yet no former assistant has returned to try his luck on his own."

"You don't know that, Cappy. You don't know that for a fact."

"Hutch, I know about every white man who has entered this jungle since I first arrived here. And every one who has left. What I'm telling you is that not every man who comes here with the colonel leaves."

"Boy, I can't believe it of you, but the colonel was right! He told me, on the steamer coming here, that people are jealous of him. That if he wasn't careful, they'd steal his connections and take his trade for themselves…"

"Hutch!"

"He said everyone was looking for a way to take advantage of him. I guess he was right."

Cappy twisted the shirt fabric tighter in his hands, drawing Hutchins closer still. From wrist to elbow, he rested on his friend's chest. They were face-to-face, nose-to-nose. But neither could really see the other's objective. Nor hear the other's objection. Each man was caught in his own world, his own obligation. Each of those spheres, each of those needs excluded the other. They simply wanted different things. Hutchins wanted to become rich, and felt he could keep his goodness in the process. Cappy wanted to be happy, and thought riches would be found in that. Neither man could surrender his plan to adopt the other's. They had met as strangers; played, then, as friends. Now, they parted as misgivings.

The sunrise brought the Ubangi River with it. Cappy docked on the south bank of the Congo, at the port of Irebu. He sent his men in search of food and supplies, and went himself in search of transport and guides up the Ubangi. He returned with his crew and another small group less than an hour later.

"Colonel," Cappy called to Byrne-Jones. "These men are on their way up the Ubangi to Impfondo and Bangui. They'll take you and your party as far as Lungala. Then you're on your own."

"Thank you, Captain Adam," the colonel chirruped in that falsely jovial way of self-righteous imperialists. "Perhaps one day I can convince you to take the whole trip with me?"

"Not fucking likely," were the last words either Byrne-Jones or Hutchins heard from Captain Pierre Adam.

Silently, Hutchins helped the retainers load their primitive scow with the gear and supplies. He never looked back to the Steamer Alysse or to its captain. He looked, instead, up the sullen Ubangi and into the brooding jungle surrounding it.

"We're off!" was all the cheery colonel offered as consolation.

And they were.

A strange band. There were eight black-skinned native polers languidly pushing the raft-like barge against the current. Byrne-Jones and his six black-skinned native porters rechecked the inventory for the trip inland. And a large empty hulk of a man, Henry Hutchins, who, through disappointment, rejection and betrayal, found himself isolated with fifteen companions. Found himself abandoned to a river teeming with strange swimming creatures. Found himself alone in a misty wilderness, its green canopy as rampant with threats as the muddy water below.

The river grew tighter as the days grew longer. The beasts from below the surface and beyond the banks grew brazen and exultant. Feathered things snapped their wings. Scaly things flourished their jaws. Furry things crept closer on the soil and swung closer from the branches. And all of them unseen, save in Hutchins' mind.

Day after day of one-sided conversation. Byrne-Jones dispensed with English and switched to Kongo, the language of the only crewmates who'd reply.

At sunset after another dreary day, Byrne-Jones made his way past the baggage and supplies, an oil lamp in one hand, a wooden bowl in the other.

"Dinner's here, Hutchins. Have some of my stew," he called out before he reached the stern.

"I can't eat, sir. I believe I'm a little under it."

"Nonsense! This is just the right—"

The little colonel stopped dead at the sight of his young assistant. Hutchins was a waxen gray in the golden light. His sodden hair was plastered to his sweaty face. His shirt had soaked through at his collar and chest, his underarms and belly. Byrne-Jones knew instantly what the matter was, but could barely say it aloud.

"Mofungo."

A simple word, but with complex repercussions.

All of the porters and all of the polers heard and repeated the word. Mofungo. The river fever. And fear swept through the small craft. Few caught the illness and lived. And few escaped the illness once they encountered it.

Byrne-Jones shouted to them in Kongo. *Come help!* But the natives huddled together on the opposite end of the boat. *Come now!* None would move. Byrne-Jones silently revealed a revolver and shot once into the air.

"The next shot will find a heart!" The colonel's stare was as steely as the sidearm he aimed.

The men came reluctantly to the colonel and the sick man. Together, he and the natives stripped Hutchins and threw his clothing in the river. They wrapped him in a sheet and then in several blankets. They added scorching habanero peppers to his stew, and Byrne-Jones fed him like an infant, dosing him intermittently with a personal remedy. His secret concoction.

For three days they repeated their unique form of nursing. Strip Hutchins, throw his sheet into the river, rewrap him, and force-feed him a soupy stew of fish meat and hot peppers. And for three days Hutchins was dosed with the colonel's potion. And he grew three days deeper into his madness.

For three days, Byrne-Jones stayed at his side, wiped his face, patted his hand, cooed softly. The colonel watched and analyzed, waited and prepared. Three days deeper into the jungle.

For three days, Hutchins labored in a personal limbo. The fever kept him blind and deaf to his benefactors and numb to their ministrations. Trapped in his private nightmare, all he saw were his own fears, all he felt were his own pains, all he knew was "Baruru."

But even in his fevered dreams, Hutchins could hear the jungle enclosing upon him. The twittering of the birds became a shrieking; the monkey's call, a scream. Each creature seemed to impinge upon him, stifling him, suffocating him. Both the tightness of his wrappings and the closeness of the humidity stole space along with the encroaching jungle and river. His own heartbeat took on the native rhythms, and he shook as if in response. In his mind those rhythms became a drumbeat; the jungle cries, a song. And that song had but a single lyric – Baruru.

From inside himself and above himself, he watched as the porters lashed him naked to a primitive stretcher. He listened to them chant as they worked. And the chant was the jungle and the river. Byrne-Jones instructed them: take care; don't harm him; don't bruise him.

From inside his mind and above his body, he watched as they moored, watched as they removed him from the scow. And he heard the drumbeat. And the beat was the darkness and the heat and the humidity. The colonel insisted: be careful lifting him; watch his arms; his legs, his teeth.

And so, with the colonel in the lead, the party descended into the darkness of an overgrown jungle trail.

Hutchins saw their progress like viewing a nickelodeon. All flickering images, oddly lit and strangely enacted. How small they seemed. How fragile. Odd, that they should carry him. He, like Gulliver to their miniature forms. And the drum grew louder. And the chant insistent. And Hutchins felt alone amid the small brown men.

They arrived at the pygmy village just before dusk. The anxious tribesmen and their overweening chieftain clamored around them. Hutchins' fevered mind saw them as miniscule, so much smaller than what the small colonel described. These tiny brown men wore small bands of fur. The young males wore nothing at all. The adults wore masks of clay pressed onto their faces, only their eyes and mouths showing. All carried weapons.

The chief was masked as well. A woven raffia mask with shells and stones tied in. The chief's raffia skirt reached the ground. Hutchins felt that same straw whip at his face. He was on the ground and they loomed above him.

Then the chanting began. A call-and-respond. The chief would yodel what seemed like a question and the gathered men would cry their answer. And their answer was always the same.

Baruru.

On and on they sang and danced, shouted and spun. They brandished their spears and grimaced behind their masks. Hutchins would have laughed, had he been well and upright. And not alone.

The porters had somehow separated Hutchins from the colonel and now, with additional help, carried his litter to the edge of the camp. Tying ropes to the litter and throwing the other ends over branches, they hoisted it upright against a denuded tree and unstrapped his hands. They retied them to the only two remaining branches, untied his lashes and pulled away his covering. The ensemble responded as one to the sight of the naked giant.

Hutchins stood weakly. He could not fall from his seeming crucifixion, yet he was still too feeble to fully lift his head. Two of the little warriors came forward and drove two thick stakes into the ground on either side of Hutchins at a little more than shoulder distance apart. They took strips of animal skin and tied his ankles to them. They brushed against him as often as they could. Hutchins could find no voice to protest.

But the others had a voice, and the voice said, "Baruru."

Naked and spread-eagled and alone, Hutchins was jolted by what happened next.

The nine adolescent pygmies approached. They were naked, but with no sense of shame. They chanted as they stroked the golden hairs of Hutchins' calves and thighs.

And all the time the clan answered the hypnotic song with the single rejoinder. Baruru.

They rubbed against him, luxuriating in his hairiness. They reached up to rub his chest hairs and armpits. Reached around to brush his hairy back. They stood upon one another's shoulders to rub against his hairy arms, his shoulders, his head. With their hands and faces they rubbed against Hutchins. With their legs and their torsos. And the more they rubbed, they faster they chanted. And the faster they chanted, they louder they got. The louder they got, the more liberties they took with their moaning, captive Hutchins. The boy on the top of the pyramid put a wadded cloth to Hutchins' face and squeezed a vile liquid into his mouth.

Repulsed and afraid, Hutchins tried to stretch away from the abnormal assault. He gagged, but could not vomit the foul potion.

And as he stretched away, he lifted open his eyes. The dimness and fog were suddenly gone. He saw all and he screamed.

"Merciful God! This is no delusion! I am not fevered, I'm drugged! Colonel, where are you? Help me, save me!"

Naked, dark bodies danced at a distance around the dull red fire that kept the dank jungle at bay. Dark, naked bodies danced against his pale, naked frame, touching and teasing. Tickling and tugging and tormenting.

"The Law of Baruru! You must be subjugated."

Hutchins heard the words in English and knew he must be imagining.

And then he saw. Just ten meters off, just past the blaze, Byrne-Jones, stripped as naked as he, was being carried upon a litter with the chieftain beside him. His skin was alternately pale pink or glinting. The chief was piling gold chains, dozens of them, on the colonel's bare neck. He was covering the colonel's naked arms and legs with more golden bands encrusted with jewels. He was encircling his bare waist with golden ropes. He was banding the colonel's fingers and toes with pure gold rings. Piling his head with golden crowns.

He'll be next, Hutchins thought. They're dressing him for some ritual. When they finish with me, they'll torture him.

"Colonel! I cannot free myself!"

"Neither am I free, Hutchins."

But even as the Byrne-Jones said it, Hutchins could sense the lie in it. The colonel was not captive.

"If you cannot free me, sir, save yourself!"

But Byrne-Jones did not move.

"I thought they were your friends, colonel. Why are they doing this to us?"

"You must be destroyed. Baruru commands it."

Slowly and deliberately, weighted down by a hundred kilograms of gold and gems, Byrne-Jones made his way over to the perverse ritual that held Hutchins as its centerpiece.

"I cannot save you, my boy. You must be consumed. It cannot be helped."

"But, why?" Hutchins cried through his mortification and pain. The rubbing and licking had become pulling and biting. "Why are you allowing this?"

"My boy, can it be that you still don't know?" The colonel just stood and stared at Hutchins in absolute disbelief as the tiny men continued their torture. The biting had become cutting and chewing.

"You, my boy, *you* are the great white ape!"

方方方

It was March the first. Victoria was queen. Women still dressed like ladies all, and men like gentlemen. Gentlemen dressed and comported themselves as such. At all times.

William Walton was a big man. Quite huge, really, for an Englishman. He stood at the dock waiting, peering left and right and left again. As if somehow he'd know on sight which member of this indistinguishable throng was his new employer. Walton was also very blond. That Saxon influence, again. Indeed, he looked very much the conqueror, standing on the wharf like a pillar of muscle. He alone was dressed in khakis. Good enough. Col. Byrne-Jones, decorated in India, remained riveted to the figure. This was a damn fine specimen of a man.

Da's Boy

"Johnny, me boy!"

The sun fell on Da like no other.

"Johnny, me boy!"

He was like those old tree stumps that could not be uprooted. Like those large rocks that could not be plowed under. He was a force of nature, better gotten around than confronted.

"No man ever got the best of me, Johnny, me boy!"

I was sure that was true. For he was a crinkly old man. A scrappy one. Hair, mostly silver, with just those few black hairs, black as his furry eyebrows. His full beard, short and mostly silver as well, seemed to grow up from his open shirtfront, and not just from his ears and nose and mouth. And his eyes.

What eyes? Sure, I know they were called emerald green. Green as the old sod. But they weren't, were they? They were black as birth, lost within the wrinkles of his leathery face. And they didn't see worth a damn. But oh, he heard everything. Every damn thing.

I'd been calling him "Da" for six years now, and I am but shy of nine. I'd been calling him "Da" since we moved here. Ma and me. To his cottage on the cliffs with his Guernsey's and his sheep. Dumb ferkin' sheep, I called them in me mind. Nasty ferkin' sheep, I cursed them between me ears and behind me eyes. Just the way me dad did.

Or, truth be told, the way I imagined that he would if he saw me – me, the son of a fisherman – forced to tend them since his death.

"Johnny, me boy!"

Stung like a new wound, those words.

"Johnny, me boy! I'm callin' to ya. Can't ya hear yer Da?"

That's how he called me. Every day. Every night. Johnny-me-boy.

Never would he just say "Johnny." Or just "John." And, saintsbepraised, never "son." No, didn't dare. Saintsbepraised. But every time called me "Johnny-me-boy." And each time, I felt cut down a bit more, even with the thing inside growing. Between me ears, behind me eyes.

"I'm just here, Da," I said to the sullen grey man on the sullen grey morning. The sodden fog aiding neither his vision nor me appreciation.

"Just where, Johnny, me boy? I can't see a ferkin' thing in this ferkin' mist."

You can't see a ferkin' thing period, old man.

"Just here, Da. Beside the old tree stump."

"Why ya runt ya! No wonder I couldn't find ya! Yer as short an' wide as the stump itself!"

I bristled at the gibe, but held me tongue as me Ma insisted. We had no place to go.

"Yes, Da."

"Too much of me fine lamb and mutton on ya. Too much of me cream and me cheese!"

I could smell the sea.

Even from way up here on the rugged cliffs, I could smell her. I could hear her. She called to me father and now she called to me. I don't remember much anymore of me father or his sea, but I do remember this one thing.

One day, I wasn't yet three, me Ma was cookin' dinner when me Dad came home, smelling of the sea. She told him to wash the stink of his mistress off before he ever thought to sit at her table. He told her she had it all wrong. She was his lover, but the sea was his love. Sad it is to say that I never truly understood these words. But still, I can't forget them. And I have to make them mine.

I smelled the sea. And then the whiskey.

"I found ya', Johnny-me-boy!" He stank.

I've given it me best, I swore then to me Ma, in silence. God-forgiveme, I've given it me best.

"No man's ever gotten the best of me, Johnny-me-boy!"

I hate you!

"No, Da," I answered obediently. "No man's ever gotten the best of you."

He wrapped me in the stink of his ancient tweeds. His sheep. Their lanolin. Feh! Lanolin and sheep. Old men and tweeds. Just stink.

Even at his age, his arms were massive. They closed like a vise. I was stuck in his stink.

"What are ya' doin' out here alone? Johnny-me-boy, there's cliff out here. Cliff that'll take ya' all the way down to the sea. The ferkin' sea."

I hate you!

All the while, as I stared at the old man who was me mother's father, I felt the warm sun on the back of me neck. I saw it on his face, in his squint. The heat of it raised the smell of him. The smell of him raised the thing. The thing that resided between me ears. Behind me eyes.

"But I'm not alone," and then I swallowed hard to continue, "Da..."

"Ya' are! Don't start yer ferkin' lyin' like yer ferkin' lyin' father! Yer alone! Out here by the cliff. All alone!"

Me ears hurt. And me eyes. Like something pushing at 'em. The thing wasn't resting anymore.

"I'm not alone and I'm not lying," I said in a voice I barely owned for its calm authority.

"I'll have no grandson of mine turn into a ferkin' lyin' sailor!"

I wanted to say, "ferk yerself," but the thing between me ears, behind me eyes, held control. I was like a puppet on a string. But not Da's puppet, nor Ma's. Not me Dad's neither. But puppet, just the same. And the puppet master, the thing between me ears and behind me eyes, instructed me. And what it said, I did.

"A lamb, Da. I was trying to figure a way to rescue the lamb."

Oh, his agitation was priceless. I don't know if it was the fog burning off, or he was actually steaming! T'was a ferkin' larf, nevertheless.

"What ferkin' lamb, ya stupid son of a sailor? No man ever got the best of me, Johnny-me-boy! I want me ferkin' lamb! Where's me ferkin' lamb?"

Blind as he was, he started tearin' around in search of a bleating baby. Priorities, I think they call it. And misplaced, I think they call that. Well, too ferkin' bad!

"Here, Da, let me help!"

"Where's the goddamn lamb, Johnny-me-boy?" He pleaded with me as he crawled hand-and-knees across the clovered lawn.

"No man ever got the best of me!"

He kept repeatin' and repeatin' it. Like it was ferkin' church or somethin'. Godforgiveme. And every time that he repeated it, the thing larffed. And each time the thing larffed, I egged him on.

"To yer left, Da. A few more meters," I shouted.

"Where, Johnny-me-boy? I can't see a ferkin' thing! Do ya' still hear it? I can't even hear it, Johnny-me-boy!"

"Yer there, Da!" *Ya ferkin' are!*

"Reach out, Da! Stand up an' reach fer it!"

He threw himself over the damn, ferkin' cliff. He did it himself.

No man ever got the best of me, Johnny, me boy!

No, Da. No man ever got the best of you. But I am just a boy.

JA Konrath writes the Lt. Jacqueline "Jack" Daniels thrillers, the latest of which is FUZZY NAVEL, *which is a lot more hardcore than the sissy title hints at. He's also the editor of the hitman anthology* THESE GUNS FOR HIRE *and the author of the horror novel* AFRAID *under the pen name Jack Kilborn, coming spring 2009. He promises that* AFRAID *will scare the shit out of you. In the past few years, Joe has had over fifty short stories published in various mags and anthos.*

Visit Joe at www.jakonrath.com.

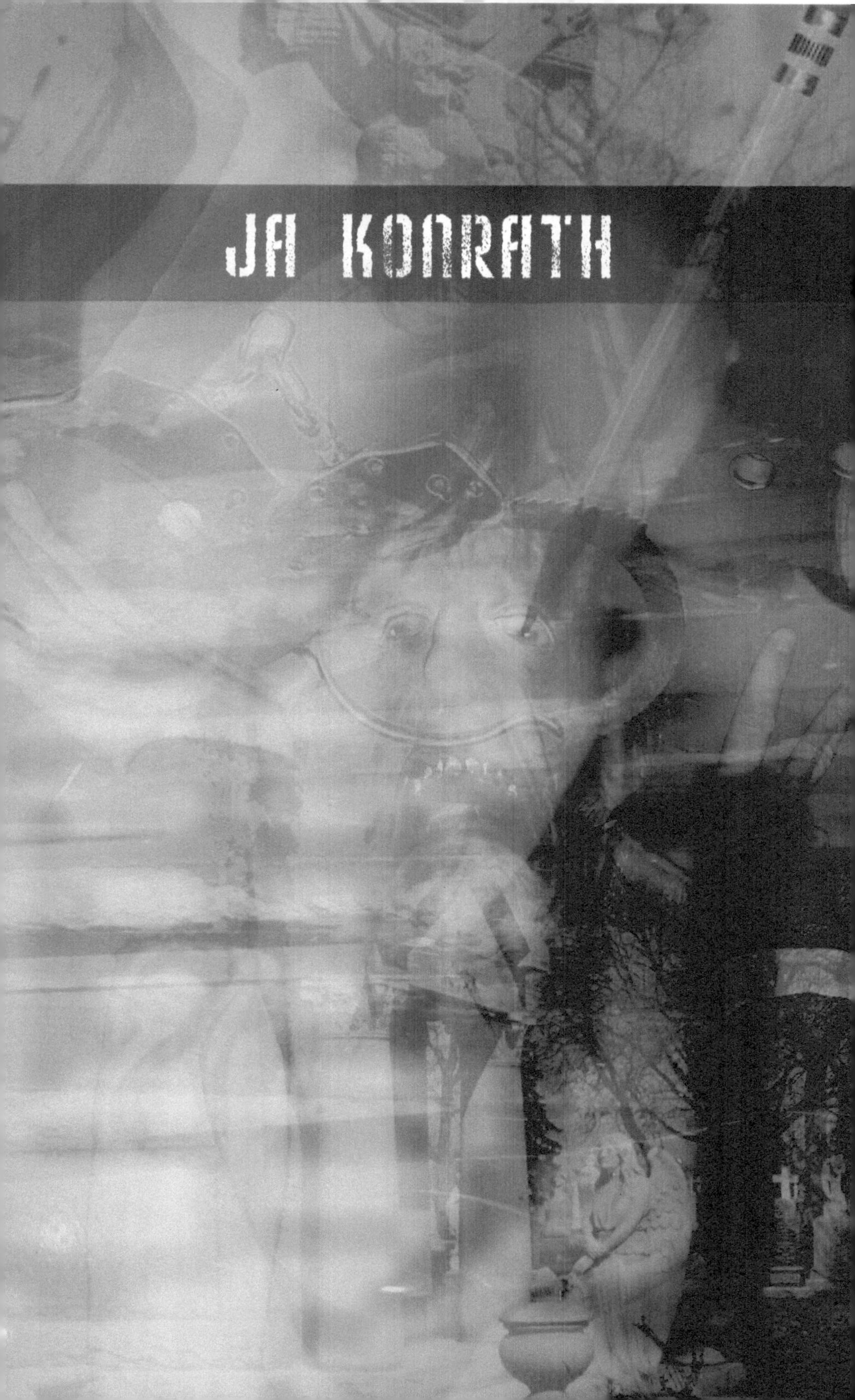
JA KONRATH

The Confession

"From the beginning? The very beginning?"

"Wherever you want to start, Jane."

"Wherever I want to start. Well. I guess you could say it all started when I was thirteen years old, when my father started coming into my bedroom."

"Your father molested you?"

"Molested? That sounds like he stuck his hand under my bra. My father fucked me. Made me suck him off. Called me Daddy's Little Whore. Used to write it on my forehead, in marker. I'd have to scrub it off before going to school. Wretched bastard. Went on until I ran away, at sixteen."

"And that's when you met Maurice?"

"That pimp fucker thought he was so smooth, busting out a white girl. Had no idea my old man busted me out years earlier."

"Was Maurice the one in the pit?"

"No. Maurice was the belt sander."

"Who was in the pit?"

"You want me to tell it, or answer questions?"

"Whatever you're more comfortable with."

"Okay. I'll tell it. Maurice found me at the shelter. Slimy pricks like him can probably sniff out teenage pussy. He talked sweet, hooked me on crack, and the next thing you know I'm blowing guys in their cars for twenty bucks a pop. Wasn't that bad, actually. I know I'm nothing to look at. Even before all the scars, I was fat and dumpy. Plain Fucking Jane, my mom called me. You got a cigarette?"

"Menthol."

"Beats sucking air. Thanks. Anyway, Maurice set me up with this freak. Guy took me back to his place, had a whole torture dungeon in his bedroom. That's how my face got all fucked up. Cigarette burns. Looks like acne scars, doesn't it? Kept me there for four days, then dumped me in a trash can."

"Did you know his name?"

"We'll get to that. You wanted this from the beginning, remember?"

"Take your time."

"Shit. I'm sorry, I can't smoke menthols. Do you have anything else?"

"No."

"Do I have to smoke?"

"No."

"I want to do this right for you."

"It's okay."

"Thanks…Mr. Police-man. Where was I? Oh yeah, after my face got burned, Maurice couldn't give me away. I wound up ass fucking winos in alleys for three bucks a pop. You ever have gonorrhea in your ass? Hurts like a bitch. And that fucking Maurice wouldn't give me money for the clinic. Whatcha got there? A picture?"

"Is this Maurice?"

"Jesus! That's disgusting! Is that real?"

"Is this Maurice?"

"Yeah. That's him. Doesn't look too good there, does he? Heard he might live."

"We don't know yet."

"Ha! Be damn tough for him to testify. But I'm getting ahead of myself. After a while, the VD got so bad I couldn't walk. Maurice beat the shit out of me, left me for dead. That's when Gordon found me."

"Reverend Gordon Winchell?"

"He's no reverend. No church would have him. He was just another preacher, screaming scripture at drunks in soup kitchens. Saved my life, probably. Got me to the hospital. Actually came to visit me during my recovery. Seemed like an actual decent guy from a while. Until I learned his kink."

"What did he do to you?"

"On the day of my release, the good Reverend took me to his apartment, tied me to the bed, and began biting me."

"Biting you?"

"Look at this—"

"You don't need to—"

"Don't get all prude on me. See? Nothing there. Bit my nipples right off. If I wasn't in handcuffs I'd show you what he did to my twat."

"Jesus."

"You okay, Mr. Police-man? You don't look so good. You want to take a break?"

"How did you get away?"

"He had it all worked out in his head that he'd kill me. But he couldn't. Didn't have the balls. So he dumped me in front of the same hospital he brought me home from."

"Did you call the police?"

"Are you fucking kidding me? I called fucking everybody. When my dad was raping me, I called DCFS, and he paid the assholes off. When that freak burned my face, I filed a complaint, and you guys didn't do shit. Gordon eats my private parts, one of your finest told me to have my pimp take care of it. Is this turning you on?"

"Stick to the story."

"This is some pretty sick shit."

"Stick to the story!"

"Okay. Sorry. Where was I? I lost my place."

"The cops didn't help you."

"Right. Okay, here it is. That was it for me. I had enough of playing the victim."

"Is that when you started…?"

"Is that when I started grabbing these sons of bitches? Yeah. When I got out of the hospital the second time, I tracked down the freak, watched his house until he was asleep, and then broke in. Used his own handcuffs on him. And his own blowtorch. It was hard to restrain myself, lemme tell you. But even holding back, his balls turned black and fell off after only three days."

"This was John McSweeny?"

"Yeah. He sure was a screamer. Screamed so much, his throat actually started to bleed. Know what the weird part is? He smelled great! Like honey baked ham. When I burned off his face I was actually drooling. Is that funny or what?"

"You stabbed Mr. McSweeny."

"The hell I did. I never killed no one. After a week or so, I uncuffed one of his hands, and gave him a steak knife. Fucker cut his own throat, and that's God's truth."

"After McSweeny came Maurice."

"Nope. Next came my father. I invited him over, got all weepy on the phone saying I forgave him. Hit him with a tire iron when he walked in the door. The freak, McSweeny, had all of these ropes and pulleys and shit, so I stripped Dad naked and hung him up. Then I lowered him down on that hat rack. Right up his ass. Funniest damn thing you ever saw. The more he moved, the lower he sunk, the higher the pole went up his poop chute. He lasted almost a month. I'd bring him food and water. That pole got about two feet up him before he finally died."

"That's murder, Jane."

"That's gravity, cop. If he stayed perfectly still, he would have lived. Blame Isaac Newton."

"Then Maurice?"

"Then Maurice. When I was honey-baking McSweeny, he was anxious to make the pain stop. Gave me all sorts of things. His bank account. His stocks. His car. I went to the dealer who used to sell me crack, bought a needle of H, snuck up on Maurice."

"You mentioned you used a belt sander."

"It takes all the skin off, but then gets real slippery. I kept buying belt after belt, until I figured out I could improve the traction if I threw salt on him."

"How long did you torture Maurice?"

"A few weeks. He'd scab over, then I'd start on him again."

"So...the guy in the pit?"

"That was the good Reverend Gordon. He got a heroin poke too, and when he woke up, he was chained up in the hole."

"What did you do to him?"

"Poetic justice. Fucker liked to bite, so I gave him a taste of his own medicine. I went to the pet store, bought a big box of rats. Put them in the pit with him. They were tame at first, but when they got hungry they began to nibble nibble. They started on the soft parts – look, do I have to read anymore?"

"Stick to the script."

"But you've still got your clothes on. You don't seem into this at all."

"I pay the money. I make the rules. I want you to finish reading."

"Look, sugar, I'm the best. Why do you want me to sit here and read when I can make you feel good?"

"Please don't..."

"Are you crying? Don't cry, baby. It's okay. Don't be afraid. Let me just get these pants off."

"I don't want to..."

"I like shy boys. Are you a shy boy? Let's see how shy you are – Jesus!"

"You...you were supposed to stick with the script."

"Where's your cock? You don't have a fucking cock!"

"You read the story."

"The story?"

"Reverend...Reverend Gordon."

"But that was all bullshit, right? Some freaky shit you made up?"

"He...liked to bite..."

"You're bullshitting me."

"I'm...a whore..."

"I'm leaving. Open this door."

"Daddy's Little Whore..."

"Open this fucking door or I'll start to scream!"

"McSweeny's house. Soundproof."

"You psychotic fucking freak! Let me out!"

"I won't hurt you. I want you to understand."

"Get the fuck away from me!"

"You're a prostitute. You're a victim too."

"Let me go!"

"Someone hurt you, right?"

"I want to leave. Please let me leave."

"You didn't choose this. You didn't choose to fuck men for money."

"I...want to leave."

"Who hurt you? Your father? Your pimp? You can tell me."

"I...don't..."

"I won't judge you. It's okay."

"No..."

"Who was it?"

"Don't..."

"Who was the monster that made you this way?"

"My...uncle."

"Your uncle?"

"He'd babysit me. Make me do things."

"I'm sorry."

"I…didn't mean to call you a freak."

"I know. It's okay."

"Jesus, I thought my life was shit. But all you went through…"

"It's okay. From now on, we're both okay. Come on, I want to show you something."

"I…I don't wanna go down there."

"Trust me. I would never hurt you."

"What's that smell?"

"I told you. Smells like ham."

"That was all true?"

"Most of it. Except they're all still alive. Meet Mr. John McSweeny."

"Oh my god…"

"Looks tasty, doesn't he? I use that wire brush on his burns. Still can coax a few screams out of him. Watch your step, there's the pit."

"Oh Jesus…"

"I see the rats finished off most of your face, Gordon. And congratulations! Looks like they also had a litter of hungry babies! You're a papa!"

"What…what is that?"

"That's Maurice. Can't even tell he's a black guy anymore, can you? That belt sander is quite a tool. Want me to pour some vinegar on him, wake him up?"

"This is all…I can't believe…"

"I know. It's a lot to take in. But here's who I really wanted you to meet. Say hello to my father. The person who turned me into the man I am today. Go on, say hello."

"Um…hello."

"He can't talk, because of the gag. But if you want him to answer, just give the pole a little shake. Like this. Hear that? I think he likes you."

"He's…crying."

"Of course he is. He's got two feet of hat rack up his ass. Probably punctured all sorts of vital stuff. You want to give the pole a little shake?"

"No…"

"Go ahead. Not too much, though. Just a little tap like this. See? You can hear him screaming in his throat.

"I don't want to."

"Yes you do. You're a victim, just like me. The only way to stop being a victim is to fight back. Go on."

"I really don't..."

"Stop playing the victim."

"But..."

"Fight back. It's the only way you'll be able to live with yourself. Put your hand on the pole."

"This isn't right."

"Raping children isn't right. Pretend it's your uncle hanging there. Remember all the things he did to you."

"My uncle. That fucking son of a bitch."

"Whoa! Hold on! You're going to kill him, shaking it that hard. Ease back."

"I'm sorry. I didn't mean to..."

"Yes you did. Felt good didn't it?"

"I...I thought of killing him so many times."

"Death is too good for men like that. He doesn't need killing. He needs to be shown the error of his ways. Oh...don't cry. It's okay. No one is ever going to hurt you, ever again. I promise. There there."

"Can we...can we..."

"Can we find your uncle and bring him here?"

"Yeah."

"Of course we can, dear. Of course we can."

The Necro File

A Harry McGlade Novella

Chapter 1

"It's my husband, Mr. McGlade. He thinks he can raise the dead."

The woman sitting in front of my desk was named Norma Cauldridge. She had the figure of a Bartlett pear and so many freckles that she was more beige than Caucasian. She also came equipped with a severe overbite, a lazy eye, and a mole on her cheek. Not a Cindy Crawford type of mole, either. This one looked like she glued the end of a hotdog to her face. A hairy hotdog.

Plus, she smelled like sweaty feet.

Any man married to her would certainly have to raise the dead every time she wanted sex. But I didn't become a private investigator to meet femme fatales. Well, actually I did. But mostly I did it for the money. And hers was green just like anyone else's.

I took a can of Lysol aerosol deodorizer from my desk and gave the air a spritz. Now it smelled like sweaty feet and pine trees. With a hint of lavender.

"I get four hundred a day, plus expenses," I told her.

I put away the air freshener and tried to sneak a look behind her large round Charlie Brownish head. When she walked into my office a minute ago, I'd been watching the National Cheerleading Finals on cable. The TV was still on, but I had muted the sound to be polite.

"I didn't tell you what I want you to do yet."

She was a whiner, too. Nasal and high-pitched. It's like God took a dare to make the most unattractive woman possible.

"You want me to take pictures of him acting crazy, so you can use them in the divorce."

On television a group of nubile young twenty-somethings did synchronized cartwheels and landed in splits. I love cable.

"How did you know?" Norma asked.

I glanced at Norma. The only splits she ever did were banana.

"It's my job to know, ma'am. I'll need your address, his place of work, and the first three days' pay in advance."

Norma's face pinched.

"I still love him, Mr. McGlade. But he's not the same man I married. He's...obsessed."

Her shoulders slumped, and the tears came. I nudged over the box of Kleenex I kept on the desk for when I surfed certain internet sites.

"It's not your fault, Mrs. Drawbridge."

"Cauldridge."

"A man is talking, sweetie. Don't interrupt."

"Sorry."

"The fact is, Nora, some men aren't meant to marry. They feel trapped, tied down, so they seek out different venues."

She sniffled. "Necromancy?"

"I've seen all sorts of perversions in my business. One day he's a good husband. The next day, he's a card-carrying necrosexual. Happens all the time."

More tears. I made a mental note to look up "necromancy" in the dictionary. Then I made another mental note to buy a dictionary. Then I made a third mental note to buy a pencil, because I always forgot my mental notes. Then I watched the cheerleaders do high kicks.

When Norma finally calmed down, she asked, "Do you take Visa?"

I nodded, wondering if I could buy used cheerleading floormats on eBay. Preferably ones with stains.

Chapter 2

Ebay didn't have any.

Instead I bid on a set of used pom-pons and a coach's whistle. I also bid on some old Doobie Brothers records. That led to placing a bid on a record player, since mine was busted. Then I bid on a carton of copier toner, because it was so cheap, and then I had to bid on a copier because I didn't have one. But after thinking about it a bit, I realized I didn't really need a copier, and those Doobie

Brothers albums were probably available on CD for less than the cost of a record player.

I tried to cancel my bids, but those eBay jerks wouldn't let me. The jerks.

I buried my anger in online pornography. Three minutes later, I headed out the door, slightly winded and ready to get some work done.

Chapter 3

This chapter is even shorter than the last one.

Chapter 4

George Drawbridge worked as a teller for Oak Tree Bank. At a branch office. It was only three o'clock, and his wife told me he normally stayed until five, so I had plenty of time to grab a few beers first. Chicago is famous for its stuffed crust pizza, and I indulged in a small pie at a nearby joint and entertained myself by asking everyone who worked there if they made a lot of dough.

An hour later, after they asked me to leave, I sat on the sidewalk across the street from the bank, hiding in plain sight by pretending I was homeless. This involved untucking my shirt and pockets, messing up my hair, and holding up a sign that said "I'm homeless" written on the back of the pizza box.

Other possibilities had been, "*Will do your taxes for food*" and "*I'm just plain lazy*" and my favorite "*this is a piece of cardboard.*" But I went with brevity because I still didn't have a pencil and had to write it in sauce.

I sat there for a little over and hour before George Drawbridge appeared.

He looked like the picture his wife gave me, which wasn't a surprise because it was a picture of him. Balding, thin, pinkish complexion, with a nose so big it probably caused back problems. After exiting the bank he immediately went right, moving like he was in a huge hurry. I almost lost him, because it took over a minute to pick up the eighty-nine cents people had thrown onto the sidewalk next to me. But I managed to catch up just as he boarded a northbound bus to Wrigleyville.

Unfortunately, the only seat left on the bus was next to George. So that's where I parked my butt, because I sure as hell wasn't going to stand if I didn't have to.

I gave him a small nod as I sat down.

"I'm not following you," I told him.

George didn't answer. He didn't even look at me. His eyes were distant, out there. And up close I noticed his rosy skin tone wasn't natural – he was sunburned. Only on the left side of his face too, like Richard Dreyfuss in that Spielberg movie about aliens. The one where he got sunburned on only the left side of his face. I think it was *Star Wars*.

Unlike his wife, George didn't smell like sweaty feet. He smelled more like ham. Honey baked ham. So much so that I wondered if he had any ham on him. I've been known to stuff my pockets with ham whenever I visited an all-you-can-eat buffet. After all, ham is pricey.

I restrained myself from asking if he indeed had any pocket ham, but couldn't help humming the Elton John song "*Rocketman*" and changing the lyrics in my head.

"*Pocket ham...And I think I'm gonna eat a long, long time...*"

I didn't know the rest of the song, so I kept think-singing that line over and over. After a few stops George stood up and left the bus. I followed him, keeping my distance so I didn't make him nervous. But after walking for a block I realized I could stand on the guy's shoulders and piss on his head and he still wouldn't notice me. George Drawbridge was seriously preoccupied.

We went into an Ace Hardware Store, and George bought twenty feet of nylon clothesline. He also bought something called a magnetron. I knew that there was something I needed to buy, but I couldn't remember what it was, and I hadn't written it down because I needed to buy a pencil. So I got one of those super large cans of mega energy drink. It contained three times the recommended daily allowance of taurine, whatever the hell taurine was.

After the hardware store it was back to the bus stop. We were the only two people there. George didn't pay any attention to me, but I was worried all of this close contact might get him a little suspicious. So I made sure I stood behind him, where he couldn't see me. Then I popped open my mega can and took a sip.

The flavor on the can said "Super Berry Mix." The berries must have been mixed with battery acid and diarrhea juice, but with a slightly worse taste. It burned my nose drinking it, to the point where I may have lost some nostril hair. Plus it was a shade of blue only found in nature as part of neon beer signs. I could barely choke down the last forty-six ounces.

The bus came. Again, the only seat available was next to George. I took it, and pulled my shirt up over my mouth and nose to disguise myself.

"Goddamn germs on public transportation," I said, loud enough for most of the bus to hear. This provided a clever reason for my conspicuous face-hiding behavior. I said it seven more times, just to be sure.

We took the bus to Jefferson Park, a northwest side neighborhood named after that famous politico, Thomas Park. George exited on Foster. I followed, tailing him up Pulaski and into the Montrose Cemetery, my mind racing like a race car on a race track, driven by a race car driver, named Race.

I never liked cemeteries. Not because I'm afraid of ghosts, even though when I was a child all the kids used to tease me because they thought I was. They would dress up like ghosts and try to scare me by visiting my house at night and threatening to hang us all because my family didn't go to church. They usually left after burning a cross on our lawn. Damn ghosts.

No, I hated graveyards for much more realistic reasons. When a person died they shouldn't be kept around, like leftovers. People had a freshness date. Death meant *discard*, not preserve in a box. What ghoul thought that one up? Fifty thousand years ago, did some caveman plant Grandma in the ground hoping to grow a Grandma Tree? What fruit did *that* bear? Saggy wrinkly breasts that hung to the ground and smelled like Ben Gay and pee-pee? And what's with neckties? Why are men forced to wear a strip of cloth around their necks good for absolutely nothing except getting caught in things like doors and soup?

As my computer-like mind pondered these imponderables, George cleverly gave me the slip by walking someplace I could no longer see him. That left me with three options.

1. Wait at the entrance for him to come out.

2. Search for him.

3. Drain the lizard. Those eighty ounces of Super Berry Taurine had expanded my bladder to the size of a morbidly obese child, named Race.

I opted for number 3, and chose *Mary Agnes Morrison, Loving Wife and Mother*, to sprinkle. Maybe the taurine would liven up her eternity.

I soaked her pretty good, and had enough left over for the rest of the Morrison family, including the *Loving Husband* and *Father*, the *Beloved Uncle*, and the *Slutty Skank Daughter*.

I made that last tombstone up, but it would sure be cool if it was real, wouldn't it? And wouldn't it be cool if someone made a flying car? One that gave you head while you drove? I'd buy one.

I shook twice, corralled the one-eyed stallion, and began to look for George. An autumn breeze cooled the sweat on my face, neck, ears, hair, armpits, back, legs, and hands, which made me aware that I was sweating. I put a hand to my heart and discovered it was beating faster than Joe Pesci in a Scorsese flick. Because he beats people in those flicks. Beats them fast.

Why was I so edgy? Had my subconscious tapped into some sort of collective, primal fear? Did my distant ancestors, with their reptile brains and their bronze weapons made of stone, leave some sort of genetic marker in my DNA that made me sensitive to lurking danger?

I did a 360, looking for pointy-headed ghosts with gas cans. All I saw were tombstones, stretching on for as far as I could see. Hundreds. Thousands. Maybe even billions.

"Easy, McGlade. Nothing to be afraid of. It's not like you desecrated their graves or anything."

Noise, to my left. I had my Magnum in my hand so fast that it probably looked like it magically appeared there to anyone watching, even though I didn't think anyone was watching.

Anyone *alive*.

My eyes drifted up an old, scary-looking tree, which had branches that looked like scary branch-shaped fingers, but with six fingers instead of the usual five, which made it even scarier. The sun was going down behind the tree, silhouetting some sort of nest-shaped mass on an extended limb that I guessed was a nest.

"Chirp," went the nest.

My first shot blew the nest in half, and two more severed the branch from the tree.

"Dammit, McGlade. Stay cool. You just assassinated a bird."

Which saddened me greatly. Magnum rounds were a buck-fifty each. Plus, I didn't have any extras on me. I needed to stay cool.

"Chirp," went the nest.

BLAM! BLAM!

By heroic effort I didn't shoot the nest a sixth time, instead walking briskly in the opposite direction. I was in a state that might be called "hyper-awareness," which was a lot like being the lone antelope at the watering hole. I could feel the stares of flying insects, and hear the grass growing. It was freaking me out a little bit, so I began to run, tripping over something on the ground, skidding face-first against a tombstone. A damp tombstone.

Mary Agnes Morrison.

I scurried away, palms and knees wet, and saw the bright red object that caused me to fall.

The empty can of Super Berry Mix energy drink.

So my paranoia wasn't really paranoia after all. It was just an unhealthy amount of caffeine in my veins. Which would have been kind of funny if I wasn't soaked with my own piss. Along with the taurine, the drink apparently contained a full day's supply of irony.

I stood up and shook out my pants legs.

"Get a grip, McGlade. And stop talking to yourself. You always know what you're going to say anyway."

I took three or ten deep breaths, holstered my weapon, and then set out looking for George.

I had no idea that in just two minutes I was going to die.

Chapter 5

I didn't actually die. I'm lying to make the story more exciting, because this part is sort of slow.

It starts to pick up in Chapter 8. Trust me, it's worth the wait. There's sodomy.

Chapter 6

It was a fruitless search, but that didn't matter – I wasn't looking for fruit. After a few minutes, I'd found him. He'd given me the slip by cleverly disguising himself as a group of three bawling women. Closer inspection, and some grab ass, revealed they really were women after all. I did my "pretend to be blind and deaf" act and stumbled away before any of them called the police or their lawyers.

Luckily, I caught sight of an undisguised George heading into the mausoleum. I never liked mausoleums. Burying the dead was bad enough. Putting them in the walls was just begging for mice to move in. And not the kind of mice who wear red pants and open up amusement parks. I'm talking about dirty, vicious, baby-face-eating mice, the size of rats.

Actually, I'm talking about rats.

Speaking of non sequiturs, I really needed to take another leak. The mausoleum was decent-sized, with a few hundred vaults stacked four high. Well lit, temperature-controlled, silk plants next to marble benches every twenty feet. It was the kind of place that would have a bathroom, I thought, while pissing on one of the silk plants. The pot it was in wasn't any realer than the plant, because all of my piss leaked out the bottom. I stepped over the puddle and commenced the search.

One of the techniques they teach you in private eye school is how to conduct a search, I bet. I have no idea, because I didn't go to private eye school. I wasn't even sure that private eye school actually existed. But it did in my fantasies. All the teachers were naked women, and wrong answers were punished with spankings. And the water fountains were actually beer fountains. If they had a school like that, I'd go for sure.

George wasn't down the first aisle. He wasn't down the second aisle either. Or the first aisle, which I checked again because I got confused.

"You do this?"

I spun around, wondering who spoke. It was some little old caretaker guy, clutching a mop. He pointed at the puddle on the floor.

"It was that other guy," I said, thinking fast. "You see him anywhere?"

"I only seen you, buddy. Did you go to the bathroom on my floor? There's a bathroom right there behind you. What kind of man does a thing like this?"

"That's what happens when you don't go to college."

"You piss on the floor?"

"You get a job cleaning up piss on the floor."

I left the guy to his menial labor and peeked down the second aisle again. Still no George. That led me down the third aisle, and I caught a glimpse of George crawling into a hole in the wall.

Closer inspection revealed it wasn't a hole. It was a vault. He'd crawled into someone's open tomb. I didn't even want to think why he'd do that, but my mind thought of it anyway, and then started thinking of it in enough detail that made me nauseous, yet oddly disgusted. Maybe a necromancer was someone who got his freak on with corpses. It was certainly a cheap date – only a few bucks for Lysol and Vaseline – and unless your game was really weak you'd pretty much always score. Still, I liked my women partially awake, and aware enough to be able to fight me off and tell me no.

Because *no* means try harder.

I crouched down, peering into the blackness, and saw nothing but the aforementioned blackness. I fished out my keys, which had a mini flashlight attached to the ring, and illuminated the situation.

This wasn't a grave after all. In the hole was a slide, like you'd find in a children's playground, if the playground was in a mausoleum, and the children were all dead. Probably wouldn't be a lot of kids begging to go to a park like that. Not the dead ones, anyway.

I gritted my teeth. There was only one way to find out where this slide went.

"Hey, old caretaker guy!" I yelled. "Where does this slide go?"

"Go to hell!"

"I told you, it wasn't me. I had asparagus on my pizza. Does it smell like asparagus?"

"Go to hell!"

I rubbed my chin. Maybe old caretaker guy was trying to tell me that this slide went straight to hell. I didn't really believe him. First of all, I didn't see any flames, and there wasn't any smoke or brimstone or screams of the damned. Second, hell doesn't really exist. It's a fairy tale taught by parents to make their kids behave. Like Santa Claus. And the death penalty.

Still, going down a pitch black slide in a mausoleum wasn't on my list of things to do before I died. My list was mostly centered around Angelina Jolie.

"This *does* smell like asparagus, you bastard!"

A glanced over my shoulder. Old caretaker guy was hobbling toward me, his drippy asparagus mop raised back like a baseball bat – a stinky, wet baseball bat that you wouldn't want to use in a baseball game, because you wouldn't get any hits, and because it was soaked with urine and stunk.

I decided, then and there, I wasn't going to play ball with old caretaker guy. Which left me no choice. I took a deep breath and dove face-first down the slide.

Chapter 7

When I was ten years old, my strange uncle who lived in the country took me into his barn and showed me a strange game called *milk the cow*. The game involved a strong grip, and used a combination of squeezing and stroking until the milk came. I remember it was weird, and hurt my arm, but kind of fun nonetheless.

Afterward, we fed the cow some hay and used the fresh milk to make pancakes. When we finished breakfast, we watched a little television. It was a portable, with a tiny ten-inch screen.

Many years later, my strange uncle got arrested, for tax evasion. So I have no idea why I'm bringing any of this up.

The slide was a straight-shot down, no twists or curve. The dive jostled my grip and my key light winked out, shrouding me in darkness, like a shroud. I had no idea how fast I was going or how far I traveled. Time lost all meaning, but time really didn't matter much anyway since I'd bought a TiVo. Minutes blurred into weeks, which blurred into seconds, which blurred into more seconds. When I finally reached the bottom, I tucked and rolled and athletically sprang to my butt, one hand somewhere near my holster, the other cupped around my boys to protect them, not to fondle them, even though that's what it might have looked like.

I listened, my highly attuned sense of hearing sensing a whimpering sound very near, which I will die before admitting came from me, even though it did.

I'd landed on my keys. Hard.

When I stood, they remained stuck in me, hanging from my inner left cheek like I'd been stabbed by some ass-stabbing key maniac. I bit my lower lip, reached back, and tugged them out, which made the whimpering sound get louder. It hurt so bad I didn't even find it amusing that I now had a second hole in my ass, and perhaps could even perform carnival tricks, like pooping the letter X. That's a carnival trick I'd pay extra to see.

I found the key light and flashed the beam around, reorienting my orientation. I was in some sort of secret lower level beneath the mausoleum. Dirt walls, with wooden beams holding up the ceiling, coal mine style. To my left, a large wooden crate with the cryptic words TAKE ONE painted on the side. I refused. Why did I need a large wooden crate?

Noise, from behind. I spun around, reaching for my gun, and a dark shape tumbled off the slide, ramming into me and causing my keys to go flying, blanketing me in a blanket of darkness.

The ensuing struggle was viscous and deadly, but my years of mastering Drunken Jeet Kune Do Fu from watching old Chinese karate movies paid off. Just as I was about to deliver the Mad Crazy Hamster Fist killing blow, my attacker got some sort of weapon between us and smacked me in the face. The blow stagged me, and I reached up and felt the extensive damage, my whole head bathed in warm, sticky liquid that smelled a lot like asparagus.

Then a light blinded me. A real flashlight, not the dinky one I had on my keys. I squinted against the glare, and saw him. Old caretaker guy. A light in one hand. His mop in the other.

I spat, then spat again. My mouth had been open when he hit me.

"I'm a private detective. My name is McGlade. I'm on a case."

"Does your case involve pissing on my floor?"

I spat again. I could taste the asparagus. And the piss. It tasted like I always guessed piss would taste like. Pissy.

"Listen, buddy, you're violating federal martial law by interfering with my investigation. Climb back up the slide and go call 911. Tell them there's a 10-69 in progress, with, uh, malice aforethought and misdemeanor prejudicial something, rampart."

My knowledge of cop lingo didn't galvanize him into action.

"Climb up the slide? How?"

"Hands and knees, old man."

"I'll get all dirty."

"You're a janitor."

"I'm a caretaker."

"You clean up in a cemetery. Dirt shouldn't bother you."

The flashlight moved off of my face and swept the area.

"What is this place? Some sort of secret lower level under the mausoleum?"

I spat again. "No duh."

"Look, there's a crate."

Old caretaker guy waddled over to the wooden TAKE ONE box, opened the top, and pulled out a brown robe.

"I guess we're supposed to take the robes."

"Obviously."

I walked over, grabbing a robe for myself. It was made out of felt, and had a large hood. A monk's robe. Or rather, a store-bought Halloween monk's costume.

Old caretaker guy put his on, and as he was tugging it over his head I gave him a Crazy Hamster Elbow to the chin. He went down, hopefully in need of some facial reconstructive surgery. I scooped up his flashlight, located my keys, and limped down the tunnel.

I followed the path a few dozen yards into the darkness, ducking overhead beams when they appeared overhead, keeping an eye peeled for rats, and giant spiders, and that guy I was supposed to be following, I think his name was Fred or George or something common and only one syllable. Maybe Tom. Yeah, Tom.

No, it was Fred.

The air down here was cool and heavy and smelled like asparagus piss, but for the most part it was clean. That meant ventilation, either in the form of an exit, or an air osmosis recirculator, and I'm pretty sure that osmosis thing didn't exist because I just made it up.

The tunnel ended at a large metal door, the kind with a slot at eye-level that opened up so some moron could ask you for a password. Which is exactly what happened. The slot opened, and a pair of eyes stared out at me, and whoever belonged to those eyes asked for a password.

"Tom sent me," I said.

"That's not the password."

"Tom didn't say there was a password."

"Tom who?"

"Tom," I improvised, "from Accounting."

"How is Tom?"

"Good. Just got over a cold, still kind of congested."

"It's great you know Tom, but I'm not supposed to let you in without a password."

I was tempted to give him a Three Stooges eye poke through the slot.

"Look," I reasoned, "why else would I be down here?"

"I have no idea. Maybe you got lost."

"I'm wearing the robe." I did a little sashay to emphasize the fact.

"Maybe you're a cop."

"I'm not a cop."

"How do I know that?"

"Because I don't have a badge. You want to frisk me to check?"

"No. You smell like pee-pee."

I set my jaw. "Doesn't anyone ever forget the password?"

The eyes shrugged. "Sure. Happens all the time."

"So what happens then?"

"I ask them for the back-up password."

I drew my Magnum, jammed it in the slot.

"Is the back-up password *open the fucking door or I'll blow your head off?*"

"Yep that's the password."

He opened the door. I considered smacking password boy in the head, and it seemed like a good idea, so I gave him a little love tap with the butt of my pistol. When he fell over, I gave him another little love tap in the stomach, with my foot. This made my ass hurt even more, so I kicked him again, which hurt even more, so I kicked him again for causing me pain, and again, and again until the pain got so bad I had to stop, but I didn't, I kicked him once more.

Then I wandered through a short hallway and into a large open area, roughly the size of a woman's basketball court, which is the same size as a men's basketball court, but a woman's court has bouncing boobs. I noticed little details like that. Unfortunately, this room didn't have bouncing boobs. It had a dozen-plus bone-heads in robes, all carrying flashlights, standing around and chanting something monkish.

I wormed my way into the group and considered the camera in my pocket. Mrs. Drawbridge had hired me to take pictures of her husband acting nutty. This qualified, but it was too dark to make out any details, and a flash might cause attention. Plus, these goofballs all had their hoods on, making positive ID pretty impossible.

I scanned the room, seeing if I could find Tom. I spotted him through my clever detective technique of looking around, and noticed his bag from the hardware store, still clenched in his hand. Maybe I could get up close, shove the camera in his face, get a quick snapshot, then run away.

"Attention, everyone!"

The chanting stopped. One of the wannabe monks had his hands up over his head, his knuckles brushing the dirt ceiling. Everyone stared at him.

"Let us form the sacred pentagon, and pray to Anubis, god of the dead, to bless the ceremony this evening. All hail, Anubis!"

"All hail, Anubis!" the monks chanted in reply.

Then we all arranged ourselves in a five-sided square around something in the center of the room. As I probably should have guessed – but didn't because I was too busy rubbing my painful throbbing ass – in the center of the room was a coffin.

The head monk shouted, "Who shall be the first to partake in the carnal pleasures of beyond the grave?"

I looked around, wondering what idiot would be stupid enough to bone a corpse, then found myself shoved into the center of the circle.

"My friend will go!"

I spun around, aiming the flashlight. It was old caretaker guy, a big grin creasing his face.

"This first has been chosen!" head monk bellowed. Two other monks – big ones – grabbed my arms and escorted me to the coffin.

"Guys, I'm new here. I'd sort of prefer to wait until next time before violating any dead people."

I tried to pull away, but these monks had supernatural strength. The weight of the situation began to weigh on me. Sex with a cadaver wasn't on the list of things I wanted to do before I died, unless the cadaver was Angelina Jolie.

Then I stopped struggling, because I realized this had to be some kind of joke. Like a hazing prank, and when the coffin opened a stripper would pop out and blow me. That made a lot more sense then a society of necrophiliacs meeting secretly under one of Chicago's largest cemeteries. Right?

I smiled, hoping the stripper had big tits, not even protesting when I was depantsed by one of the hulky monk guys. They also took my gun. I figured that was okay – I only needed one type of gun to handle a hot stripper. You know what I mean.

My penis. I'm talking about my penis.

"Okay." I clapped my hands together. "Let's do this."

Another monk opened the coffin, and I stared in grinning expectation at a naked dead man.

"That's a guy," I said.

Head monk came in close and whispered. "Couldn't find girl this time. It doesn't matter. Death is death. It's all a turn-on. You're here to get laid, right?"

I eyed the body. A chubby bald white guy, late fifties. The Y cut across his chest indicated he was autopsied. Death was probably a heart attack, based on the size of his gut.

"I'm actually not really feeling it right now," I said.

"We can flip him over, if that helps."

"I don't think it will help."

"How fresh is it?" someone in the crowd yelled.

"Planted eight days ago," head monk answered.

The crowd cheered.

"I got sloppy seconds!"

"I got thirds!"

"I want to go last, when he's so full he's leaking out of his nose!"

I tried to step away, but the inhumanly muscular monks held me firm.

"I'm really not horny right now," I insisted. "In fact, I may never be horny again."

"My friend is shy!" That damn old caretaker guy again. "He doesn't like to pitch! He prefers catching!"

"No problem. Fetch the bicycle pump!"

Someone brought over a bike pump, complete with needle tip. The head monk fussed around with the poor dead guy's junk, then pushed the needle into the pee hole at the shriveled tip. I had an anti-erection, my dick actually retreating into my body as I watched.

He began to pump. And, incredibly, the corpse's johnson responded by filling out in length and width, until it stuck up like a tent pole. The monk kept pumping, and then the scrotum inflated. First apple-sized. Then grapefruit. Then soccer ball. I winced, waiting for the *POP*, but he quit before it got to medicine ball proportions. Which is a good thing, because balls that big would be bad medicine indeed.

"This is wrong on so many levels," I said.

Someone stuck a tube of KY into my hand, the head monk said, "Have fun," and then I was tossed onto the corpse, the coffin lid slamming closed above me with devastating finality.

Chapter 8

I lied. There isn't any sodomy in this chapter. Instead, there was a good minute of mindless screaming panic, followed by a minute of mindless yelling terror, and another two minutes of unmanly begging.

"We're not opening up until you finish," head monk spoke through the coffin lid.

"I'm finished." I hoped I sounded sincere. "It was fantastic. Best dead sex I ever had."

He wasn't buying. "The only way you're getting out of there is by embracing your necrophilia. That's why you came, isn't it? That's why we're all here. To make our fantasies come true. To taste the forbidden."

"I tasted it. It's like rotten meat, and disappointingly unresponsive."

"We can stay here all night if we have to."

I collected my thoughts, the sum total of which were *Get me the fuck out of here.* Then I calmed down a little. Then I started screaming again. Then calm. Then more screaming. Then even more screaming.

Finally, I took a deep breath, and really started screaming.

Being hysterical is pretty exhausting, so I took a time-out and tried to rationalize what to do next, other than scream.

Unfortunately, clearing my head made me even more aware of my current situation, and how disgustingly horrible it was. I was trapped in a coffin, lying on top of a naked dead guy with nuts the size of a basketball. A curly-haired basketball with a bratwurst glued onto the top. It pressed against my pelvis in a way that could only be described as awful.

My upper half wasn't any happier, with my face inches away from a dead man's. He didn't really smell like rotting meat. Not exactly. It was more like meat that was about to go bad, but dunked in formaldehyde first. His flesh was waxy, sort of stiff, and cold in a way that only dead people get. I moved my hands up across his nude, hairy chest, fighting the urge to vomit, and then pressed my elbows into his gut to force some distance between us.

It was a mistake. His autopsy meant his ribs had been cut away, and no ribs meant no internal support. My elbows ripped through the stitches and my arms disappeared into his still-moist body cavity.

I felt things. Horrible things. Squishy things. To prevent the organs from leaking, the clever embalmer had placed them in plastic bags, like some sort of lunch snacks from hell. I thanked the darkness that it was dark and I couldn't see anything, because I had no light. But I screamed anyway.

When the screaming finally stopped, I screamed a little more, and then realized the only way I was going to get out of here is to do what women have been probably doing with me ever since I'd been sexually active.

I'd have to fake it.

Unfortunately, the only way to fake a sexual movement is to perform a sexual movement. So I locked my knees on either side of his hips, his giant scrotum tucked beneath my legs like a fleshy bicycle seat, and began the humping motion. I also began to cry.

The coffin went with the rhythm, back and forth and back and forth, and it was a high end model which meant springs in the cushion which meant this felt even more like the real thing. Even though I couldn't see I squeezed my eyes shut and invented gods in my imagination so I could pray to them to make this end. I tried to think back on happy times, but too many of my happy times involved sex and that didn't help me block out the unhappy fact that I was fake dry-humping a corpse. I tried thinking about happy times when I was a kid, and unwillingly focused on the time

I was six years old and my mother bought me a Hoppity Horse for my birthday, and how I used to love bouncing up and down the neighborhood and, oh goddamn it…

I threw up in my mouth. Energy drink and pizza mixed with stomach acid. I swallowed it because adding puke to this situation was possibly the only thing that could make it worse.

Scratch that last thought. My pelvic gyrations had loosened up some trapped air in the nether regions of the cadaver, prompting extreme flatulence. He ripped one so loud it sounded like a trumpet. But it sure as hell didn't smell like one. You think you know stink? Dead guy farts are number one on the stink-o-meter. It was so bad, I'm sure if I could see I would have seen green gas.

"Do it! Give it to him!"

I wasn't sure who the head monk was cheering on, me or the dead guy. But I knew in order to properly fake it, I had to add some vocals to the rhythm.

"Oh, daddy!" I moaned, trying not to breathe. "Oh, yes, daddy!"

Someone slapped on the top of the coffin, urging me on. There was more corpse farting, more crying, more humping, and finally I couldn't handle this anymore without a complete nervous breakdown and I cried out "Oh, god!" and then went still.

Eventually, miraculously, the coffin lid opened. I made it. I was alive. Amazingly, wonderfully alive. Now I needed to find my gun and eat a bullet.

The strongarm monks pulled me out of the coffin, my arms slupping from the dead man's chest cavity, glistening with guck.

"Congrats!" head monk said, giving me an *attaboy*! slap on the back. "You really rocked his dead world!"

I wiped my hands on his fake robe.

The rest of the perverts queued up for their shot at playing Megaball, and I managed to stumble into my pants. I even got my gun back. I cocked the hammer and stared deep into the blessed release promised by the inside of the barrel, and then remembered I only had one bullet left, and if anyone should die, it was old caretaker guy.

I looked around for the bike pump, flitting with the idea of filling his nads up with air before sending him to hell. Or maybe I would just pump him up and let him live. Live out the remainder of his pathetic life with unusually large testicles. The humiliation he'd suffer. The stares. The laughter. Plus, it would be impossible to find pants.

Regrettably, the bike pump was nowhere to be found. Neither was old caretaker guy. And I'd apparently won the loser trifecta, because Bill, the man I'd been hired to follow, was also MIA.

Some pinhead hopped into the coffin with Frankengroin, and I picked up the flashlight and made my way to the exit before the groaning began. I needed some fresh air. I also needed a hatchet and some steel wool, so I could access and scour the last half an hour from my brain.

Conveniently, the exit was a large door marked EXIT, which opened up to some concrete steps. I took them up, and they ended in a maintenance closet, which opened up into the mausoleum. It was an easier – and faster – entrance than the nightmare slide, but lacked the dramatic effect.

I pulled out my gun, did a quick search for old caretaker guy, scared the hell out of some grieving old man, mourning his dead wife or some similar maudlin bullshit, and then made my way through the cemetery, across the street, and into the first place that sold liquor.

Three shots and two beers later, I called the police.

Chapter 9

The cop I called was a somewhat tasty little morsel named Lieutenant Jackie "Jack" Daniels. So-so face, great legs, nice rack, especially for an older broad. I knew her back in the day, when we were partners in blue, and she continued to have a crush on me almost two decades later.

"I don't owe you shit, McGlade. And if you bother me again I'm going to send some uniforms over to trash your apartment and beat you with phone books for so long you'll have area codes embedded in your skin."

"Pay attention, Jackie. I'm offering you a prime bust here. As we speak, there's a group of perverts running a train on a dead guy with gonads the size of a Thanksgiving turkey."

"Let me guess. Is it a *Butterball*?"

"They have to be stopped. Would you want some loonies digging you up and poking your cooter after you've been laid to eternal rest?"

"Sex with a corpse, disgusting as it is, isn't a crime, Harry. Didn't you read *Bloody Mary* by JA Konrath? There was a character in there, did the same thing."

"I listened to part of the audiobook. The author thinks he's funny, but he's not."

"It's a he? I thought a woman wrote those books."

I tried to make my voice sound soothing, a tough trick because I had screamed myself raw.

"Jackie, partner, be a good cop and send a team over to the cemetery. You'll get brownie points from the Captain, a little TV spotlight, and the satisfaction knowing that you got a bunch of lunatic perverts off the street."

"What do I charge them with, McGlade? Public indecency? You want me to waste manpower on a minor misdemeanor?"

"Aggravated sexual assault. Trust me. It was aggravating."

"Who's going to press charges? The cadaver? You want to bring a corpse to trial? The cross examination would be riveting, I bet."

I clenched my fist. "Dammit, Jackie! I was violated in ways you can't even begin to understand. I'll never be the same. My sex life might very well be ruined, and I won't be able to ever watch basketball on TV again. And I love basketball. If you don't arrest these assholes I'm going to go on a killing spree and when they bring me in I'll tell them you could have stopped it just by doing your job."

She sighed big, but I knew I'd won. "Cut the melodrama, McGlade. I'll send a few uniforms over to check it out."

"If you arrest a creepy old caretaker guy, call me. I'm going to impale him on his mop and make him clean all the floors in Union Station."

"I got extra tickets to the Bulls game tomorrow. Want them?"

"You can really be a mean bitch sometimes, Jackie."

I hung up, ordered another tequila, drank it, ordered another, drank it, then called a taxi to take me back to my condo to really start drinking.

Chapter 10

My plan had been to drink so much I didn't dream. And when I peeled my eyes open, I thought it worked. I couldn't remember a single nocturnal image, let alone any nightmares.

Then I realized I was lying naked on the kitchen floor, straddling a head of lettuce.

"Oh hell no."

Like any freaked-out person, I needed answers. So I searched Google, using the terms "post dramatic stress disorder sex with corpses and giant testicles" which linked me to a bunch of unhelpful porn sites. I dutifully surfed them anyway, but there were no answers there.

Then I went to eBay, and I was still the top bidder on everything. Lousy eBastards! I decided I just wouldn't pay if I won, but then I'd get negative feedback, and negative feedback was permanent. I'm proud of my 99.4% positive score. My only bad mark came from some jerk who didn't read the whole product description, only the header. I sold him a mint Babe Ruth baseball card for $260. The card had some tears and a few bends, but I'd stapled some mint leaves to it. Which I mentioned, in two point font, at the bottom of the listing. Some guys can't take a joke.

Next I checked my email, where I discovered I'd won the Irish lottery, inherited eighty million dollars from an unknown relative, and was asked to shuffle funds into my bank account from the President of Rwanda. They all got my standard response: enthusiastic replies with an attachment supposedly containing my routing number. The attachment really contained an email bomb, which once opened would bombard their computers with tens of thousands of naked pictures of actress Bea Arthur. I called it the Maude Virus.

I had a bit of a hangover, my ass still hurt from where I'd fallen on my keys, and I was hungry. But the only food I had in the condo was that head of lettuce, which I wasn't going to eat even if I were starving to death, so I changed into a slightly less dirty suit and hit the corner convenience store for an overpriced cup of joe, a dose of Advil, and a prepackaged cheese Danish.

It was a gorgeous Chicago day, the sun shining, the lakeshore breeze blowing, the pigeons singing their lovely song. I leaned against the storefront window and called my client.

"Hello?"

"Is this Maxine Drawbridge?"

"It's Norma Cauldridge."

I rubbed my nose. "Hi, Maxine. It's Harry McGlade. I need more money."

"Did you find something out, Mr. McGlade?"

"I did. And it's ugly. Real ugly. Plus, I was gravely injured during my surveillance." I smiled at my unintentional pun, which was actually intentional. "I'm not going near him again without more cash."

"I've already paid you twelve hundred dollars."

My nose still itched, so I scratched it. On the inside.

"I want double that. Think of it as an investment. When the lawyers see the dirt I've got on old Roy, you'll take the freak for every dime he has."

I removed my finger, noted something gray and waxy stuck to the end. I'd been picking my nose for years, and this was the strangest booger I'd ever seen.

"Who's Roy?"

"Whatever the hell his name is."

I took a closer look. Sniffed. It smelled familiar.

"Do you have pictures?"

"I will. Send the money to my PayPal account. My email is… oh god…"

The odor was rotten meat and formaldehyde. Somehow, while I was in the coffin, I'd gotten a hunk of dead flesh up my nose. Dead flesh covered in boogers. And a nose hair.

I leaned over and puked up the coffee, Danish, and Advil. Eighteen bucks and change, shot to hell.

"Mr. McGlade? Are you there?"

I wiped a toe through the puke, looking for the Advil. They were probably still good. Instead, I saw something that made me want to quit eating forever.

Part of a human ear.

I got closer, sure it had to be some coincidentally-shaped chunk of chewed Danish.

No, it was an ear. The upper, cartilagey part. I often nibbled women's ears when we were fooling around. I must have got caught up in the role-playing and bitten off a hunk.

"Mr. McGlade?"

"Scratch that. I want triple."

"That's outrageous."

"Lady, I went to third base with a dead guy last night, all because of your husband. Pay me, or find some other schmuck to do your dirty work."

"You did what with a dead guy?"

"Don't believe me? You want to talk to him?"

I held my cell phone over the ear. Then I realized I was acting a bit hysterical. Maybe I was still asleep, and this was just a dream.

I felt my backside, wondering if the pain in my ass was truly from sitting on my keys, or from something that was *still up there*...

I stuck my hand inside my pants, reaching down the plumber's crack...

It's a dream, it has to be a dream...

A pigeon waddled over, pecked up the ear, and ran off. My fingers crept closer...

"Mr. McGlade?"

A dream, all a dream, just a harmless dream...

And then I touched the severed end of something that shouldn't be there. Something that felt like a Pepperidge Farm County Style Breakfast Sausage Link.

"Please!" I cried out. "If there's any decency left in this cruel world, Let this be a dream!"

Chapter 11

It was a dream.

I woke up in bed next to an empty bottle of tequila. Blessedly, there was no head of lettuce between my legs. And the puddle of puke on my pillow didn't contain anything resembling human flesh. I did a nose check and an ass check, and they were both free and clear.

So much for drinking away the nightmares.

I rolled out of bed, padded to the can, showered, dressed in a slightly less dirty suit than yesterday, and visited the local convenience store for a coffee, Danish, and some Advil. That should have been my tip off I'd been dreaming – paying eighteen bucks for those three items. I forked over the real-life money – twenty-six bucks – then called Mrs. Drawbridge and demanded quadruple my rate. She reluctantly agreed, and mentioned her husband was in bed, still asleep. I decided to stakeout her house and tail him. And this time, I'd be taking some sophisticated equipment.

I returned to the condo and entered my Crime Lab. It was actually an extra bedroom that I converted into a crime lab by stocking it with spy stuff and writing *Crime Lab* on the door. The modern private detective had to stay current with modern gadgetry, so I bought all of the latest high-tech stuff. Phone tappers. Listening devices. Infra red things. A remote control tank with a miniature video camera hooked up to the turret. Cell phone jammers. A set of brass knuckles with a microchip inside that played Pat Benatar when I socked somebody.

All the essentials.

I popped the SanDisk memory card out of the tank and plugged it into my computer, to check the footage I'd recorded during my practice run. The video was a little choppy, but more than acceptable.

The first scene was of a dog in Grant Park, urinating.

Cut to the same dog, pooping.

Cut to another dog, pooping.

Cut to the first dog, eating the second dog's poop.

Cut to a third dog, trying to hump the first dog, who was still munching on the poop.

Cut to the poop, which didn't look like it warranted being eaten.

Cut to some gangbanger punk, running off with my tank.

Cut to me explaining to the cop why I fired my gun in a populated area, and then me getting arrested.

With some editing, and the right soundtrack, the footage could be the backbone of a really good documentary about urban crime, and the amusing social lives of dogs.

I opened up a fresh SanDisk card, put that in the tank, and loaded everything into in a gym bag, along with a digital camera that could shoot night-vision, a Bionic Ear listening cannon, and a little wind-up nun that shot sparks out of her eyes. Thusly equipped, I high-tailed it over to the long term garage, jumped in my stakeout car – an inconspicuous green Chevy El Camino with yellow racing stripes on the hood – and drove to Jim Drawbridge's house.

The key to any successful stakeout is three-fold: Food, tunes, and a pot to piss in. The food should consist of chips and snack cakes. Sugar and carbohydrates jack up the insulin level, which leads to a heightened sense of awareness, probably. The music should be high energy, like heavy metal, but shouldn't include the power ballads. The piss pot can be an old milk jug or thermos. Try to avoid cellophane potato chip bags – as I've learned from experience, they tend to leak.

Since I never knew when I'd have to go on a stakeout, I kept my car stocked with everything I needed. But once I found a suitable vantage point – on the street directly in front of Jim's house – I realized I was less stocked than I should have been. I was way low on sugary snacks, but had a surplus of urine in an old apple juice bottle. Unless it was, perhaps, actually apple juice. A quick sniff would tell me.

It was urine. And I needed to stop eating asparagus.

I took a moment to muse about the gratuitous amount of bodily fluids that seem to have come up in this case, and cracked open the door and dumped the piss onto the street, where it made a foamy little river down the curb and to the sewer drain.

Then I cranked up the Led Zepplin, licked the crust out of some old Twinkie wrappers, and waited for Jim to show up.

After half an hour, the coffee needed to be set free, so I filled up half the apple juice bottle. The secret to zero splatter is aiming for the inside edge, and then squeezing dry rather than shaking.

After an hour, Mrs. Drawbridge came out of the house and knocked on my window.

"George left before you got here."

"Do you have any snacks?"

"No."

I noticed she had some orange powder in the corner of her unattractive mouth.

"You have cheese curls," I said.

"No I don't."

"Bring me the cheese curls."

She folded her arms. "I don't have any."

"You have Cheetos dust on your lips."

"I was eating carrots."

"Were they powdered carrots?"

"Maybe."

"Bring me the goddamn Cheetos, or I'm off the case."

She frowned and waddled off. I called after her, "And anything Hostess or Dolly Madison!"

I air guitared in perfect synchronization with Jimmy Page until the ugly wife returned with my treats. The Cheetos bag only had a few left in the bottom, and Mrs. Drawbridge's cheeks were puffed out chipmunk-style. She also brought me half a raspberry Zinger.

"You ate them," I said, stating the obvious.

She shook her head. "Mmphmtmummuffff."

"Don't lie. You did. You're still chewing."

"Ummurrfumamamm."

"Are too."

She swallowed, and I watched the large lump slide down her throat.

"I think my husband went to his parents' house," she said, smacking her lips.

"What am I supposed to do with half a Zinger? It's like the size of my thumb."

"I said I think my husband went to his parents' house."

"Who?"

"My husband. After his parents died, he refused to sell it. I'm not allowed to go over there. He's got all kinds of locks and security devices. I think he may be hiding something."

I scarfed down the rest of the cheese curls, then washed them down with the remaining half a Zinger. It wasn't even half. Maybe a third, at best.

"I'm the detective, lady. I'll decide if he's hiding anything. Gimme the address."

She gave it to me. It was in the neighborhood of Streeterville, less than a mile away.

"I'll call you in exactly two hours. If you don't hear from me, I want you to call Lt. Jacqueline Daniels in District 26 and tell her where I am. Tell her it's an emergency. Did you get that?"

"Yeah. Is that apple juice?"

I glanced at my pee bottle.

"Yeah. But it's warm."

"I have ice in the house."

"Help yourself."

She took the piss, and I started the car and drove off. Little did I know I was about to face the darkest moment of my entire career. A moment so dark, that had I known it was coming, I would have done something else instead, like see a movie, or go to the zoo and bang on the windows in the monkey house. But I didn't know what was going to happen, because I couldn't predict the future, because if I could I would have predicted the lottery numbers and been super-rich and never would have needed the money that caused me to go to that house in Streeterville, which was the darkest moment of my entire career. So that's where I went. Unbeknownst to me.

In hindsight, I really shouldn't have gone.

Chapter 12
aka The Darkest Moment Of My Career

So I had no idea I was heading into the darkest moment of my career, but I went anyway.

Before going there, however, I stopped for red hots at Fat Louie's Red Hots on Clark and got a dog with the works. It was terrible, and I have really low standards. In my humble opinion, hot dogs shouldn't have veins. Or anything resembling a foreskin. I could barely choke the third one down.

Uncomfortably sated, I pressed onward to Phil's parents' house. The house was unassuming enough. Split-level, single family, red brick exterior. There was an oak tree out front, and a chain-link fence partitioning off the tiny backyard. I parked on the street, then took out my remote control surveillance tank. After double-checking the batteries, servos, memory card, remote sensor, camera focus, tread alignment, and wireless frequency, I gingerly set the tank down in the street and a taxi ran it over.

Damn taxi jerks. I decided to charge it to Mrs. Drawbridge's bill.

My next course of action was to figure out my next course of action. I played a little more air guitar, broke an air string, put on a new one and spent a minute air tuning it, and then decided on my approach.

I could put on my ghillie suit – a mesh shirt and pants with real and fake grass and shubbery sewn into it that I ordered from PsychoSniper.com – and then slowly belly-crawl across the lawn, traverse the fence using a carbide steel bolt cutter, inch my way into the backyard, creep up the porch in slow increments stopping often to pretend to be a potted plant, trick his surveillance system by recording a loop from his outdoor camera and feeding the playback into the main line, drill into his door frame using a cordless screwdriver to disable the burglary alarm sensor, pick the pick-proof Schlage deadbolt, and sneak inside his house using my Invisible Voyeur NightVision Goggles, which I bought at CautiousStalker.org.

Or I could knock on the front door and ask what's up.

"What's up?" I asked when the front door opened.

Since I'd seen him yesterday, Ken had gone from half a sunburned face to a full sunburned face. The smell coming from his house was real bacon, which sure beat the smell of fake bacon, which my mother used to make out of soy and library paste and brown Crayons.

"Who are you?"

"Housing inspector." I flashed him my PI badge, too fast for him to read it. "I'm here to check for gas leaks. Are you leaking any gases?"

"No. Can I see that badge again?"

"I smell something. Are you cooking in there?"

"No, I'm not."

"Is it bacon?" I smacked my lips. "I love bacon. I read somewhere that you could shave with bacon. Rub it on your face raw, and it lubricates better than shaving cream. Have you every heard of that?"

"No."

"I tried it once. Closest shave I ever had. But I got an E. Coli infection and they had to remove eight yards of my large intestine. Can I come in?"

"No. Hey, you look kind of familiar."

I flashed an aw shucks grin. "I get that a lot. I've made a few videos. You might know my screen name, *Sir Dix-A-Lot.*"

"I don't think that's it."

"Ever see *Snow White and the Seven Blowjobs?*"

"No."

"*Robin Hood, Prince of Anal?*"

"I don't think so."

"*The Empire Strikes Scat?*"

"Maybe you should come in. I may have some gases for you to check on."

I nodded, stepping into his humble abode. It was no surprise he let me in. Fast talking is one of my special skills. That and being able to swallow pills. If I had a super power, it would be the ability to swallow a whole handful of pills at once. Big pills too. None of that baby aspirin crap for babies. I secretly hoped that one day I'd get cancer, and the doctor would prescribe me a lot of pills, and he'd tell me to space them out throughout the day because there were so many, but I'd tell him no need to and grab the whole handful and swallow them up right there while he watched, amazed.

That's what I was thinking about when Phil hit me in the head with the hammer.

Chapter 13

I awoke from a terrible dream that I was trapped in a coffin with a inhumanly large-testicled man, to the terrible reality of being tied to a chair in some freak's basement.

Said freak was standing over me, staring.

"You're awake," he said.

"No I'm not."

I shook my head, which caused a spike of pain. My left eye stung, and I looked down my nose and saw some dried blood on my cheek. The freak still held the hammer. He waved it in front of my face in a way I'm sure he thought was menacing, which actually was pretty menacing.

"Yes you are! And I know what you want! That whore hired you!"

"Which whore? I know a lot of whores."

He poked me in the chest with the hammer. "She hired you to spy on me! To find out what secrets I had hidden in my parents' house! Well, now you'll be privy to those secrets, Mr. Private Eye! Because I'm going to show them to you!"

I checked my bonds, noted he had used the same clothesline he'd purchased at the hardware store. The knots were tight, expert. My legs were bound as well, tied to the steel chair legs of the steel chair, which was made of steel. The basement was unfurnished, concrete floor, I-beams and joists exposed in the ceiling, menacing curtains sectioning off the area we were in.

"Got any aspirin?" I asked. "Some asshole hit me with a hammer."

"Silence!"

"And can you please stop shouting? I'm right here. It's not like I'm in another part of the house and you're calling me for dinner."

The freak chuckled, the nostrils on his large nose flaring out.

"Oh, funny you should mention dinner. Because the main course…" He cackled.

"Yeah?" I asked.

"The main course…" More cackling.

"What's the main course, Emeril?"

"The…main course…is…" Hysterical laughter now.

I interrupted him. "I got it. The main course is me. You're going to eat me. Scary. What a scary guy you are."

"Not me, Mr. McGlade. You're going to be a snack," cackle cackle, "for my…zombie wife!"

I waited for the giggles to die down before I said, "Dude, your wife isn't a zombie."

"Yes she is."

"She's not even dead. I just saw her like an hour ago."

"Not that hag. I mean my first wife. The love of my life, tragically taken from me after only one year of marriage."

"So what about that ugly chick back at your house?"

"Her? I married her for the money."

I smiled. "Thank god. I thought you were totally nuts there for a minute."

"No kidding. She's a real heifer, isn't she?"

"I said in the first chapter that it was like God took a dare to make the most unattractive woman possible."

"Yes, that's Norma."

"Who?"

"My second wife! But now it's time for you to meet my first wife! And to feed her! Do you know what a necromancer is, Mr. McGlade?"

I shrugged. Not an easy task when tied up. "Nuts, and I meant to look it up."

"It's someone who has the power to raise the dead. Since Roberta died…"

"Who?"

"My first wife."

"This is a lot of names to keep straight. Can you write them down on a sticky pad for me?"

He didn't take the bait. I'd hoped he would have gone off in search of a sticky pad, which would have given my time to scoot my chair over to the menacing curtains hanging from the ceiling and hide behind them. He'd never think to look for me there, and would probably go watch TV or something.

But he was too smart to be tricked.

"Since Roberta died, I've been searching for a way to bring her back. Now, through a combination of magic and science – something I call sci-magic – I have finally gained mastery over death! Behold, Mr. McGlade, the living dead!"

He cast aside the menacing curtain. Hanging from the ceiling was a dead body.

"Is that her?" I asked.

"That, indeed, is Roberta, my Zombie Wife!"

He spread out his hands, as if waiting for applause. Even if I wasn't tied up, I wouldn't have applauded.

"That's not a zombie," I said. "That's a dead chick hanging on a rope."

"Really, Mr. McGlade? Really?"

"Yeah. Really."

"Well, watch this then." He turned to face the corpse. "Roberta, my love, come to me!"

Phil grabbed an overhead rope, and Roberta swung forward using a system of weights and pulleys. He made her wave at me.

"You're butt nuts," I said.

"She lives, Mr. McGlade! And she thirsts for your flesh! For nothing else can quell the hunger of the living dead! Isn't that right, Roberta?"

He tugged another rope, and she nodded. Actually, it was more of a sideways flop then a nod.

"Look, buddy, this has all been tremendously entertaining, but what do you say we untie me, I go to the cops, and you get put in a nice room with soft rubber walls so you don't hurt yourself?"

"I'm not crazy! Roberta is one of the walking dead!"

"More like the swaying dead."

He got in my face. "Admit she's undead!"

"No."

"But she moves! See!"

He made her do a little dance.

"You're making her move using pulleys and ropes, like some strange sad puppet."

He raised the hammer, aiming for the same spot where he hit me before. "Say she's a zombie!"

"She a zombie," I said quickly. "You're a genius who has conquered death. I'm in awe of your brilliance."

He stared at me hard, and then spun and yanked the dead chick closer. I realized she was naked, and her boobs were missing. I always notice little things like that. Her skin had become dark brown and wrinkly, like a giant raisin. Whack job had also cut some blue eyes from a magazine or poster, and stapled them over her eye sockets. Her teeth were bared, the corners of her mouth turned up. Twist ties, to make it look like she was smiling.

It was kind of endearing, in a raving psychotic way.

"Roberta does seem sort of tired today." He caressed what was left of her cheek. "Perhaps she needs another treatment. I shall fetch the Rejuvenation Ray!"

He scuttled insanely off, and I wondered what time it was, and if his butt ugly whore of a second wife had remembered to call Lieutenant Jackie when I failed to check in. Then I remembered I'd given her a bottle full of piss and told her it was apple juice, so I probably couldn't count on that particular horse to come in.

Like it had happened so many times before, the burden of saving my own skin rested on my own skin. I needed to figure out some sort of ingenious plan to escape. If I could only do that, then I'd be free.

Freak boy returned, pushing a wheeled wine cart stacked with electronic equipment. He shoved it in front of his living undead zombie wife who was really just a putrefying corpse.

"Behold the Rejuvenation Ray, Mr. McGlade!"

"How do you know my name, anyway?"

"Your wallet."

"I had eight bucks in there. It better still be in there."

"I didn't take your money."

"And a Blockbuster Video card. They charge you five bucks if you lose that."

"Silence! Through magnetron technology, I have harnessed the life-giving properties of ordinary microwaves, coaxing the spirit back into the body!"

"That's a big microwave?"

"Behold!"

He hit a switch, and the stack of electronics hummed and whirred, throwing off a huge amount of heat. Most of it was directed at Roberta, the undead living zombie wife. Some of it came my way, and it hurt like a bad sunburn.

Then the smell hit me. Honey baked ham and bacon strips. I watched through squinty eyes as Roberta sizzled and popped and exuded a scent that was downright mouth-watering.

Now it all made sense. Phil's sunburn. Why he smelled like ham. Why his first wife's skin was so brown and wrinkly. Why his second wife smelled like sweaty feet.

Actually, this didn't explain why his second wife smelled like sweaty feet. But I guessed that to be a hygiene thing.

Blofeld finally turned off the microwave stack, then embraced his hanging wife. The embrace became a kiss. The kiss became a nibble. The nibble became a corn-on-the-cob chow-down, and I realized what happened to the zombie's breasts.

"And now!" He wiped the grease off his mouth with his sleeve. "Now it is time for Roberta to feast!"

Fred reached under the cart, pulled out a meat cleaver. You don't see too many meat cleavers, outside of a butcher shop.

"What shall we start with, Roberta? The leg? Yes, I agree. The leg looks delicious. Do you prefer the left on or the right one, dear? Yes, the left one."

He raised the cleaver. There are few things more terrifying than being tied to a chair about to be hacked up by a lunatic so he could feed the pieces to his dead wife who he thinks is actually a zombie and is hanging from the ceiling using an admittedly clever series of weights and pulleys.

"Stop!" I yelled.

Incredibly, he stopped.

"What?"

"Your parents!" I said, speaking quickly. "What would your parents think?"

"Why don't we…ask them!"

He stepped over to the menacing curtain, and with a flourish drew it back. Mom and Dad were hanging there, roped together so it looked like Dad was giving it to Mom, doggy-style.

"Oops!" Fred said, tugging on ropes and making his parents bump uglies. "Daddy! Why are you hurting Mommy?"

He pulled the cord again and again, Dad's hips rising and falling. A shrink would have a field day with this guy. Field days were fun. I liked dodgeball best.

"Say that again, Daddy? You're wrestling? What wrestling move is that?"

It looked, to my untrained eye, like a sodomyplex. I tore my eyes away and pointed at something with my chin. "What's that hanging next to them?"

"Fluffy. My cat."

"And those tiny things?"

"My goldfish, BA and Hannibal. Fluffy loves to chase them around. Don't you, Fluffy?"

More manic pulling of ropes, and the three dead animals knocked into each other. While he was preoccupied, I called out in my best falsetto, "Honey, it's Roberta!"

John turned his attention back to Roberta the zombie living bacon wife.

"Dearest? Did you say something?"

"I said," I said, "We should let Mr. McGlade go. I'm not hungry right now."

Nut job was buying it. He wrapped his arms around her, nuzzling against her tasty ribs.

"But you need to eat, honey. You're getting thinner and thinner."

"Tack a couple of tomatoes to my chest. I'll look a lot better."

Bert began to laugh. A chilling laugh that chilled me. He spun, pointing the cleaver at my nose.

"You idiot! Do you think I'm that stupid?"

"Yes."

"What good husband doesn't know the sound of my wife's own voice?"

"You, I was hoping."

"Enough of this tomfoolery! This ends now!"

He launched himself at me, screaming and drooling insanely, his probably very sharp cleaver raised for the killing blow.

Then Lieutenant Jackie Daniels shot him in the head.

Chapter 14

"You're an idiot, McGlade," Jackie said, using the cleaver to cut away the ropes.

Carl was dead on the floor. He was finally with his wife. Because she was dead on the floor too. Jack had made me sit there until the Crime Scene Unit arrived, taking pictures and gathering evidence. They cut the bodies down before they freed me.

"So how did you know I was here?" I asked.

Jack wore a short skirt and heels that probably cost a fortune but still looked kind of slutty, just how I liked them.

"Norma Cauldridge," she said.

"Who?"

"George Cauldridge's wife."

"Who?"

"She called me, wanted me to arrest you for trying to poison her. I asked where you were, and she said probably here. After we nabbed those necrophiliacs at the cemetery last night, I needed to find you anyway to get your statement. Lucky I heard your girlish screams which gave me probable cause to bust in here without a warrant."

I wasn't listening, because it sounded like a boring infodump.

"Can I give you my statement tomorrow?" I asked. "I gotta take a monster dump. I had some hot dogs earlier that are going to look better coming out than going in."

Jackie leaned in close. I braced myself for the kiss. It didn't come.

"Did you give Norma a bottle full of your urine and tell her it was apple juice?"

"Maybe. Did she drink any?"

"She said the second glass went down rough. She's going to sue you, McGlade."

"She can take a number. Seriously. I've got one of those number things. I swiped it from the deli." I grinned. "You can come over later, and watch me cut the cheese. You know you want to."

"I'd rather gouge out my own eyes with forks."

"Don't be coy. This could be a way to pay back what you owe me."

She cocked her hips, hot and sexy. "Excuse me? I just saved your ass, McGlade."

"Are you kidding? This is front page news. You'll probably get a promotion. There's no need to thank me. It's all part of the service I perform."

"I really think I hate you."

"Really, Jackie?" I raised an eyebrow. "Really?"

She nodded. "Yeah, really. Be in my office tomorrow morning for your statement. And try to stay of trouble until then."

I stood up, stretched, and gave her one of my famous Harry McGlade smiles.

"I'll try. But trouble is my business." I winked. "And business is good."

Punishment

Dominick Pataglia tried to block out the screaming coming from the Punishment Room, but the ceiling-mounted speakers were at maximum volume.

The screams came at regular intervals – animal cries, sharp and shrill, only identifiable as human because they were punctuated with pleas for mercy.

Mercy was not known here.

Dominick clamped his fists over his ears, but the terrible sound penetrated the flesh and bone of his hands. From the creaking noise that underscored the screaming, Dominick guessed they were using the screws; wooden clamps, tightened on joints until the bones almost cracked.

Sometimes bones did crack, causing political bedlam in the form of inquiries and written protestations from sympathy groups.

This usually resulted in a sharp fine.

The Law plainly stated that the punishment couldn't inflict permanent damage. The Government was a stickler on that. It interfered with the education process.

Another scream, like a pig being butchered. Dominick squeezed his eyes shut. He had felt the screws before, and other things that were even more horrible.

Dominick had been a guest of the Punishment Room three times since he came here. Each time it had gotten worse.

His first visit had been just after he arrived. Two men in hoods and uniforms grabbed him before he'd even gotten off the bus. They dragged him to the Waiting Room and locked him in, confused and afraid.

There were no windows in the Waiting Room, no furniture, and the floor was cold, gray concrete. It had a sharp, acrid odor, beneath the scent of antiseptic. Dominick would later identify it as the smell of fear.

On the walls of the Waiting Room, tacked up in ranks and files and covering every inch of space, were photographs.

Pictures of people being tortured.

Thousands of photos, thousands of faces, each depicting a moment of grotesque agony.

Dominick opened his eyes and they locked onto a picture of himself. He looked so young in the picture, even in the grip of agony. It was taken only a few months ago.

They had used the rack the first time.

He hadn't done anything to warrant it. It was just to get him acquainted with the way things were done here.

He had screamed until his voice gave out.

That was what seemed to be happening to his comrade in the Punishment Room. The screams were becoming hoarser. Not because the pain was lessening, but because he had been in there for over an hour. Poor bastard.

Dominick let his eyes wander around the room until he saw the photo of the second time he'd visited the Punishment Room. For talking to an instructor out of turn. Dominick couldn't even remember what he had said to him.

Dominick's face in the picture was tear-stained and manic.

They had used the screws on him. On his thumbs, his knees, his testicles.

It had taken him ten days in the infirmary to recover.

His third visit to the Punishment Room was the worst, and warranted three Polaroids, all of which hung on the wall. During a two-hour period he was strung up by his feet and beaten with a rubber whip over every inch of his naked body.

Then he was beaten again.

And again.

And again.

The pain reached such an intense level he kept blacking out, and a doctor had to be called in to give him amphetamine shots to keep him awake.

That's what the Torture Man thrived on. There was a rumor one poor girl had been in the Punishment Room for fourteen hours, simply because she kept passing out from the pain.

The Torture Man loved that.

What he loved even more was breaking someone tough.

The Torture Man glowed when someone showed anger or hatred; anything other than total submission. Because then the Torture Man got to break the spirit along with the body.

Where they found people like the Torture Man, God only knew.

Another hoarse cry. It would be ending soon, and then it would be Dominick's turn.

This was his fourth visit. That meant the electricity. From what others had told him, electricity made everything else look mild.

He would have current driven into his teeth, and his ears, and up his anus. The Government had not banned this torture, even though it resulted in burns on the contact points. Burns weren't considered permanent damage.

The screaming stopped. The silence that filled the Waiting Room made Dominick dizzy.

It would be only moments now.

He hugged his knees to his chest and touched the bottom of his left heel for the hundredth time. Rules required he strip before he came in, but Dominick had managed to tape a stubby pencil to the bottom of his bare foot.

He tapped the sharpened point, but it offered him no courage. Even if Dominick somehow found the guts to use it as a weapon, he didn't think it would get him very far. The Torture Man would probably be amused.

And after the amusement would come anger.

Thinking about it made Dominick nauseous. But he thought about it anyway.

Maybe it would work, if he was quick. Maybe it would work, if he stabbed the Torture Man somewhere vital, like the face. Maybe…

The door opened.

The Torture Man filled the doorway, steeped in the stench of body odor and fear. He stood almost twenty inches taller than Dominick, a monster of a man, with a barrel chest and strong, thick fingers.

"Nice to see you again, Mr. Pataglia." His voice was like raking leaves. The black cowl left his mouth uncovered, and his crooked brown teeth smiled with power and certainty. There were stains on his gray shirt from his armpits to his flanks, and a large wet spot soaked the front of his black pants.

Though sexual abuse and rape weren't allowed by the law, the government allowed him to masturbate while torturing.

Dominick palmed the pencil and fought to keep his sphincter closed. He could hardly breathe. The Torture Man produced a clipboard and glared at it with little rat eyes.

"Attacked a hall monitor, eh Dominick? Haven't you got the balls? We'll have to hook them up to the generator, see if we can light them up."

The Torture Man giggled like a young girl.

Dominick stood on rubbery legs and backed into the corner of the room. Dread soaked him to the core. The Torture Man closed in, huge and looming. He grabbed Dominick by the wrist.

"Please," Dominick pleaded. The pencil felt like a strand of spaghetti in his hand, slick and useless.

The Torture Man brought his face close, so close Dominick could smell his rancid breath.

"You're my last assignment of the day, so we'll have plenty of time together."

Dominick looked away, catching a glimpse of his photo on the wall.

"No we won't."

Dominick's voice surprised him. It was low and hard, steely with resolve.

The Torture Man was surprised as well. He went smiley and wide-eyed.

"Why, Mr. Pataglia, did you just contradict—"

Dominick's hand shot out and plunged the pencil into the center of the Torture Man's right eye.

It went in hard, like stabbing a tire, and there was a sucking-slurping sound.

The Torture Man screamed. He released his grip and stumbled backwards, his meaty hands fluttering around his face like birds afraid to land. Blood and black fluid seeped down his face in gooey trails.

Dominick took three quick steps after him and swung his fist at the pencil, managing to knock it deeper into the socket.

The Torture Man made a keening sound, and then crumpled into a large, fat pile on the concrete. His mouth hung open like an empty sack, and his good eye rolled up into the socket, baring the bloodshot white.

Dominick stood over him for a moment, shocked. Had he done it? Had he killed him?

Run! demanded the voice in his head.

But Dominick remained rooted to the floor.

He had to make sure. He had to make sure the bastard was dead.

The adrenalin was wearing off, leaving Dominick sick and shaky. He forced himself to kneel, and then tentatively stretched out a hand to check the Torture Man's pulse.

It was like willfully putting his hand in a fire.

After an eternity of inching closer and closer, Dominick touched the Torture Man's wet, clammy neck. He probed beneath the fat and the stubble, seeking out the carotid.

There was a pulse.

Dominick yanked his hand back as if shocked.

Run, you idiot! If he wakes up…

But Dominick couldn't run. He embraced a chilling certainty; even if he didn't escape, he couldn't allow this evil man to live. Not just for himself, but for all the others.

He chewed his lower lip and reached for the pencil.

The Torture Man groaned.

Dominick sprang to his feet. He needed a weapon of some kind. Side-stepping the Torture Man, Dominick raced out the door and into the hallway. To the left, the door to the courtyard. To the right, the Punishment Room.

Dominick's reaction was visceral – he didn't want to go in the Punishment Room ever again. But there were weapons…

He went right.

The Punishment Room was straight out of his nightmares. Dark and filthy, illuminated by two bare bulbs hanging from the ceiling by greasy cords. The walls were black, and an underlying stink of urine and excrement fouled the moist air. Chains and shackles were bolted to the floor and walls, a rack sat in one corner, and a cabinet full of the Torture Man's hideous instruments yawned open, revealing his tools of pain.

Dominick heard a noise like wind whistling through the trees. He looked back and saw the Torture Man standing in the doorway, wheezing. The pencil was still poking from his eye, and gooey red tears streaked down his face. He pointed a huge finger at Dominick, and took another labored step forward.

Dominick reached into the Torture Man's cabinet and removed a can of lighter fluid. He popped the top and squirted it at the Torture Man's face.

The Torture Man screamed when the alcohol hit his punctured eye. He stumbled backwards and tripped over the generator.

"You little bastard! When I get you…"

Dominick grabbed the nearest object – a digital camera sitting on the cart – and fell upon the Torture Man. He brought the weapon down on his tormentor's face, again and again, the plastic case cracking and splintering as he used it to knock out teeth and break bone.

The Torture Man lashed out, connecting with the side of Dominick's head. Dominick fell onto his back, landing hard. His vision blurred, and something was poking him behind his left shoulder.

Next to him, the Torture Man sat up. He grabbed the pencil and pulled. His eye slurped out of the socket, looking like a tiny red jellyfish trailing its tentacles. The Torture Man howled, dropping the pencil. The eye swung freely down at cheek level, hanging by a coil of optic nerve.

Dominick reached behind his back, seeking the source of his discomfort. He pulled it into view.

It was a steel clamp, almost the size of his hand. He squeezed the ends and it opened its jaws, baring tiny teeth. A cord was attached to the bottom, and Dominick followed it along the floor to where it plugged into the electric generator.

He glanced at the Torture Man, who had managed to find his rubber whip. He smacked it against Dominick's face, the pain instant and staggering.

Dominick rolled onto his side, still gripping the clamp. The whip lashed across his naked back, and he cried out.

"You think you know pain?!" the Torture Man bellowed. "I'll show you pain!"

Dominick spun around onto his bottom, taking another whip stroke in the face. He thrust the clamp at the Torture Man, securing it to his ankle.

Then he stretched out his hand and hit the switch on the generator.

The reaction was instant.

The Torture Man doubled in half like a book slamming shut, and pitched head-first to the floor. A strong whiff of ozone plumed around him as his grotesque body shook in wracking spasms. Blood sprayed from his mouth and a piece of tongue escaped his clenched teeth and tumbled down his chin.

Dominick crab-walked backwards, putting distance between them. He watched, wide-eyed, as the clamp on the Torture Man's leg began to smoke, and then ignited the soaked-in lighter fluid.

The Torture Man burned like kindling.

Dominick pulled his gaze away and found the drawer next to the cabinet that held his clothes. He tried to ignore the popping sound of blistering flesh and the Torture Man's gurgling moans. By the time he'd tied his shoes the moans had died along with the monster.

The can of lighter fluid was on the cart, next to a pair of tin snips. Dominick shoved the snips in his back pocket and squirted fluid onto the rack. Then he did the same to the Torture Man's dreaded cabinet and the instruments it contained.

They burned well.

Finally, he went back into the Waiting Room and doused the walls, staring one last time at the picture of himself on the rack, watching it burn.

They would be coming. Soon. He had to get away.

The door to the courtyard was open, and amazingly, no one was around. It made sense – the Hall Monitors hadn't expected to escort him out of there for another few hours.

Dominick stepped out into the fresh air. The sun winked through the trees like an old friend. A light breeze cleared the stench of urine from his nostrils.

The fence was just beyond the basketball courts, locked and topped with razor wire. Impossible to climb over.

But he wasn't climbing.

Two minutes with the tin snips, and he was though the fence.

Freedom enveloped him like a mother's love.

He ran off into the woods, giddy, yet knowing that someday he would return.

But not as a victim.

Dominick had read the forbidden history books. He knew

that a hundred years ago there was no torture in America's Public Schools. There was once a time when eleven-year-olds like himself went to school to learn. When education wasn't Government indoctrination. When children were free.

The Torture Man, evil as he was, was just a symptom of the disease. Both a part of the system, and a product of it.

But Dominick knew there were others like himself. Fighters, who sought change.

He would meet up with these people. Grow strong. And in time, when he returned to this place, it wouldn't be as a victim.

It would be as a liberator.

Dominic Patalglia ran through the woods, not looking back at the Elementary Camp. His footfalls were sure and strong, and as he ran he could swear that he heard the sound of a thousand boys and girls behind him, cheering.

www.ingramcontent.com/pod-product-compliance
Lightning Source LLC
LaVergne TN
LVHW091134080826
845145LV00008B/2147

* 9 7 8 0 9 7 7 9 6 8 6 3 3 *